P9-DHD-952

CHICAGO PUBLIC LIBRARY

TEEN

VOLUME

Teen Volume is made possible
by a grant from the
McCormick Tribune Foundation
through the Chicago Public Library Foundation

McCormick
Tribune
Foundation

CHICAGO PUBLIC LIBRARY
EDGEWATER BRANCH
1210 W. ELMDALE 60660

LAST DANCE
AT THE FROSTY QUEEN

LAST DANCE AT THE FROSTY QUEEN

richard uhlig

Alfred A. Knopf New York

THIS IS A BORZOI BOOK PUBLISHED BY ALFRED A. KNOPF

This is a work of fiction. Names, characters, places, and incidents either are the product of the author's imagination or are used fictitiously. Any resemblance to actual persons, living or dead, events, or locales is entirely coincidental.

Copyright © 2007 by Richard Uhlig

All rights reserved.

Published in the United States by Alfred A. Knopf, an imprint of Random House Children's Books, a division of Random House, Inc., New York.

KNOPF, BORZOI BOOKS, and the colophon are registered trademarks of Random House, Inc.

www.randomhouse.com/teens

Educators and librarians, for a variety of teaching tools, visit us at
www.randomhouse.com/teachers

Library of Congress Cataloging-in-Publication Data
Uhlig, Richard Allen.
Last dance at the Frosty Queen / Richard Uhlig. — 1st ed.
p. cm.
SUMMARY: In the spring of 1988, as his high school graduation approaches, Arty Flood worries that he will never be able to escape his tiny Kansas town.
ISBN 978-0-375-83967-2 (trade) — ISBN 978-0-375-93967-9 (lib. bdg.)
[1. Coming of age—Fiction. 2. Interpersonal relations—Fiction.
3. Family problems—Fiction. 4. Kansas—Fiction.] I. Title.
PZ7.U32578Las 2007
[Fic]—dc22
2006024355

Printed in the United States of America

August 2007

10 9 8 7 6 5 4 3 2 1

First Edition

R0411912751

CHICAGO PUBLIC LIBRARY
EDGEWATER BRANCH
1210 W. ELMDALE 60660

For Dad, who didn't insist I go to medical school,

and for Heather, who insisted I write.

———

With thanks to Irene Kraas for championing the book

and to Cecile Goyette for making it happen.

CHICAGO PUBLIC LIBRARY

PART ONE

1

I wheel the Death Mobile onto Broadway, my hometown's main drag, and head west. Pierre, my bosses' standard poodle, sticks his delighted-doggie head out the window, his tongue flapping. The digital thermometer on the savings and loan blinks 93 degrees—and it's only May 6. They say it's going to be a scorcher this summer, and the air-conditioning in my hearse is fatally busted.

A big white banner flutters overhead: HARKER CITY, KANSAS—CELEBRATE OUR ONE HUNDRED YEARS MEMORIAL DAY WEEKEND! Celebrate what? Here it is 1988, and if you're in the mood for McDonald's, Chinese food, a movie, or even a stoplight, you'll have to drive thirty miles north and swing a right at Junction City.

Our Broadway might not have much in the way of shows, the cheesy promotional brochure in City Hall tells you, *but we make up for it in our traditional small-town friendliness.*

Harker City's slogan is "1,700 smiling faces—and yours!" Of all the things this burg lacks, dateable girls would have to be at the top of my list. My class, the seniors, has twelve girls in it, right? Three have children, two are pregnant (say what you will, but we yokels know how to entertain ourselves), one is my cousin, one is becoming a nun, one is morbidly obese, and the decent-looking remainders date football players. If you don't play football in Harker City, you don't exist (I don't exist).

I drive past our house, the plain-looking two-story white clapboard with a big front porch. Carrie, my sister, wants to paint the exterior Victorian rose with sky blue trim, but Dad'll never go for it. Way too flashy. The sign on the lawn says FLOOD & SON FUNERAL HOME, SERVING HARKER CITY SINCE 1922. Dad added this a few years ago, when those awful Larsons moved to town and built a sprawling new Southern Colonial–style funeral home across the street. The Larsons, beaming yuppies with giant white teeth, live in a big house with a swimming pool out by the country club. The "son" in Dad's sign is my big brother, Allen, whose official title is assistant funeral director, a position that allows him to lie on his bed all day and smoke pot.

My dad, the bald guy who looks like he might be expecting twins, is in our driveway washing his new used hearse. He's growing that grizzled beard for the Centennial.

Five minutes later, hot wind whips my hair as we zoom past the rusted marquee of the old Chief Drive-in Theater. Town soon gives way to wheat fields as my speedometer hits seventy. The stand-up twenty-four-karat-gold wreath-and-crest hood ornament reminds me that I am driving a genuine Caddy. A gift from Dad on my sixteenth birthday, this black 1965 hearse, with its rusted frame and chrome-draped grinning face with dual headlights, accelerates like a cement truck going up Pikes Peak and gets about eleven miles per gallon with a stiff breeze behind it.

Gleaming in the sun, lined with cabins and trees, Harker City Lake stretches out before us.

I pull off the lake road into the rutted drive next to where we used to live. The mailbox leans way over, the M. FLOOD stenciled on top just barely visible. I see that swallows have nested inside, and that cheers me up a little. The driveway is overgrown with weeds, and I worry that after last night's rainstorm I'll get stuck. But the earth feels solid under my tires as I park beside the foundation of our old house. You can still see the char on some of the stones. The fireplace is all that stands and a tree grows out where the kitchen once was. I think about Mom cooking in there and I try to remember her face, but the picture is too hazy. I'm amazed at how small the house must've been—seemed so much bigger then. It's been nine long years since it burned down.

I grab a Snickers from the glove compartment. It's soft from the heat and when I tear it open, the chocolate runs. It's been raining like crazy all spring and the water is nearly up to the road. I amble down to the small floating dock with Pierre and sit and nibble the Snickers while he marks the cattails.

It's windier out here than in town, and the bouncing platform makes me horny. I lie back and stare at the cotton-ball
clouds and listen to the water slap the wood. I imagine I'm on
a giant water bed with Olivia Newton-John rocking and riding me. My eyelids grow heavy.

2

Arf! Arf! Pierre's barking jolts me back.

How long have I slept? My hard-on is about to tear out of my jeans and I consider crawling into my car and beating off, but Pierre is barking at something in the water. There's a splash, and I turn and see a face in the water staring at me not two feet from the edge of the dock. It's alive and the cheeks dimple with a half-smile.

It's a girl, about my age, in swimming goggles, with a small, freckled, slightly sunburned nose. Her long dark hair clings to her head and neck like seaweed.

"Jesus!" I bolt up, my heart pounding. "You scared the shit out of me."

She grins as she stares at the bulge in my crotch. I pull my legs up and attempt to cross them. I can feel the blood flaming to my face. She pushes off from the dock and backstrokes out several feet, slicing through the water like a mermaid, graceful and effortless. Next, she arches and does a backward somersault. Her long, tan legs are suddenly all that's sticking out of the brown-green water. They disappear. No more girl.

I sit there, shocked and embarrassed, my blood pounding,

mad at her for spying on me, mad at myself for having such an obvious boner.

She doesn't surface and now Pierre is going crazy. Still no girl—not even a bubble! Just as I think about diving in, she pops up at the edge of the dock again. She lifts her goggles to her forehead and I suddenly take in the full glory of her sparkling blue eyes. Her lashes curl upward. As her gaze meets mine, my heart turns way over.

Pierre pads up and sniffs her face while she rubs her long fingers between his ears. Her smooth skin isn't so much tanned as it is a natural olive. Then she grabs my Snickers, takes a bite, puts it back, and takes off across the lake.

I open my mouth to say something, but she's so fast. I watch as she becomes smaller and smaller until she's a mere dot. I grab Pierre and dash to the Death Mobile. It grinds to a start on only the third try. We speed down the gravel road that outlines the lake and circle it three times. Defeated, I park on the grassy dam, sit on my hood, and scan the rippling water for over an hour. Where could she have gone? Did she drown? And most of all—who *is* she?

3

Back in town, I roll the Necro-Caddy into the gravel parking lot at my after-school job, Stiles' Styles. It's supposed to be a garment manufacturer and I'm supposed to be a design assistant. Not one stitch of clothing has been made since yours truly started here over a year ago. I park beside my bosses' white Toronado, the only car in the lot.

Inside, Pierre and I pass the rows of dusty sewing machines. You'd think I'd welcome a job where I get paid to take the bosses' dog to the lake. I agreed to only half my wage (a princely three dollars an hour) because my bosses, Mr. and Mrs. Stiles, aren't bringing in any money right now. The deal I made with Mr. Stiles is that when I graduate in three weeks, he'll pay me the other half, plus interest. I have $1,437.17 coming my way. And the moment—no, make that the second—I get it, I'm gone. So long, job. *Auf Wiedersehen*, Harker City. *Au revoir*, Kansas.

A wall of smoke hits me when I enter the office. Mr. Stiles, hunched behind his bill-heaped desk, holds one cigarette, while two more burn in the beanbag ashtray. He looks constipated and worried, his thick face and bulging, blood-shot eyes partially hidden by the veil of smoke, his toupee noticeably off center. Mrs. Stiles puffs on a Virginia Slims she holds daintily between her yellowed, skinny fingers. You can't make out her eyes behind her huge sunglasses. Amber-colored pill bottles clutter her "design table." On the wall behind her hang five large professional photographs of Pierre modeling various Doggie Joggie outfits, a line of canine sweat suits designed by Mrs. Stiles and yours truly. The Stileses used to be upbeat, nice people, but their business isn't taking off and I've watched their moods grow darker by the day.

I clear my throat. "Mr. Stiles, I, uh, wanted to remind you that today is payday."

He puts down his cigarette. "Oh, I forgot. Have it for you on Monday."

Though I really need the dough, I pat Pierre on the head and say: "Okay, Monday, then. Have a nice weekend."

Mrs. Stiles just smiles her vacant, drugged-up smile while Mr. Stiles lights another cigarette.

On the drive home, I can't stop thinking about Mrs. Stiles smiling into space like one of the pod people in *Invasion of the Body Snatchers*. Just a year ago, she was wearing a towering red wig (not that dingy turban she now sports), colorful outfits, and glittering earrings and bracelets that matched Pierre's jewel-studded Doggie Joggie. Once she was perky and joking all the time. A real hoot, and even the occasional object of *moi*'s lustful fantasies. Nowadays, all she wears are gray sweats and sunglasses. She used to dye Pierre different colors for each season, with sculpted puffs on his hips, tail, and legs. Now he's a faded magenta in need of a trim. Although I suppose she's pretty tacky, I liked Mrs. Stiles right away. She hired me based on my drawings; I helped illustrate the clothes she was going to manufacture, and learned a lot from her. She said she thought I had a future in design and if she got a big order for Doggie Joggies, she'd help pay my way through art school. When you have nine dollars to your name like I do, it's dangerous to set your heart on something like art school. I still can't help thinking about it a lot. Who knows, maybe Mrs. Stiles will come through. But it's kind of scary—my future hinges on the sale of velour jogging suits for dogs.

4

I walk through our back door and the aroma of permanent solution stings my nostrils. Shear Expressions by Shirley, my stepmom's beauty shop, is located in our enclosed back porch off the kitchen. In here the beehive and the bouffant not only are alive but thrive and rise to dizzying heights. Every day Shirley erects varnished spires and cotton-candy cylinders of petrified hair for Harker City's glamourpusses. Shirley, her own hair a Darth Vader helmet, Aqua Nets a pile of teased, frosted curls. I make a beeline to the fridge, take out Miracle Whip, baloney, and Wonder bread.

"Aren't you going to say hello, Arthur?" Mrs. Kaye asks.

The woman in the chair is my high school drama teacher—and then some. Two hours ago, in class, she had long, straight black hair. Now she has some sort of teetering, curly bird's nest.

Mrs. Kaye spins around in her chair. "Well, what do you think?"

"It looks . . . real nice, ma'am," I lie, then turn back to making my sandwich.

"I was inspired by Cyndi Lauper," she says, and flashes her gap-toothed smile. "After all, girls just wanna have fun."

Shirley and Mrs. Kaye laugh at this like it was the wittiest thing ever said.

I nod and head to the living room.

Dad's in his La-Z-Boy, puffing his pipe and watching *Wheel of Fortune*. On the end table, the CB radio crackles. Dad leaves it on the Harker City emergency band in case he might need to prepare the hearse.

"Hi, Dad," I say as I pass through.

"Evening, son."

In the upstairs bedroom, I find my brother where he always is: lying on the bottom bunk, listening to John Cougar Mellencamp, KISS, or Megadeth.

"Hey, bro," Allen says in his squeaky, I've-smoked-way-too-much-and-stretched-out-my-vocal-cords voice.

I carefully place the remains of the Snickers the girl bit into behind Allen's Coors cans in our small refrigerator.

"Allen, don't eat this Snickers bar, understand?"

He nods.

"Allen, repeat what I just said."

"Allen, do not eat the Snickers bar."

"Okay, thanks. So . . . you heard about any new girls in town?"

Allen shakes his head. His reddish brown hair sticks out Einstein-like. He hasn't shaved in a couple of days and despite being six feet two inches tall, he's getting a notice-able gut.

I kick off my shoes and leap up on the bunk. "If you hear of any, let me know right away, okay?"

"Uh, sure. Hey, speaking of girls, guess who's coming back for the Centennial?"

I drop my head on my Superman pillow. "Suzanne Somers."

"C'mon, don't you even wanna guess?"

"Y'know, that *Juggs* you loaned me isn't bad," I say. "Can you get some more?"

"Not unless I have to pick up a stiff—I mean, a client—outta town. Too broke to go anywhere just so you can jack off."

It's impossible to purchase special-interest periodicals in Harker City, with its twelve churches and League of Concerned Lutherans.

"So, you gonna guess who's coming back for the Centennial or not?" he asks.

I stare at the cracks in the ceiling.

"Renee!" he says. "Isn't that awesome?"

Renee is the only girl Allen ever dated. Their prom portrait hangs in a silver frame next to his beloved Metallica poster. She dumped Allen when she went to flight attendant school after graduation six years ago. Allen's never gotten over it.

"So I guess she flies all over the world and meets all kinds of men," he says. "But you know what they say—there's no one like your first true love."

Allen checks in with Renee's mother daily. He mows her lawn, shovels her snow, and runs errands for her. Sometimes he'll say something like, "Renee and I prefer the old Coke to the new Coke." It really creeps me out.

He goes on about how he plans to take Renee for an "elegant" Italian dinner in Wichita and, to show her that he's not a Harker City hick, he'll order an "expensive European wine." Then he's going to take her to play miniature golf.

"You know, little brother, I know how to make an impression. She used to love that about me."

Speaking of impressions, my mind returns to the girl at the lake. If it weren't for her teeth marks in the Snickers bar, I might think I dreamed her up.

5

Although the Centennial meeting starts in fifteen minutes, I make a quick stop at the Frosty Queen. It's the only twenty-four-hour business in town. Vernadell, the owner, also runs the attached ten-room motel. Were it not for the railroad, she says, she couldn't afford to run the FQ. They pay her to keep it open all night so train crews have a place to eat and get coffee. Pretty much everyone in town eats at the brand-spanking-new Dairy Queen out on the highway. Has a drive-up window and big asphalt parking lot. The employees wear headsets and are rigorously trained to smile and say, "Welcome to the Dairy Queen. My name is Cindy. How may I help you this fine day?"

But the Frosty, unchanged since the forties, with its crusty chrome, giant ice-cream-cone-shaped neon sign, sagging roof, and haggard and grumpy Vernadell, is the real thing. In my humble opinion, its Zip Burgers, sloppy Joes with Colonel Sparks' barbecue sauce, cannot be compared to the Big Mac knockoffs at DQ. After the lake, it is my favorite hangout.

I park between a pickup and the yellow Mercedes that

belongs to Hal Denton, the town banker. (It's the only Benz in town.) I kill the engine, but the Rigor Motoris still rattles, chokes, and farts for a good half minute.

The cowbell above the door clangs at my entry and I inhale the great smell of grease and onions. Dennis Dickers' hairy butt crack greets me, exposed by his sagging Levi's as he slouches over the counter to sip his coffee.

Dennis swivels around. "Sounds like your engine's on its way out, Flood."

"Don't think so, Den," I say. "Remember, she's a Caddy."

"Your girlfriend, Barry, been waitin' for ya." Dennis smirks, turns back around, and watches his moustached wife, Darlene, clean the grill. When he's not fixing railroad track, Dennis is always here because he thinks every man in Harker City lusts after the frumpy and furry Darlene. I suspect Vernadell even hired my friend Barry to be a waiter so Dennis wouldn't worry about him being around Darlene. Everyone assumes Barry's got to be gay, despite his going steady with Ladonna Stover.

Vernadell is sitting across from Mr. Denton in a red leatherette booth. She glares and points her crooked index finger at him. I can't hear anything because "Dancing on the Ceiling," Barry's favorite song, blares endlessly on the Rock-Ola. God, how I hate Lionel Richie. In the neighboring booth, the Datweiler sisters—ninety-year-old twins in matching pastel outfits and white gloves—share a gooey banana split.

Barry comes out from behind the counter in his starched white uniform, a shiny drama/comedy-face brooch pinned conspicuously to his lapel.

"You didn't come in after you got off work," he says. "What the heck happened to you?"

"Busy. Say, Bar, have you seen a new girl in town? Real cute, kinda exotic-looking, blue eyes?"

He shakes his head.

I sit at the Ms. Pac-Man machine, the tabletop type, which two people can play facing each other. Every day after work I come in for a game with Barry. I'm pretty good. Actually, I hold the all-time Harker City high score.

Before I can fish a quarter from my pocket, Barry takes the seat across from me, hands me a Dr Pepper, drops two quarters in the slot, and pushes the doubles button.

"Read my script yet?" he asks as the Ms. Pac-Man theme kicks in.

"Not yet, too busy at work."

I grip the joystick and guide the yellow, crescent-shaped, lipsticked body through a maze of dots while the four ghosts fervently pursue me.

"I know you'll just love it," he says. "I mean, it all came to me last night—in a fabulous burst. I was in the bathtub, staring at my feet, when the entire pageant hit me in a moment . . . of efiffany."

"Epiphany."

"Right. See, it starts off with me in age makeup as Mr. Harker, on my deathbed singing 'Memories.' You know, from *Cats*."

I nod, sip my cool, sweet Dr Pepper, and keep eating dots—*whoka, whoka, whoka*.

"Then we go back in time. I'm twenty-five years old and riding my horse across the prairie—I haven't built the town yet—and I'm singing 'Oh, What a Beautiful Mornin'.' Then an Indian chief rides up—"

"Barry!"

"Huh?"

"Please, man, don't spoil it for me."

"Okay. Sorry. You're absolutely right. It's just, well, you know how much it would mean to me if I could play Mr. Harker in the pageant. It would be a real boost for my career."

"Even if they do use your ideas, I can't guarantee they'll let you play the lead."

"But you're on the Centennial committee."

"Doesn't mean I can just hand you the part."

"Still, you've got clout, Arty. And I know you'll help your best friend. Ever since the whole *Peter Pan* disaster, I've been in the dumps. I want to leave my fans with something special to remember me by. I owe them a great final performance."

Barry was supposed to play Peter Pan in the spring production but, due to our drama teacher Mrs. Kaye's lack of directing ability and failure to show up for rehearsals, the thing never came together and Principal Swedeson canceled the play. Barry has been out of sorts ever since.

"It'll make my senior experience complete," he adds.

I've been hearing about Barry's "senior experience" all year. Suddenly everything is a big, meaningful event: "This is our last forensics tournament," "our last prom," "our last frog dissection."

Astonishingly, Barry has received a scholarship to attend Kansas State for musical theater.

"I'll do what I can," I say.

I let all four ghosts line up behind me and, just when they're about to eat me, I chomp a power pellet. It's my move. Now I'm chasing them down: Inky—dead. Pinky—dead. Blinky and Sue—history. Arty Flood knows when to pour it on.

6

The tinny Ms. Pac-Man theme plays and I wait for the next screen to come up.

I used to hang out with Barry because he was practically the only guy around who wasn't into macho jock crap. And he loves my caricatures. But then, last year, Mrs. Kaye cast him as Curly in *Oklahoma*. He found "the theater" and has been a nutcase ever since.

Ms. Pac-Man is off and running when a ghost eats me.

"You're up," I say, and sip my pop.

I hear Vernadell arguing with Mr. Denton in muffled tones.

"Told ya, you'll get your money when the Missouri Pacific pays me," red-faced Vernadell says, nervously tapping her glasses on the tabletop.

Barry says, "I know this town is just a backwater place to you but it's where my talent was discovered. Nurtured. It gave me my first audience and I can think of no better way of saying thank you than to play Mr. Harker in the pageant."

"Said I'll do what I can."

"One more thing," he says.

"What's that?"

Barry looks at me flatly. "Don't let Mrs. Kaye direct the pageant. She'll ruin it just like she ruined *Peter Pan*."

I shrug a little.

"You know as well as I do that she *will* ruin it."

"Not my call to make, really." *What does he know?*

I'm relieved when a customer, some farmer in a Co-op Feed cap and overalls, lumbers in and Barry moves over to his booth.

I jump back and forth from Barry's seat to mine and almost make it to the third maze before a ghost ambushes me, the little fucker.

A harried-looking Mr. Denton grabs his briefcase, slides out of the booth, and charges out. Vernadell removes her glasses, rubs her eyes. She looks at me and says, "Swear to God, I think it's entirely possible that the Frosty Queen will be the ruin of both me *and* Hal Denton."

"Don't let that bean-countin' SOB wear ya down, Vernadell," offers Dennis Dickers.

"You're just pissed off 'cause he repossessed your Chevy," Vernadell retorts.

Dennis buries his face in his coffee mug.

"Hell, the man's just doin' his job," she continues. "To tell you the truth, I feel sorry for him. He believed in too many people in this town and, if anything, was too damn generous. Wish I had the money I owe him." She takes an aspirin bottle from above the grill, shakes out two, washes them down with a gulp of coffee.

Vernadell lives in the small apartment connected to the motel office. I remember she used to be married to Jesse, a mean drunk, but she kicked him out years ago. "When I dumped Jesse," she likes to say, "is when I became the Frosty Queen." They say she has a daughter who is grown and lives in Arizona or Nevada, but Vernadell never talks about her.

"Why I ever took on this grease pit I'll never know." She looks up at the RC Cola clock, its face shaped like a bottle top, which shows seven o'clock. "Arty, we're officially late," she announces, and heads out the front door.

"I'm comin', V."

7

As I park in front of the Legion Hall, alongside Verna-dell's white Datsun pickup and four other cars, I suddenly feel antsy about this meeting. Inside, the wood floor creaks under my Nikes and the members of the Centennial commit-tee look up.

"Arthur, must I remind you that we start at seven P.M. sharp?" Mrs. Fudge, committee chair, mayor, and my fifth-grade teacher, says in the same voice she used when I failed a pop quiz.

"Sor-ry, Mis-sus Fudge." I take my seat between Verna-dell and Gale Schneider, who's filing her long red fingernails. Gale, who is sporting a matching red hat and low-cut dress, is the wife of a rich hog rancher. Rumor has it she's had one of those face-lifts.

"You're just in time, Allen," Flea Jones says to me in his bullfrog voice. "We're about to vote on who's gonna direct the pageant."

"At our last meeting we discussed Beulah Mann's oldest boy, Mitchell, the big-time Hollywood movie director," Mrs.

Fudge says. "But he wants two thousand to do it. And we only have four thousand in the entire budget."

"I hear he makes pornographic films," Reverend Hanky says.

"Well, that oughta spice up the pageant," Vernadell huffs, snuffing out her cigarette in a yellow and green ceramic ashtray shaped like a sunflower.

"As a servant of the Word, I'm very concerned. And you all should be too." Reverend Cindy Hanky, minister at New Life Church, a nondenominational group of born-again Christians, petitioned her way onto the committee, pushing out the more traditional, soft-spoken ministers in town.

"Who knows, maybe he could get some real stars to be in it," Mrs. Fudge says.

Gale looks up from her nails. "Imagine Tom Selleck as Horace Harker."

"Joan Collins could play Mrs. Harker," Flea says lustily.

"Or Chesty Morgan," I mutter. Vernadell gets my reference and kicks me.

I'm comforted by the certainty that this meeting won't run late. Like everyone else in town, Mrs. Fudge is a *Dallas* fan, which means we'll be out of here not a minute later than ten till eight.

"Maybe he'll make a movie out of our pageant," Gale adds.

"Call it," Vernadell says, *"Nowhere over the Rainbow."*

"Those Hollywood types are all smut promoters and everyone knows the movie industry is run by Jews, the same people who killed our blessed Jesus," Reverend Hanky intones. "Besides, we don't need outsiders. There's more than enough good Christian talent right here in Harker City."

"Maybe we should agree to disagree," Larry—Mr. Offend No One—Larson says with raised eyebrows and a shrug.

How would I tell the story of Harker City? It would be an empty stage with a toilet on it. Someone—maybe Vernadell?—comes out, takes a crap, and bows. Applause, applause. Curtain.

"I suppose Carole Kaye will do it," says Mrs. Fudge. "And I'm sure we can get her on the cheap."

"Carole Kaye's a dope-smoking hippie," Reverend Hanky says. "And she don't attend church. . . ."

"And she ruined the last high school play," Gale adds.

"What do you think, Allen?" asks Flea, who always confuses me with my brother. "You were in her plays. Be honest. It won't get back to her."

"Uh . . . what if we have Mrs. Fudge direct it?" I say, just to stir things up.

Everyone looks at me as if I just told them Mrs. Fudge is carrying my child.

"Me?" Mrs. Fudge turns bright red.

"You directed me in the Thanksgiving pageant, remember?"

I say. "Dad said it was so realistic he completely forgot he was watching a bunch of fifth graders."

"Oh, I don't know." Mrs. Fudge blushes and fingers the back of her globe of curls.

"Well, no offense, Francine," Flea says. "But there's a big difference between a fifth-grade pageant and an epic event like this."

The discussion continues for the next few minutes. How did I end up being the youth representative for the Centennial committee? Mrs. Kaye nominated me because she figured she would direct the pageant and wanted to dictate what sort of show was chosen. Barry seconded my nomination because he thought I could see to it that he starred in it. Dad, hoping I could upstage Larry Larson, urged Mrs. Fudge to accept my nomination.

"I say we take this to a vote right now," Flea says.

"All in favor of asking Beulah Mann's son to direct the pageant for two grand, raise your right hand," Mrs. Fudge says.

All hands, except Reverend Hanky's, shoot up.

Mrs. Fudge pounds her damn gavel. "Motion passed."

"That does it!" Reverend Hanky slaps her hand on the red Formica tabletop. "I refuse to sit by and watch our community fall into the hands of Sodomites and Christ-killers. When Jesus returns—which is any day now—I want the record to show that I voted against the Hollywood degeneracy. I resign, effective immediately."

"So recorded," confirms Mayor Fudge.

Collective relief wheezes across the room as Reverend Hanky storms out.

"Thank God," Gale says, and pulls out a silver flask from beneath the table. "Now let's have some fun."

8

Driving out of town on Highway 76, to my other event of the night, it occurs to me that my life is loaded with obligations. I turn into the Von Boscom farm, where several cars—including Barry's baby-blue Chevy Nova—are parked in front of the sprawling ranch-style house.

In the living room, the members of Ichthus, our high school's born-again Christian club, are seated on the brownie-colored shag carpeting in a big semicircle facing Frank Von Boscom. The fish is the symbol of Christ, and *ichthus* means "fish" in Latin or Greek or something. I normally wouldn't waste my time with these dorks, but my fake girlfriend is deep into it. I normally wouldn't spend time with her either—but fate has decided otherwise.

"All the signs are right here, kids," Frank Von Boscom screams. He waves the Bible in his right hand. "Armageddon is coming. You can read it for yourselves in Revelations!"

Geraldine waves me over. I sit beside her, and she kisses me on the cheek, then grips my hand. Barely five feet tall, Geraldine Bottoms, whose inch-thick pancake makeup is unsuccessfully concealing her constellation of zits, has been experimenting with her hair since I saw her in school today. At this moment, her bangs stand on end, frozen in a wave-about-to-crest position over her forehead—kind of like the symbol on the Ocean Spray cranberry juice cocktail bottle. She rests her head on my shoulder. Love's Baby Soft emanates off her in waves.

"The Antichrist is coming," Frank booms. "Look what's going on in Libya right now. Couldn't that Colonel Qaddafi be the face of the devil himself?" He opens a book and reads, " 'The Master of Evil will wear a turban and arise from the east.' "

"Mrs. Stiles wears a turban," I whisper to Geraldine with a cocked eyebrow. "And she lives east of the railroad tracks."

Geraldine sniffs and says, "Hush."

It's amazing—Frank Von Boscom was once a fit, well-to-do farmer. The bank foreclosed on him a few years back, taking everything but his house and barn. Then his wife left him and he spent a month in bed, eating Pringles and drinking beer. Apparently that's when Jesus showed up and warned him the end of the world was a-comin'. Frank gained two hundred pounds and three chins and he started his own doomsday church in his basement, where he preaches to anyone who will sit still and listen.

"All right, kids," he says as he closes the book and dims the lights. "Tonight's video is the informative *The Late Great Planet Earth*. Take heed, my children." Frank takes his seat and, within minutes, is deeply snoring.

Immediately, Danny Carlson, a freshman A/V geek, switches the videotape to a porno: *Pink Clam, Part 11.* A few couples disappear into the bedrooms. Geraldine removes her gum and shoves her tongue down my throat. French-kissing Geraldine is what I imagine kissing Pierre must be like. It's well known that the Ichthus girls are easy.

Geraldine pushes me onto my back and is crawling on top of me. I'm politely stifling a grunt when Barry comes over to us and whispers: "Hey, have you read my script?"

"Shut up and leave us alone, Barry," Geraldine barks. "Can't you see we're trying to watch the movie?"

As we make out, I keep one eye on the TV, where a naked, giant-boobed blonde is getting it from behind by an Afro'd black man with a stallion-sized pecker. Geraldine feels my growing hardness against her leg and whispers, "Honey-bunch, let's go to the barn."

9

In the barn, we climb up the ladder and into the dusty-smelling hayloft. Our eyes adjust to the darkness and I, ever the gentleman, remove my jacket for Geraldine to lie on. As I settle in beside her, I hear the breathing of another couple somewhere up among the bales.

I push my hand through her hair, which is bristly as steel wool. "Watch the 'do, darlin'! It took me over an hour to get this look."

We make out for a century and, finally, Geraldine slips off her sweater and bra.

Mercury light comes through the vents, throwing patches of blue across her doughy stomach. Her crinkled nipples look like pepperoni slices.

For the next few minutes, we go through our kissing routine, and while I fumble with her tits, Geraldine pulls back and hisses, "Why don't you ever look at me when we're making out?"

"I *do* look at you."

"No, you *don't*. I want you to look me in the eyes when we're kissing."

We kiss a little more and she checks to see if my eyes are open. I'm trying, but they keep snapping shut.

She pulls away again and asks, "What's the matter?"

"Nothing."

"You're not putting anything into it. You act bored."

She gropes me and notices I'm completely limp.

"Arty, why don't you wanna make sweet love to me?" she whines.

"Oh, I do." I'm going to burn in hell for the zillion lies I tell. Very soon.

"Then why haven't we?" She snaps on her bra. "I'm the only virgin left in Ichthus and it's downright humiliating."

"But sex before marriage is a sin."

"We'll pray for forgiveness and it'll all be fine. Jesus is a forgiving Lord."

"But your dad ain't."

"Ya know, I'm starting to think you're one of those gay-wads."

She buries her face in her hands and sobs. I do feel awful, for both of us. I go to put my arm around her but she throws it off.

Then she lifts her skirt, slips off her panties, and splays herself out on her back like a starfish.

"Prove you love me, Arthur Flood," she says. "Make me a woman."

She lies there with her dimpled white thighs spread far apart. Her pubic hair reminds me of the Afro of the guy in *Pink Clam*.

"But I didn't bring any protection."

"If you loved me, you would want to get me pregnant," she cries. But when I go to touch her, she slaps my hand away. "Don't touch me! Take me home! Right now!"

God almighty.

10

We don't speak walking to the Stiff Wagon. The first thing Geraldine does is turn the radio dial to the Christian station. She sings along with Sandi Patty, something about how the Lord is her strength.

I'm beyond relieved to see the red pulsing light on the Harker City water tower come into view.

She repairs her makeup-smeared face in the rearview mirror. "The least you could do is buy me a hot fudge sundae."

Geraldine is *always* trying to get me to buy her food.

I drive to the Frosty. As I get out, Geraldine calls, "Extra fudge sauce and sprinkles, honeybun!"

I place the order with Darlene.

"Geraldine need something sweet?" Vernadell says from her booth, where she's reading Louis L'Amour and sipping coffee.

I drop my head and nod. "You have no idea."

"Don't be so sure about that." Vernadell just shakes her head and returns to her novel. I pay for the stupid sundae and ask Darlene to add some stupid sprinkles. I'm down to my last two dollars for the weekend and I'm more depressed than I care to measure.

Geraldine rolls down her window and I hand her the sundae. Not even a thank-you. Just rolls up the window.

I'm speeding toward Geraldine's house when she says, "Let's cruise while I eat my sundae."

I turn onto Broadway and thus we are cruising. About a dozen cars drag, among them Allen's Dodge Charger. Dragging Broadway is what most kids in Harker City do on Friday and Saturday nights, that or go to keg parties. The turnaround points are Clement's IGA parking lot at the north end and the U-turn spot in front of Mrs. Kaye's house on the south. I spot the blue glare of her TV through the living room window. We make the loop three times.

At the corner of Walnut and Broadway, I turn on my blinker.

"Not yet, sweetie," Geraldine says. "Go around one more time. For me."

Geraldine has the sundae good and hoovered by the time I park in front of her house, right behind her dad's police cruiser.

"I can never stay mad at you. I wuv you too much," she says, and hungrily kisses me. She tastes like fudge and peanuts.

She looks at me and says, "Good night, my Arty-schmarty."

"Right."

"And I know you love me too, don't you. Say it, Arty. Say you love me."

"I. Love. You." The temperature in hell just soared.

"Someday when we're married, with a big batch of kids, we'll look back on how silly we acted when we were in high school."

Maybe hell won't be so bad?

I'm dying to open the car door and push her the hell out.

"Tomorrow night," she says huskily. "And bring the protection."

Before I can respond, I'm choking on her tongue again and the front porch light comes on. Geraldine breaks off our kiss.

"My heart's set on it, Arthur."

Sheriff Bottoms steps out of the house in his undershirt.

"And I'd just hate to think what Daddy would do if you broke my heart."

She pecks me chastely on the lips and finally climbs out of the car. I squeal backward out of the drive as Sheriff Bottoms glares into my headlights.

11

I roll down the windows to get rid of her perfume. Drive downtown.

Sheriff Gerald Bottoms refers to Geraldine, his only child, as "the sunshine of my life." I've known that Geraldine has had a crush on me since junior high. She claims it's my blue-green puppy dog eyes that do it for her. I guess I'm not an awful-looking guy—no Rob Lowe or Tom Cruise, though. Anyway, I always successfully avoided Geraldine. Then, a couple of weeks ago, I was driving down Walnut when police cherries flashed in my rearview. I pulled over just west of the old Rock Island railroad tracks. Sheriff Bottoms swaggered up to my window, leaned in, and stared at me till I felt my balls leap into my stomach.

"Something wrong, sir?" I squeaked, appalled at the frightened image of myself reflected in his tinted glasses.

"Hot, ain't it?"

"Yes, sir, it sure is."

He reached into his shirt pocket, removed a container of Copenhagen, pinched out a wad, and stuffed it in his lower lip.

"There's a rumor goin' 'round that your brother is growing marijuana out at your granddad Kohl's place. You know the penalty for growing marijuana in this state?"

"No, sir."

"Up to ten years. I'm talking state prison, hard time."

"I can assure you, sir, the rumor's not true." My voice quavered as if I were riding a bucking bronco.

In response, he whirled, spat tobacco juice at the curb, then turned back to me. "By the way, son, my Geraldine don't have a date to the prom."

"Uh, that's too bad, sir."

He removed his tints and fixed me with his bloodshot gaze. "Tell ya what I'm gonna do. I'm gonna ignore that rumor 'bout your brother so long as you don't give me a reason to do otherwise."

That night, I asked Allen, who was high, of course, about the rumor.

"Why? You in the market?"

"I'm serious, Allen. Sheriff Bottoms asked me about it."

"Why'd he ask you?"

"His precious Geraldine. If I don't take her out, he's going to arrest your sorry ass. Now, is it true?"

"I plead the Fifth."

"Get rid of it, 'cause I am *not* going to date Geraldine Bottoms."

But it turns out I am. Oh, Lord, how I am.

Another reason I haven't broken it off with Geraldine is

Sheriff Bottoms' scary-ass temper. Last summer when he pulled over a drunk driver, the man puked on Sheriff Bottoms' boots. Bottoms, claiming self-defense, beat the guy till he begged for death.

Once, when the sheriff was a mere deputy, he shot a shoplifter in the aisle of the IGA. He's been known to rough up guys in jail, punch wetbacks, and shoot stray dogs from his cruiser, using the leash law as an excuse. After numerous complaints, he was investigated by the county attorney, Mr. Elden, for excessive violence. When the windshield of the attorney's car was shot out and the tires slashed, the case was declared officially closed.

12

It is 11:04 P.M. by the glowing clock of the Harker City Savings and Loan. I make a U-turn in front of Mrs. Kaye's house and flash my brights at her living room window. I then proceed past the railroad yard and the Co-op grain elevator and head out of town to the cemetery road, up the hill, and through the gate. The shiny faces of the upright gravestones reflect the lights of the town below, each marker flashing with eerie familiarity as I drive past. I park beneath the gigantic oak tree and turn off the engine. The Death Mobile sputters and coughs.

I crawl into the back and clear off the empty Dr Pepper cans, Snickers wrappers, and other junk before stretching the sheet out. Once the "bed" is ready, I climb back into the front seat and turn to the oldies station in Abilene. "Our Day Will Come" is playing, a song I happen to like.

I can see my whole town from up here. The water tower, the high school, the sloping rooftops, my house, the bank clock flashing 11:15 and 72 degrees. I can even make out the tip of the red neon cone atop the Frosty. Every single person I know lives within this little cluster of mercury lights.

Being here late at night always makes me feel more alive. Maybe because I'm surrounded by dead bodies. Most of the town's live ones, except for Vernadell, are asleep. I'm not dead and I'm not asleep. Arty Flood won't be doing his final countdown stuck in Harker City. Nuh-uh.

I've only been out of Kansas a whopping once, for less than an hour actually, when I rode with Dad to pick up a stiff at a nursing home in Missouri. But after my graduation, everything is going to change. Once I have my money from the Stileses, I'm driving to Colorado to see the Rockies. Then it's on to the Grand Canyon and the Petrified Forest. Think I might spend a few days checking out Las Vegas and, time permitting, Death Valley. Finally, Hollywood. See where they make the movies, and spend a week on the beach admiring those famous California girls. I'll sleep in the Death Mobile the whole way, to make my money last.

On June 18, a little over a month from now, my new job starts. I'm going to be working on a freighter called the *Murray* that leaves from Long Beach, California. I've already sent in my application, been accepted, and got my passport and visas in the mail. I read about the job in the classifieds of *Outdoor Life* magazine. It doesn't pay a lot, but I'll get to see the Fiji Islands, the Philippines, New Zealand, and Australia. Imagine that. I'll be gone for *six whole months*.

No one knows about my specific plans. Why? You could say my family are experts in finding reasons why a person shouldn't go after whatever it is he desires. For the don't-get-your-hopes-up Floods, passion is a dangerous thing that leads upstanding citizens to do irresponsible and embarrassing things. If only Cousin Sally hadn't up and quit her job at the post office to be a barmaid in New Orleans. New Orleans! With its drunken, immoral crowds and crime-ridden streets. Now look at her: thirty-five, unmarried, and without a pension plan. A life wasted. And then there's Dad's old high school pal Wilbur, who refused to marry the nice Schlesinger girl right next door and threw away a perfectly good career as a Farm Bureau agent to work as a scuba instructor in the Florida Keys. Word has it he votes Democratic now and has stopped going to church. We sure wouldn't want to be in his flippers come Judgment Day. The Flood philosophy: avoid risk at all costs, stick close to home, and if it's not fun it's probably good for you.

I'm also hoping that by the time I return in January, Mrs. Stiles will have the money from the Doggie Joggie order to send me to art school, like she's always promised.

The song ends, and Mrs. Kleinstadt's nightly appeal comes over the radio: "On the night of October third of last year, my son, Douglas, a senior at Harker City High, left a party at Harker City Lake and drove off in his car, and no one has seen him since. Douglas has short blond hair and hazel eyes. He is six foot one, weighs a hundred eighty-five pounds, and drives a '78 Cutlass Supreme. If you have seen my beloved son or know of his whereabouts, please call the Harker County sheriff's office. We are offering a two-thousand-dollar reward. Douglas, if you're listening, please come home. We miss you terribly."

I start to tear up and I turn off the radio. I look down the hill at the Kleinstadts' trailer home, right at the base of the grain elevator. The porch light is on, as it is every night. Most unfortunately, Doug was an asshole. In the eighth grade, he beat the crap out of me because I liked to draw. He even gave his girlfriend, Gina, a black eye. A real creep. Now a missing creep.

I speculate: what if Doug just got fed up with being a badass football player and moved to California or Mexico to start a new life? That would take guts, and I kind of reluctantly admire the guy for it. Even though his being gone is cruel beyond words to his mother.

Headlights appear and begin moving through the cemetery. I start to get hard. Moments later, her VW Bug pulls up and my drama teacher turns and stares at me.

13

We are lying naked side by side on the mattress in the back of the Death Mobile. My ears are still ringing from Mrs. Kaye's screeching when she came. The thing is, why don't I ever feel better after we do it? Every time, I swear that this is going to be the last. Then I get stupid—stupid and horny. So here I am, lying with Mrs. Kaye while Mom and Grandpa Flood are buried just yards away.

"You were late tonight," she says. "How come?"

"Couldn't get rid of Geraldine."

She picks at her hair. "You really like my new hairdo?"

"Sure. Looks great."

If I've learned one thing living in a beauty shop, it's that women never want to hear anything the teensiest bit negative about their hair.

"I did it for you, baby," she says. "Can you believe I first modeled for you six months ago tonight?"

I want to say, *Feels more like a life sentence.* Instead, I say, "Gosh, isn't that something?"

"Happy anniversary, darling," she says, and gives me a smooch on the mouth.

She raises herself on one elbow, reaches into a small plastic grocery bag, and hands me a Tupperware container. "I baked brownies, your favorite."

"Thanks, Mrs. Kaye—I mean Carole." I can never get used to her first name.

The edges of her mouth curling upward, she pops open the container, removes a warm, moist hunk, and places it between my lips. Mrs. Kaye does make the best brownies.

"I love to make you happy." She watches me eat. "I want to *always* make you happy."

The brownie lodges in my throat. I can't breathe or swallow. Panicked, I grip my neck.

"Oh, my God!" she yells. "Oh, my God!"

I sit up, trying to retch. Her hands pound my upper back. "Baby! Oh, my God, baby!"

A spasm of coughs dislodges the chunk. I swallow painfully and fall back, gasping.

"Oh, thank God." She throws her arms over my chest and squeezes. "I was so scared!"

From a thermos, she pours me some cold milk and watches me drink several cupfuls.

"What's the matter?" Mrs. Kaye says as she lightly strokes the back of my head. "You've hardly said a word tonight."

"Geraldine expects me to pop her cherry tomorrow night."

"So what's the big deal? Just screw the heifer."

She's quite the poet, my Mrs. Kaye.

"I . . . I just don't want to."

"Close your eyes and pretend it's me."

"I think I'm going to break up with her."

"You do that and Sheriff Bottoms will kill you. Besides, your relationship with that girl will kill any suspicions people might have about us."

Mrs. Kaye rolls over, takes a joint out of the plastic bag, and lights up. She expertly inhales from her doobie, and I find myself getting big again. With my foot, I unlock the back door and kick it open to let in some fresh air.

"So tell me," she says, exhaling smoke, "when do I start directing the Centennial pageant?"

"Sorry, Mrs. Kaye, they're gonna pay some big-shot Hollywood guy to do it."

She spins to me, her gray eyes full of hurt. "You stood up for me, didn't you?"

"Of course!"

"I don't believe this!" she says. "I've been nothing less than generous with my talent, and look what I get in return!"

She rants for the next ten minutes, eventually convincing herself that she never wanted to direct the pageant in the first place. I awkwardly pat her bare shoulder and try to figure out a way to get her out of my car.

A train whistles in the distance.

"Must be the midnight from Kansas City," I say, to make her realize how late it is.

She sits up and grabs her bra. "Dale's supposed to get back from Tulsa tonight."

Mrs. Kaye's husband, an army recruiter, is on the road all the time.

She slips on her Playtex Cross Your Heart and her blouse, then kisses me. "Happy anniversary, sweetie."

"Happy anniversary, Mrs. Kaye—I mean Carole."

I walk her to her car. And now here I lie staring at the torn fabric on the ceiling of my hearse. Mrs. Kaye's diesel engine turns over and rattles off, the sound of her tires crunching on the gravel fading away as a cool wind rustles the leaves in the oak tree and dries the last of the sex sweat from my body.

Believe it or not, slutty little me was a virgin until six months ago. What precipitated my fall from grace? It started with a notebook I had misplaced backstage during our school's production of *Barefoot in the Park*. When I sauntered into language arts class on Monday morning, Mrs. Kaye, who up till then had never shown particular interest in me, said, very innuendo-y, "I think I have something you'd like," and handed me the notebook.

I instantly felt my face redden and my hands and neck heat up. Despite the cover marked "Biology," the notebook was chock-full of drawings I had done of naked women—

facsimiles from my various special-interest periodicals. It was under a pencil drawing of the legendary Chesty Morgan that I saw Mrs. Kaye's handwriting, in her red grading ink: *Perhaps you should draw a real woman sometime. Need a model?*

What to make of this? Weeks passed. Around school I caught Mrs. Kaye glancing at me more and more, giving me a bit harder time in class, like calling on me when she knew I didn't know the answer to a question. I also noticed she was wearing more cleavage-exposing blouses and higher-cut skirts, and she was crossing her legs a lot. Then one afternoon, she passed back my book report. On the bottom of the second page she had written, *See me in the dressing room today at four. Bring your pad and pencil.*

At four o'clock sharp, I gingerly opened the dressing room door. And there was Mrs. Kaye reclining on the dusty props trunk, smoking a joint.

"Close the door," she commanded. I felt my heart and groin pounding.

With her half-mast eyes she peered at me through the veil of smoke for the longest time before uttering, "Don't you think it's time you drew me?"

And right then and there she stripped naked. I couldn't believe it. This was the first time I had seen a real woman in her very flesh. Breasts plump but well formed. Hips not firm but still sexy, and her black pubes were neatly trimmed.

For the next two hours she sat perfectly still on the props trunk while I sweated and sketched. Drawing a real completely naked human being—and not just some lady's big knockers out of a magazine—turned out to be a lot harder than I had expected, especially below the waist. My eraser was a nubbin by the time I finished. I thought the picture embarrassingly awful, with Mrs. Kaye's cranium entirely too large for her body, like one of those bobble-head dolls you see in the back windows of cars.

She motioned for me to show her the drawing. "Let me see."

"It needs work—"

She snatched it out of my hand. I expected a laugh, but instead she said, "You've captured my eyes perfectly."

Setting the drawing aside, she leaned forward, unzipped my fly . . . and I've been sucked in ever since.

A few months ago, after a romp that was particularly devastating to my car's shock absorbers, I asked Mrs. Kaye why she chose me out of all of the guys in school, and not some football player.

"When I saw the drawings you did of those women's breasts, I saw a curious, sensitive young man in need of an education," she said as she stroked my hair. "Now, haven't I taught you well?"

That explanation aside, I'm still not entirely sure why Mrs. Kaye does what she does with me. She says that I'm a good listener and that I make her feel young. And I know her husband's gone a lot, and that they argue when they are together. But I worry about what she'll do when I leave town. She's become pretty dependent on our . . . sessions, or maybe on me?

The mournful train whistle sounds again. I am lonely beyond words.

14

Broadway is deserted and not helping my state of mind. I head down to the Frosty.

Vernadell is ensconced in her favorite booth, reading Louis L'Amour's *Sitka*. Darlene watches a black-and-white Vincent Price horror movie on the small TV above the grill.

I pour myself a Dr Pepper at the fountain and sit at the Ms. Pac-Man machine. I'm about to drop a quarter in when I notice my all-time high score has been topped, by more than two thousand points!

"Hey, Vernadell?"

She looks over the rim of her little glasses.

"Who's the guy that beat my score?"

"Why d'you think it's a guy?"

This brings me up short.

"The only person to play that game since you were in here last was definitely a female," she says.

"Yeah? Who was it?"

"Never seen her before. She was tall, with black hair and blue eyes. Real pretty."

My pulse quickens. "You catch her name?"

She shakes her head.

"You talk to her?"

She shakes her head again.

"What do you know about her?"

She dog-ears the page and, with a cocked eyebrow, motions me over to her table. She leans forward and in a whisper says, "You best watch yourself, Arthur Flood. This is a real small town."

I shake my head, confused.

She holds up her bony, hardworking hand. "What you do is your business, young man. All I'm sayin' is, if you're gonna engage in that kinda behavior out in the cemetery, you best do it with one eye open."

The cowbell clangs, and Sheriff Bottoms ambles in and sits at the counter. I feel the nausea and panic rocket from my groin up to my eyebrows.

15

I'm in the cabin on the lake. It's just like before the fire, with the knotty pine walls and thick red carpeting. Dad, Carrie, Allen, and I are seated around the circular kitchen table; the Flood family coat of arms that Dad received as a gift from a coffin salesman stares down at us. Mom's at the stove in her pink apron, flipping pancakes. She's still young and beautiful, and wears her long light brown hair in a bun. I look out through the glass sliding doors and see the girl swimming up to the dock. Mom hands me a towel and tells me to invite her in. I walk outside and offer the girl the towel. She grabs my arm and shakes it.

"Wake up, son," she says in Dad's voice. "We've got work!"

Dad stands beside my bed. I roll onto my stomach to hide my morning wood.

"Elmer Kandt was taken to the Abilene hospital DOA," he says. "I need you to help Shirley prepare the chapel."

Somebody dies and my dad springs to life.

An hour and a half later, we are waiting in the living room for the call to pick up Mr. Kandt. Shirley, in her black dress, her black swelling hair moussed, checks her lipstick in the mirror above the TV. Allen and I sit on the couch in our good black suits. The hearse idles in the driveway. The chapel has been dusted, the embalming room prepared. Dad, also in a black suit, paces in front of the picture window that looks onto Broadway.

"Maybe they saved him?" Shirley asks.

"I heard Sheriff Bottoms say over the scanner that he was brought in cold," Dad answers.

"Doc Hayes is probably doing an autopsy," Allen says.

"Maybe the Kandts didn't request us," I say.

I feel the collective glare.

"We've buried all the Kandts," Dad says calmly. "The family's always been pleased with our services."

"Like I said, we're probably waiting on the autopsy," Allen says.

Then Dad stares out the window at the stunning sight of the Larsons' hearse creeping up Broadway.

Shirley, Allen, and I look to one another with pinched mouths and creased brows.

"This can't be," Dad says weakly. "I'm calling the hospital."

He dials the phone.

"Hello, this is Milton Flood. I was sorry to hear about Mr. Kandt's passing. Should I pick up the body?"

There is a long pause. Dad's mouth droops into a deep frown.

"I see. . . . Thank you." He hangs up.

For years, Dad didn't advertise, because he didn't have to. He was the only mortician in town. Then, three years ago, the Larsons moved to town from Florida. Dad still wasn't worried; he was the native son who offered quality embalming and funerals at fair prices.

But the Larsons' mortuary is part of a national chain called the Golden Rule. Their PR training course taught Larry Larson how to be a grade-A public ass kisser. He's a Shriner and a Jaycee, sings in the church choir, and is a volunteer fireman. His wife, Terry Anne, chairs the PTA and volunteers at the nursing home and hospice. Together, they formed Meals on Wheels and Carolers for Shut-ins. What better way to meet future clients? Dad, who's never had to have a knack for self-promotion, belongs only to the Harker City Odd Fellows.

In addition to having a new hearse and a fancier funeral home, the Larsons have a stretch limousine. Dad dismissed the limo as a gimmick, but I know that people in town love it. I guess it makes them feel like a movie star or a Kennedy when they're chauffeured to their loved one's final resting place. Dad was certain that the good folks of Harker City would eventually see through the Larsons' flashiness, but so far they have not. Everyone loves the Larsons, who are young and energetic and jog together down the center of Broadway in their matching velour jogging suits, waving to everyone. They parade their twin boys, Jerry and Larry Jr., at every event in town. Last year, the Chamber of Commerce even voted Larry citizen of the year.

Dad sings in the church choir now, volunteers at the senior citizens' center, and drives old ladies to their doctor appointments. The thing is, he's not comfortable doing any of it, and not because Dad isn't a generous guy. I'm not sure he will ever get over losing the families he and Grandpa served for three generations to a fancy-pants poseur like Larry Larson.

"Uh, Dad," I say, "want me to put the hearse back in the garage?"

He shakes his head. "I'll get it, son."

16

Around three o'clock in the afternoon, I'm sitting on the dock with Dad's old army binoculars. No sign yet of the Loch Ness Girl. If I hadn't seen her legs, I would be convinced she was a mermaid who lived at the bottom of Harker City Lake. A fresh Snickers bar lies on the dock's edge, but it's turning into chocolate soup in the merciless sunlight. I'm finishing the sketch I started of her last night.

A honk. Barry's Chevy Nova rolls to a stop behind the Death Mobile. He waves, climbs out, and walks over. I close my tablet.

"I've been driving all over looking for you," Barry says. "I can't believe you didn't tell me the big news."

"What big news?"

"Only that a big-shot Hollywood director is coming to direct the pageant! Do you phanthom what this could mean for my career?"

"Fathom."

Barry removes his Docksides, sits, and sticks his feet in the water. "Geez! Water's freezing!"

I'm not used to seeing Barry in the stark sunlight. "You

know, Bar, you could pass for an albino. Could land you a lot of interesting character roles."

He ignores me and rushes on. "Just last week, I was reading Gene Kelly's autobiography and he said that every successful show-business career comes down to one chance meeting, one big break that launches a star. Hey, you gonna eat that Snickers?"

"Don't even think about it."

He grabs my can of Pringles and starts munching.

"I believe in fate," he says, spewing Pringles bits into the water in his rhapsodizing. "And I believe there's a divine reason why a Hollywood director is coming to my town."

"Ugh. Don't talk with your mouth full."

He chews while I peer across the lake. What if she were to swim up now and see me sitting with Barry, who's in his waiter uniform and sporting his comedy/tragedy pin?

He looks over at the ruins of the old home place. "Hey, isn't this where your family used to live?"

"Why do you ask?"

"Doesn't it creep you out being here by yourself after what happened?"

"What is it you want, Barry?"

"You haven't said anything about my script. Did you read it?"

"Yep."

"It's great, isn't it?"

"It's a great excuse for you to sing your favorite show tunes. I have to ask, why would Mr. Harker sing 'Life Is a Cabaret'? And the ending is stolen right out of *The Music Man*. You even called it River City instead of Harker City."

"Oh, right. Well, it's a home-age."

"Homage."

He sips from my Dr Pepper bottle. "I was thinking, for the audition, I'd do the Stella scene from *Streetcar*. . . ."

"You'd make a terrific Stella." I'm not kidding.

"Stanley, you card!" He pokes me in the side.

I watch a flock of geese fly over the dam and come to a graceful landing near the cattails while Barry prattles on about playing Mr. Harker and empties my Pringles can.

"Heard you're going to deflower Geraldine tonight," Barry says.

"She tell Ladonna that?"

"I will not disclose my sources. So, is it true?"

"I don't want to talk about it."

"You should also know there's a rumor going around about you and Mrs. Kaye. I'm defending you, because I'm your best friend. But people *are* talking."

"Well, it's a damn lie."

"Whatever you say, boss." Barry pulls his feet out of the water, slips on his Docksides, and stands. "Stop by the Frosty later. We'll play some Ms. Pac."

"Sure."

17

At home, Shirley is in the kitchen dyeing Gale Schneider's hair. Dad, in the living room, slouches in his recliner and stares vacantly at a fishing show on TV. I step into Dad's little office off the chapel, shut the door, and dial the phone.

"Hello," Geraldine says on the other end of the line.

"Geraldine," I gasp into the receiver.

"Honeybunch? What's the matter?"

I fake four tortured coughs. "I'm sick as a dog. I have a fever and I just know I'm contagious."

"You were fine last night."

"It hit me this morning." *Cough-cough.* "I'm afraid we won't be able to go out tonight. I'm so sorry." *Cough-cough.*

"Shoulda figured you'd pull a stunt like this."

"There's nothing I want more than to be with you tonight, but I simply don't have the strength." *Cough-cough.* "Trust me, you don't want whatever it is I got."

"Well, this is just great. Just great," she says. "What am I s'posed to do tonight? I would've signed up to go to the Ichthus roller-skating party in Salina, but they've already left town. Guess I could come over and we could watch *The Golden Girls.*"

"I could never subject you to this grotesque illness." I rasp this as if these are my dying words. "I'm going to pass out the moment we hang up."

"Well, don't think for a second that you're going to get out of you-know-what. There's always next weekend. Wait!" she says. "Next Friday is prom. That's perfect! You'll be in your tux and I'll be in my new dress. We'll do it then. I have to call Ladonna and tell her the news. Bye." *Click.*

An hour later. I'm lying on my bunk studying the bite marks in the Snickers bar. Allen, on the bottom bunk, drags on his bong and tells me about how he just knows Renee is going to fall back in love with him. The Snickers bar is starting to melt in my fingers. I climb down, put it back in the fridge, climb back up.

"Forgot to tell you," Allen says. "About that new girl you were askin' about yesterday."

I lean over my bunk.

"I don't know if it was her or not, but I saw some hot girl, who wasn't from here, go into the library."

"When?"

"This morning, 'round eleven."

When I get to the library, the front door is locked. Through the glass, I see Mrs. Beavers, our blue-haired librarian, at the checkout desk. I knock. She mouths the words "We're closed." I knock again. Again, she mouths: "We're closed." More knocks. She sighs, walks around the desk, and unlocks the door. She peers at me through her thick glasses.

"We close at four o'clock on Saturday," she says.

"I just have a quick question," I gasp.

"Who is this?"

"Arty Flood, Mrs. B."

"You better be here to return *A Night to Remember*."

"I lost that book back when I was in the seventh grade."

"You don't want me to call your father and tell him you stole a book."

This is the reason I avoid the library.

"Look, a girl came in here this morning. . . ."

"Who?"

"That's what I'm asking you. I don't know her name. She's not from here. She's tall, long dark hair, blue eyes. . . ."

"Charla Klobes."

"Charla's short and blond."

"You must mean the Reader."

"The Reader?"

"She's read almost everything in here, except for the romance novels. And she returns books on time, unlike some people I know."

"What's her name?"

"Zelda."

"Zelda what?"

"Fitzpatrick, I believe."

"Do you know where she lives?"

"Why do you need to know?"

"Because I have something of hers I urgently need to return."

"Her address is on the information card inside but we're closed."

"May I please see the card?"

"I have to get to Mass. Come back on Monday."

She closes the door. I block it with my Nike. "It's real important, ma'am."

"Just what's the emergency?"

"I . . . found her catechism book at the Frosty Queen."

"Oh. Well, in that case . . ."

She lets me in, and I follow her to the checkout desk. I haven't been inside this library in probably five years. It smells the same: musty books and Lemon Pledge.

Mrs. Beavers goes through her Rolodex, removes a card, and hands it to me.

Zelda Fitzgerald. Address: *Bellevue Hospital, New York City.* Phone: 911.

Her handwriting is angular and hard, not curlicue cursive like that of the girls around here. I wonder why Mrs. Beavers let her get away with this address, then I remember that she's nearly blind.

She snatches the card from me. "I really must get to Mass."

"May I see the last book she checked out?"

"Arthur . . ."

"Please. Then I'll go."

She sighs and examines the three books in the book bin, pulling them to her face.

She hands me *My Ántonia*. I remove the card from the checkout sleeve: *Zelda Fitzgerald*.

"Do you know when she's coming in next?"

"Her next book is due back in two weeks."

"I want to check this out."

"Not until you return *A Night to Remember*."

"It's for Shirley. She wants to read a good book tonight."

She stamps the circulation card and hands back the book. "You better find that *A Night to Remember*."

On the walk home, I flip the pages in search of clues as to who this Zelda is. Suddenly, I recognize the sound of a certain approaching car engine. Geraldine's Chevette is rattling up Broadway! I duck into Franklin True Value Hardware just in the nick of time. Way too close.

"There you are." My sister walks up the aisle with two cans of varnish in her arms. "Why are you sweating?"

"Uh, just out getting some exercise."

Carrie, who is almost thirty, has had the same hairstyle since she was sixteen: parted down the dark-rooted middle and majestically feathered. With her caked mascara and lined pink lips, she hopes to look like a Kansas version of Farrah Fawcett. On her sweatshirt two teddy bears hug above the caption FRIENDS ARE FRIENDS FOREVER IF THE LORD'S THE LORD OF THEM.

"I just called Allen," she says, and sets the cans on the counter. "We're having a family meeting tonight at six. My place. You *will* be there."

Yet another obligation.

18

It's twenty after six and raining when I park in front of my sister's small pink house with white gingerbread trim and purple heart-shaped window shutters. The attached two-car garage has been converted into her home business, Carrie's Christian Crafts and Cuddlies. Allen's ten-speed leans against the front porch. He *never* drives his beloved Dodge Charger in bad weather.

The place reeks of cinnamon and nutmeg potpourri. Carrie is big on faux Victorian furniture, cloth bunnies, demonic rag dolls, and embroidered pillows that say HOME IS A SCHOOL WHERE THE HEART LEARNS TO LOVE and LOVE ABOUNDS IN SMALL TOWNS.

At the dining room table, Carrie hot-glues a bonnet onto the head of a wooden goose in a frilly dress while Allen sits across from her and sips a Coors. He pretends to be listening, glancing furtively at the baseball game on TV in the living room. Carrie's big, silent, bushy-moustached husband, Rod, is sprawled on the couch in front of the TV. He's *always* there.

"I've called this family meeting because I'm worried about Daddy," Carrie announces.

I am drawing Carrie in my notebook on my lap. It's impossible to exaggerate my sister, the poster child for overstatement.

"You know he's been real down in the dumps lately. And his not getting Mr. Kandt this morning was another terrible blow." The tears well up; they always do. She sets down her glue gun, grabs a Kleenex, and wipes her eyes, smearing their vibrant purple coating.

Once, I saw Carrie cry over *The Dukes of Hazzard,* the episode when Bo and Luke got into a fight. It was the Dukes at their most sensitive and vulnerable.

"So," Carrie says, blowing her nose, "we need to figure out how we can cheer him up."

"Maybe we could knock off the old farts who've prearranged their funerals with him," I suggest. Allen cracks up.

"That's not funny! Get serious! All Daddy does is sit in that chair all day and watch TV."

I can't help pointedly glancing at Rod lying in front of their Zenith nineteen-inch TV.

Between sobs, Carrie utters, "It just breaks my heart. . . . We have to get him to *believe* in himself again."

"Maybe we oughta get Shirley's opinion," Allen says.

"No!" Carrie says. "This should stay in the real family."

You'd think that since both Carrie and Shirley are big Bible-thumpers, they'd be best friends, but that is most assuredly not the case. Carrie views Shirley as the woman who "moved in" on Dad. And Shirley sees Carrie as a weak spoiled brat, a troublemaker. Hardly sisters in Christ.

"I thought we could send him on one of them Carnival cruises," Carrie says. "You know, get him out of town, get his mind off things, so he'll come back refreshed. But you know Daddy, he'd never take a gift like that from us."

"True," says Allen.

"None of us has enough to send him any further than the Frosty Queen anyway," I say.

"I suggested he go to church with Rod and me, but he declined."

Good. My dad is still sane.

"I've volunteered to spice up the funeral-home decor," she says, "so Dad can compete with the Larsons, but he's not interested in that either."

I picture Carrie painting the funeral chapel baby pink, with a paisley border, and hanging an embroidered sign reading DEATH IS WHEN THE HEART STOPS above a casket.

"Arty, I want you to make sure Daddy gets a part in the Centennial pageant," she says. "If he gets involved in the community more, he'll feel better and make more business connections."

Whenever I get together with my brother and sister, I become the little brother, a jokester no one takes seriously but everyone orders around.

"Look," I say, "there's nothing I can do about the fact that the Larsons have stolen Dad's business."

"If Mommy were alive, she could pull him out of this. Mommy was always there for Daddy. She understood him," Carrie says, and here come the tears. "I miss Mommy so much. She loved us all. . . ."

"Mommy was a drunk," I say.

"What a horrible thing to say about your own mother." Carrie's bottom lip quivers. "You ought to be ashamed."

And actually, I am.

19

"**L**ook!" Carrie shouts. "On TV! Rod, turn it up!"

On the tube, some cheesemeister with a Joker smile addresses the camera: "Do you feel frustrated? Depressed? Has life been a disappointment? I'm Pat Powers, author of the bestselling *Power People, Power Results*. I've transformed millions of lives and I can do the same for you. Come to the Topeka Civic Center, Friday, May 13th. Let me, Pat Powers, put the power back in your life!"

Pat Powers runs around a stage, waving his arms, while his rapt audience hysterically cheers. "Tickets are going fast. Order now!"

"Rod, call and see how much it costs!" Carrie turns to Allen and me. "It could be a sign from God. Pat Powers may be just what Daddy needs."

"That phony windbag?"

"Shut up, Arty! Pat Powers is the top motivational speaker in America today. A friend of mine went to hear Pat Powers. It changed her life."

"What friend?"

"A friend."

"Who?"

"Darlene Dickers," she murmurs.

"Darlene Dickers! Pat Powers obviously did wonders for her. Why, at this very moment, she's cleaning the grill at the Frosty."

Rod hangs up the phone. "Tickets are a hundred and fifty."

"So, what do you say we each chip in fifty?" Carrie gives us a smile.

"You've got to be kidding," I say.

"You got a better idea? Daddy could be out of business by the end of this year."

"But that might be the best thing for him," I say. "He could finally leave town, like he's always wanted. . . ."

"I can't believe I'm hearing this!" she gasps.

"Geez, Arty, you don't mean that," Allen says.

"Dad wanted to be a doctor, not a mortician, but when he knocked Mom up—"

"That's enough!" Carrie shoots out of her chair, veins pulsing in her temples, and points to the door. "Get out! Right now!"

"I'm going!"

"Oh, now, Arty didn't mean that," I hear Allen say as the screen door slaps shut behind me.

I gun the Death Mobile and peel out. At home, Dad is slumped in his La-Z-Boy, watching a Dick Clark blooper special while Shirley knits an afghan on the sofa.

"Arty," Shirley says, "Geraldine stopped by a little while ago looking for you."

"Thanks." I head for the stairs, then stop and turn around. "Say, Dad, would you want to go with me to the Frosty for a Coke or something?"

He shakes his head. "Not tonight, son."

"Sure."

Upstairs, I fall into my bunk and open *My Ántonia*. If I ever meet the Loch Ness Girl, I *will* have something to talk about. I haven't completed a novel since I had to give a report in sophomore English, and even that book, *The Count of Monte Cristo*, I skimmed. *My Ántonia* starts out a little slow. It's about this boy, in the last century, who goes to live on a farm in Nebraska. I soon grow to like this kid and the harsh world he's thrown into, and I read until almost five in the morning— a personal record.

20

Monday, after school, I tap on the Stileses' office door.

"Come in," I hear Mr. Stiles say.

I open the door and peer into the haze. Mrs. Stiles smiles catatonically into space from behind her design table. Mr. Stiles hunches over an open box of powdered doughnuts while two cigarettes smolder in his beanbag ashtray beside a pile of bills. Pierre sleeps at the feet of the mannequins.

"What is it, Arty?" Mr. Stiles says.

I step inside. "I, uh, wanted to talk about my thousand dollars. . . ."

He bites into a doughnut. White powder sticks to his lips and chin.

"I know you said you'd pay me in full on my last day. But I was wondering if maybe I could get it early."

"Let me see what I can do," he says with his mouth full.

"I'd appreciate it. You can just add last week's paycheck to it."

"Finish sweeping out the cutting room?"

"Sure did."

"Then why don't you take Pierre out for some fresh air?"

Soon I'm driving to the lake with Pierre. It's a cloudless scorcher. I asked Mr. Stiles for the money because I'm paranoid that Mrs. Kaye's husband might find out about us and I'll have to split before graduation.

No sign yet of the Loch Ness Girl. Pierre sniffs for frogs in the cattails while I stretch out on the dock in the warm sunlight. I'm about to drift off to the sound of a dragonfly when Pierre barks at something in the water. I'm instantly wide awake. The sun reflecting on the lake is so bright I can't make anything out. More splashing. I place my hand across my forehead and squint. In the glare, I see a figure swimming toward me. My pulse skitters, my palms sweat. Yes! It's her. I swallow hard and sit straight up.

She is swimming up to the dock, she is grabbing hold of the wood with her long fingers, she is lifting her goggles and peering at me with those blue eyes. I feel a prickling in the pit of my stomach and I open my mouth, but my throat tightens and closes. I'm frozen. I'm mute. Pierre runs over and licks her chin. Her irresistible lips curve into a smile and she giggles—the most adorable sound I've ever heard.

Pierre's long pink tongue laps the water from her forehead and freckly, wrinkled nose. She closes her eyes and continues to laugh. I'm a goner.

Suddenly, she disappears under the surface. I leap up and peer into the dark water. Pierre barks like crazy. Then she pops back up, her eyes shut, and lets Pierre lick the new layer of water from her face. Oh, to be Pierre right now.

I stammer for a moment. "Pierre, he—he sure likes you" is the sparkling line that finally escapes my witless lips. And my voice—it sounds so high-pitched and strained.

Pierre falls onto his back and she rubs his tummy. Her wrists are delicate and her finger movements are the most sensual thing I've ever seen. What would happen if I lay on my back and stuck my legs in the air? Should I go for it?

What to say? Sweat drips down my nose, and my hands clench with resolve.

"You're not from around here, are you?" Now my voice is far too low! *God, help me to not screw this up.*

The girl's eyes tilt from Pierre to me and she kicks off from the dock. She floats on her back and I take in her bikini-clad body. Her breasts aren't huge but they're smooth and a perfect fit for my hands, her nipples outlined in the wet fabric. Her waist is slim, her hips nicely curved. Should I jump in?

She swims back again and pats Pierre's tummy some more.

"My name's Arty. What's yours?" *Please, God, steady my goddamn voice.*

She shrugs her slender shoulders, lowers her goggles, turns, and swims effortlessly across the lake.

But the Loch Ness Girl has underestimated Arthur Flood.

21

I jump into the Cadaver Caddy with Pierre and race around the lake road, my car rocking and skidding on the gravel. I keep a constant eye on her as she swims toward the other side. I slow down when I come across a 1950s boy's bicycle leaning against a tree. A big orange towel hangs from one of the handlebars, a pair of cutoffs on the other.

I wait on the shore as she swims toward us. Pierre jumps into the water to meet her. She removes her goggles and looks startled.

"Imagine running into you here," I say with a smile, and hand her the orange towel.

She steps out of the water slowly. Taller than I thought. I try not to gape at her shiny, wet body while she dries off.

"Actually, Pierre insisted we come over."

She tilts her head and knocks the water from her right ear.

"Does the swimmer have a name?"

"Lucia," she says with an accent of some kind, then wrings the water from her long black hair.

"A pleasure to meet you, Lucia." *Lu-ci-a.*

She removes her shorts from the handlebars and slips in

one slender, tan leg after the other. I look away, to prevent further embarrassment. When I turn back to her, she's towel-drying her hair. Why does she sign out her library books as Zelda Fitzgerald? Is this the same woman? She eyes the Death Mobile.

"Don't worry," I say. "There are no clients in it."

She smiles. "Too bad."

Her pronunciation sounds European. French, maybe? Wait, did she just say what I think she said?

"Where are you from?"

"Italy," she says, and scratches Pierre's head while he rubs against her leg.

Italy. The blue eyes, the sexy accent, the graceful way she moves—how can such a perfect human specimen appear in muddy ol' Harker City Lake? Did God drop her in there from heaven? Every second of my life has led up to this crucial moment. Never have I felt so alive, and so petrified.

"You're a long way from Italy," I squeak.

I might as well have slapped my knee and said, *Well, shucks, sweetheart, you're a real 'Eye-talian, ain't ya?*

She kneels down and rubs her nose with Pierre's.

"Can I give you a lift?" I ask.

"I have my bike." Mmm, that sexy accent.

"There's plenty of room for your bike in the back."

She throws me an uncertain look.

"Pierre doesn't bite and neither do I." I grin. "Besides, how often do you get to ride in a hearse?"

"Only if I drive." She says this with a serious expression.

"Uh, okay."

She stands. *Thank you, Jesus!* I run around and swing open the driver's door for her, she falls in behind the wheel, and I gently close the door behind her. Lu-ci-a is in my car! Lu-ci-a is in the Death Mobile! I fetch her bike and stuff it in the back, where I see the white Tupperware container that holds the brownies Mrs. Kaye made for me. I forgot all about them.

22

I climb in after Pierre. Lu-ci-a is behind the wheel, holding the drawing I did of her with the caption "Waiting for the Loch Ness Girl."

"You drew this?"

I nod.

"*Bella.*"

"Thanks."

She sets the picture on the dusty dashboard and I'm struck by how filthy the car is. Smashed pop cans, Snickers wrappers, and my drawings are everywhere. "Sorry about the mess."

"Yank tank," she says, and taps the steering wheel.

"She's kind of hard to start," I say. As I reach over, shove the gearshift into neutral, and turn the key in the ignition, my left arm brushes her thigh. She smells kinda froggy from the lake. I suddenly love the smell. So natural. So sensual.

On the second attempt, the engine kicks in. She presses the gas pedal and we jolt forward.

"The accelerator is a little sensitive," I say as I lean back.

We bounce down the gravel road, a little too fast, but I say nothing. I switch off the CB before Dad calls and embarrasses me.

She reaches down and picks up the CB mic. "Boss Hogg, this is Daisy Duke."

It sounds hilarious with her Italian accent. She drops the mic to the floor.

"You watch *The Dukes of Hazzard* in Italy?" I say over the wind and crunching gravel.

"No, here."

I'm about to offer to take her to the Frosty when I remember I'm broke.

She takes the curve by the spillway faster than I ever have. Maybe her dad is a race car driver.

"How do you like Kansas?" I say, and glance at her. She looks smaller and more vulnerable behind the giant steering wheel. Her hair, fast drying in the wind, is more brown than black, with a natural curl. The skin around her eyes looks as if she never wears makeup. It's rare to see girls go without makeup around Harker City.

She flies past the stop sign, then fishtails onto the blacktop highway. I watch as the speedometer climbs to seventy . . . seventy-five . . . eighty. . . .

"Kansas must be a lot different than Italy," I offer.

She switches on the radio and jacks up the volume. It blares, "We built this city on rock and roll." She sings along.

The speedometer hits ninety! My drawings are flying everywhere and the Death Mobile shimmies like an old washing machine.

"I'm afraid my car is a little out of alignment." The music drowns out my voice, which shakes like Katharine Hepburn's.

Pierre crawls onto the floor and curls around my feet. I switch off the radio.

"You might wanna slow down." My voice is staccato. "Police on this road."

She slows—thank God—and whips onto a gravel road.

"I've always wanted to go to Italy. Pompeii sounds awesome."

She has the car back up to seventy and we're shaking and rattling again. The sound of flying, crunching gravel is deafening. The fence posts blur, they're going by so fast.

"Do you drive much in Italy?"

She shakes her head.

My hands sweat. She's driving at speeds a 1965 hearse is not designed to go, on roads she knows nothing about. I think about all the people Dad buried who were killed on gravel roads.

"Cars flip easily on gravel," I say.

She honks the horn, sticks her head out the window, and hollers something I can't make out. This woman is crazy.

Ahead is a curve on a hill. She's going way too fast.

"You might want to slow down," I say, and press my foot on an imaginary brake.

We crest and are airborne. We scrape bottom coming down. My head hits the roof. Suddenly, Pierre is in my lap.

She laughs and honks the horn.

"Look, I'm glad you're enjoying yourself—"

A hay truck pulls out in front of us from a side road.

"Shiiiit!" I grip the dashboard. She hits the brakes, but we don't stop. We slide on the loose gravel, careening sideways toward the truck. I feel the car lifting. I see my funeral. Larry Larson is gloating as he dumps my mangled, decapitated body into the casket.

We don't flip. The car skids to a stop inches from the hay truck. We sit, breathless. Gravel dust blows in the windows.

"Sorry," she says.

I'm too dazed to say anything. Pierre whimpers. She coughs dust.

At a sane speed, we head down the road in silence. I am pissed off at how she's treated my car. If there's any damage, she'll damn well pay for it. She finally parks in front of a mailbox marked R. HOLTZ and throws the car into park.

"Thank you for the ride. *Arrivederci*, Pierre." She pats him on the head. "*Arrivederci*, Arturo."

She climbs out.

I unload her bike, then watch her ride up the long driveway to a white wood frame house with a red barn and detached garage. I recognize this place—it's the Christmas tree farm. It was a family tradition to drive out here with Dad, Mom, Carrie, and Allen to select our tree. A nice old man in overalls, who lived in that house, would chop it down, wrap it in chicken wire, and tie it to the roof of our station wagon. After Mom died, Dad bought an artificial tree, and we haven't been back since.

Lucia stops, turns around, smiles, and waves. I wave back weakly, simmering and dazed.

23

"All you need to know about history is that America has never lost a war," Coach Hass, the dumbest and laziest teacher in school, says. He "teaches" sitting at his desk while he oils and winds his fishing reel. Today's lecture is "How America Beat the Commies and Won the Vietnam War."

In my notebook, I caricature Coach Hass: I attach his buzz-cut, unibrowed, Neanderthal head onto a ballerina's body.

On my right, Geraldine highlights her zipper Bible. My name, in hearts, is written all over her notebook. On my left, Barry does some jock's algebra homework. Barry is so consumed with being liked that he does all the football players' homework. They don't even have to threaten him into doing it.

Coach Hass lumbers over to the TV and VCR in the corner. "All right, people, we're going to watch an educational film. Turn your chairs around and face the TV." He turns out the lights.

The Kansas City Chiefs versus the Green Bay Packers lights up the screen. We watch at least three tapes of old football games a week. When Coach Hass heads outside for a cigarette, Kristy Lynn Kline and her boyfriend, Kevin Schmidt—the popular couple—start making out. Geraldine leans over and whispers to me, "I'm living for prom night."

I have just three weeks left at Harker City High. People keep telling me that the high school years are the best of your life. I'm betting my whole future on them being dead wrong.

Next hour, dramatic arts class. My fellow classmates and I are being treated to Barry and Mrs. Kaye's performance of a scene from *A Streetcar Named Desire*. If Stanley Kowalski were an eighteen-year-old fruit, then Barry's performance might be convincing. Mrs. Kaye, with the phoniest southern accent ever, plays Blanche DuBois. If you're wondering why Mrs. Kaye and not one of her female students is performing, it's because, as she claims, "it's important you people study a real professional."

Mrs. Kaye goes out of her way to ignore me in class. I never get anything over a B on papers, and she rarely calls on me.

"Western Union?" Mrs. Kaye drawls into the prop phone. "Yes! Ah want to— Take down this message! 'In desp'rate, desp'rate circumstances! Hep me! Caught in a trap. Caught in—' Oh!"

Barry's skinny Mr. Pretzel arms, protruding from a white

sleeveless undershirt, struggle to take the phone from her when the bell rings. Curtain! Applause, applause.

I spend the better part of the rest of the day in the library, feverishly memorizing facts about Italy.

After school, I head to the lake but when I see that Lucia's not there, I drive to the farm. I step onto the front porch and knock on the door, my hands sweating and my heart pounding. The door behind the screen door is open, but I can't see much inside. It smells like my great-aunt Alma and uncle Vernon's house: mothballs, coffee, and chewing tobacco.

A large, familiar-looking, gray-headed man, his face and neck creased by years in the wind and sun, peers out at me from behind the screen door.

"May I help you?" he says in a booming voice.

"I'm looking for Lucia."

He presses his face to the screen and squints. "Who?"

"She might go by Zelda."

He leans on the screen door and looks at me suspiciously. "You're zero for two."

An awkward silence. I shuffle my feet.

"Is there an Italian girl staying here?"

"Nope."

"Right. Well, sorry to bother you."

"What's your name?"

"Arty Flood."

"You must be Milton's youngest. You're not here on official business, I hope." He motions toward the hearse with his head.

I smile at this.

"How is your old man?"

"He's good, thanks."

"Was the fastest runner in school, Milton was. Broke the hundred-yard-dash record his sophomore year."

I nod and try to imagine Dad having the energy to walk a hundred yards.

"Now, 'bout this girl," he says, leaning forward. "Y'sure she's Eye-talian?"

"She said she was. . . ."

"Where'd you meet her?"

"The lake."

He nods knowingly, unlatches the screen door, and invites me inside with a tilt of the head.

The living room holds a large pea green sofa and a console TV in the corner. Except for a cuckoo clock, the place feels manly and sparse.

"Vanessa!" he calls up the stairs.

Vanessa? What if this is the wrong girl?

"Yeah?" a girl's voice answers.

"You've got company!"

"Be right down." No Italian accent.

"I was just about to have some iced tea," he says. "Y'want some?"

"Thanks," I say.

I follow him into the kitchen. The round-topped white refrigerator, aqua-colored walls, and chrome dinette are right out of the fifties.

"I probably woke her," he says, and pours two iced teas. "She keeps strange hours, that girl. No schedule whatsoever. Stays up all night reading. She'll wake up at two or three in the afternoon and go for a swim or take pictures. What a life."

I thank him for the tea. It's strong, almost bitter, and bracingly cold.

"I ain't complaining," he says, and takes a giant gulp of tea. "She keeps this place spotless. Not a bad cook, neither. I'll sure miss her when she leaves."

I hear feet on the stairs.

"Uncle Roger?"

"In here, hon."

Sure enough, you-know-who saunters into the kitchen, barefoot, wearing cutoff jeans and an oversized black T-shirt. Her hair is staticky and there are pillow creases across her face. Her eyelids have that heavy I-just-woke-up look.

"Hey, Arty," she says, without an accent.

"Hi."

She pours herself a glass of iced tea.

"This your Italian girl?" Roger asks.

"That'd be her."

Mr. Holtz gives Vanessa a disapproving look. She shrugs

and sips her tea. Mr. Holtz drains his glass in one swig and puts it in the sink.

"I got chores. Good to see you, Arty." I shake his thick, callused hand. "Tell your old man hello from Roger Holtz."

"Will do, sir."

24

She sits beside me at the dinette, drumming her fingers on the red Formica tabletop. "Okay, so my name isn't Lucia and I'm not from Italy."

"No shit?"

"Don't be angry."

"I'm not angry. Being made a fool of is my favorite pastime."

I had to buy in to her act, had to memorize all those stupid statistics about Italy, had to dream about the two of us riding in a gondola through the canals of Venice. All for a damn liar.

"I wasn't trying to make fun of you—"

"And your Italian accent, very impressive."

"I thought I'd never see you again," she said. "Besides, you have to admit Lucia from Italy is more interesting than Vanessa Said from Marin County."

"Sure."

She raises her right hand and looks at me. "I swear my name *is* Vanessa Said and I *am* from San Rafael, California."

"And I'm Dmitry Smirnoff from Moscow."

"You don't believe me."

"Should I . . . Lucia?"

She opens her mouth, then closes it, and levels those blue almond-shaped eyes at me. "I give you my word I'll never lie to you again."

"And your word is supposed to mean something to me?"

"Look, I'm sorry. I *really* am. What more can I say? May God strike me dead if I ever lie to you again."

I taste my iced tea, bite into an ice cube. It feels good making her squirm.

"I'm glad you stopped by," she says.

"Oh, this isn't a social call," I say. "I'm here because you broke the axle on my car yesterday."

She covers her mouth with her hand.

"It's gonna cost eight hundred dollars to fix it."

She shakes her head and mutters through her fingers, "I'm *so* sorry."

"Gotcha." I smirk and slap my right hand on the Formica. "Now we're even."

She shoves my right shoulder, those lips stretch into a grin, and I begin to lose all my resolve.

"Where's Pierre?" she asks.

"At his home. My bosses' dog."

She stands and slides back her chair. "Let's go sit on the porch."

Her bare feet smack on the hardwood floor. The screen door bangs shut behind us as we step out on the front porch.

Fishing in her back jeans pocket, she extracts a skinny brown joint. "It's not what you think. It's called a bidi. An Indian cigarette. Want one?"

I shake my head.

She lights up as she settles on the top step. I sit beside her. Those tanned legs. *Mmm-mmm.*

"You're looking at me funny," she says.

"Guess I'm surprised you smoke."

She shrugs. "Why?"

" 'Cause you swim so much."

"Can't I do both?"

"You just hit me as the health nut type."

"That kind of nut I am not."

Stretching out my legs, I lean back and rest on my elbows. "Just what is it you do out here, aside from impersonating Italians, swimming, and smoking stinky cigarettes?"

"I go to my sessions in Topeka."

"Sessions?"

"At Menninger's. You know, the loony bin."

I throw her a look. Dad thought of sending Mom to Menninger's for treatment but he couldn't afford it.

"I swear to God I'm not making this up," she says. "I'm certifiably crazy."

"Oh, I believe that wholeheartedly. It's the Menninger's part that I'm having trouble buying."

"I promised you no more bullshit."

"So why're you living on a farm so far from Topeka?"

"I'm an outpatient. I'm staying with my uncle Roger."

"He's your real uncle?"

She nods. "My mom grew up here. You live in Harker City?" she asks.

"Only for a few more weeks."

"Y'mind if I hitch a ride? Have to return some library books. We can put my bike in the back, so you won't have to drive me home."

I can't find a worthwhile reason to say no.

She takes a final drag on her cigarette, flicks it, and runs into the house. "Be right back!"

I shove her bike in the rear of the Autopsy Auto and wait for her, all stirred up inside. Am I a fool? An errand boy? She emerges from the house in flip-flops, an expensive-looking camera swinging from her neck, carrying a stack of books.

She leans in my window. "Scoot over, I'll drive."

"Not a chance," I say as I stare straight ahead and start the engine.

She sprints around the front of the car to the passenger side, moving with deerlike grace.

"What's the camera for?" I ask.

"Maybe I'll find something worth photographing," she says. She drops into the passenger seat and pulls the door closed.

"In Harker City? Best of luck." I shift into drive and we're off. Her long brown hair blows in all directions.

She opens my notebook and looks at the drawing I did of her.

"Can I have this picture?"

"No." I snatch the notebook from her and toss it in back.

"Meant what I said yesterday," she says, and places her bare feet flat on the dusty dashboard. "I think you're a gifted illustrator."

"Thanks."

"Where'd you learn to draw?"

"My mom taught me a few things."

She aims her camera at me and clicks.

"No pictures of me," I say. I roll up my window so that she can hear me over the wind. "Why do you go to Menninger's?"

"Told you, I'm crazy."

"But why Menninger's? California's got to have plenty of nuthouses."

"Menninger's is the closest thing there is to a Ralph Lauren nuthouse. That's what's important to my parents. Pedigree, labels. I only agreed to it because it's far away from my parents, and besides, I love Uncle Roger. He's a sweet old guy who lets me do my own thing."

We drive past the old Chief Drive-in and she snaps a picture of the marquee.

"Your parents rich?" I ask.

"They like to appear richer than they are."

"How long you been going to Menninger's?"

"Let's see . . . I started two weeks after my accident, which was in late March."

"Accident?"

"I slammed my jeep into a tree."

"You hurt?"

"Just a concussion. I don't remember much about it."

I glance at her and see that she's pulled her hair into a ponytail. That slender neck is so kissable.

"Explains your driving yesterday," I quip.

"The judge ordered me to get treatment—I was high when it happened. My histrionic mother saw the accident as a suicide attempt, so it's off to Menninger's for Vanessa."

"Was it a suicide attempt?"

"Nah, not that I'm aware of. I was just pissed off at my parents. My shrink thinks it was a subconscious suicide attempt, though. Of course, shrinks think everything is subconscious. Menninger's is Camp Freud."

"Shrinks do think they know everything."

"You been to one?"

I deflect with "Why were you mad at your parents?"

"In a nutshell, they have a total disregard for who I am and what I want. They care about me only so far as I reflect well on them, Michael and Diane Said, members of the San Rafael Golf and Tennis Club. One night things came to blows. I smoked too much weed, crashed into a redwood.

Next thing I know, I'm living out in God's country, being psychoanalyzed and churning butter."

I wonder what "things came to blows" means. I eye the rearview to see if Sheriff Bottoms might be tailing me, but the highway is empty.

"You like Kansas?"

"It's good for me," she says, and stares out at the flat, treeless prairie. "I need to be somewhere that's a little dull right now."

"With the Centennial celebration coming up, all that's going to change," I say with a smirk. "This'll be excitement central."

She smiles at this, and I ease up on the gas as we enter town. Soon I'm parking in front of the library.

"Want me to get my bike out?" she says as she gathers her books.

I shake my head. "I'll take you home."

"Thanks. Be right back."

25

Books in hand, she flies up the library steps and I'm suddenly happy. I wonder if she's a sex machine? Seems like the kind. I start thinking of scenarios I'd like to play out with her when I hear a honk. The honk of doom.

Geraldine's Chevette rattles into the parking space beside me. God, I have brilliant timing. She waves me over to her car. I shake my head. She starts to climb out. I throw the Death Mobile into reverse and peel out. I'd rather Vanessa think I split on her than have her see me with Geraldine.

I race down an alley and a side street but the Chevette stays right on my tail. Then I hear a train whistle. I swerve onto Walnut, speed up, and shoot across the railroad crossing as the gates come down—yes!

As I pull up to the library, you-know-who waits on the steps, books stacked on her lap, smoking her funky cigarette.

She climbs in. "What happened to you?"

"Sorry about that," I say. "Quick errand."

"Thought maybe you'd ditched me." She sets the books down on the seat.

"That's quite a stack you got there. You one of those speed-readers?"

"Say, I got you a book!" she says, and hands me one. *Main Street* is printed on the tattered binding. "Thought you might like it. It's about a free spirit in a small town."

"So someone's written my biography."

"Thought it might give you some perspective."

"You think I need perspective?"

"Everyone needs perspective. By the way, you don't have to return it. I lifted it. It was last checked out in 1947, so I don't think anyone'll miss it."

I take the book, but I'm not sure what to make of her comments and her thievery. I head south on Broadway.

"You didn't answer my question," I say. "Are you a speed-reader?"

"No, I just love reading. You have any good books I can borrow? I've exhausted that dinky library."

I shake my head.

"You live here your entire life?"

As much as I want to shake my head, I'm forced to nod.

"How about a town tour?" she says.

"You're pretty much looking at it."

"I want the Arty Flood tour."

"Huh?"

"Show me where the monumental moments of Arty Flood's life unfolded: where you were born, where you went to kindergarten, where you lost your virginity."

"What makes you so sure I'm not a virgin? This is a good Christian community."

She throws me an oh-come-on look out of the corner of her eye along with a huge smile. I'm tremendously flattered.

"Let's go in chronological order," she says. "Were you born at home or at the hospital?"

"Hospital."

"Then let's go there."

We come to the corner of Walnut and Broadway. I am preparing to turn left when she spots our funeral home. In the front yard, Dad, in a tight-fitting sleeveless white undershirt and plaid shorts, black knee socks on his stork legs, waters the Bermuda grass.

"Dad?" she asks.

I nod and speed up, wishing I wasn't embarrassed.

She aims and snaps. "Cute legs."

I am about to turn left when a car pulls in front of me. I slam on the brakes, narrowly missing Mrs. Kaye's VW Bug. She peers at us as she creeps past. I know I should be worried . . . but for some reason I'm not.

26

We drive past the rodeo grounds and up the hill to the clapboard one-story building with the peeling paint that once was Harker City Hospital. Because of dwindling population, the town couldn't afford to keep it running. Everyone goes to the modern Abilene or Junction City hospitals now, thirty miles away. I haven't been here in ages and it makes me sad to think me, my brother, and my sister were born in this boarded-up shed with grass up to the windows.

"Here's where I made my grand entrance."

Leaping from the car, she jogs up to the building. She has more energy than anyone I've ever met. Is it those weird cigarettes? Or is it just that she's nuts? I watch her stroll around the building and peer through the broken windows.

"Before this was a hospital," I say as I approach, "it was an old World War Two airfield barracks. After the war, they trucked it into town and—presto!—instant hospital."

"Which room were you born in?"

"In the old emergency room 'round back. That's where Doc Hayes delivered almost everyone I know."

She trots across the grass and disappears around the side of the building. I round the corner and see her squinting into a small window. "What's your birth date?" she asks.

"January 18th, 1970."

"Aquarius. You're trustworthy. What time of day were you born?"

"I just remember Mom saying it was early in the morning. Supposedly I was born in a blizzard. Dad barely got Mom to the hospital in time."

She pulls on the door, but it's padlocked. Pushes up the wooden frame of a half-open window. "Help me up?"

Placing her right foot in my cupped hands, she springs up. Although her long legs seem very muscular, I'm amazed at how light she is. She positions her right leg on the windowsill. Her shapely ass is mere inches from my face and I very much want to bite it. With ease, she slips inside.

What if this is leading somewhere? What if she gets off on taking guys to their birthplace and seducing them?

I strain to pull myself through the window. I can picture Sheriff Bottoms shooting us for trespassing. I'd no doubt get an extra round in my nuts for cheating on his precious flower.

I teeter in the window and drop onto the floor. The building is dark and my eyes take a minute to adjust. The place is musty, yet still has that antiseptic hospital smell. Empty boxes are strewn about on the maroon tile floor, which I always remember being so shiny and bright. I haven't been here since Mom was a patient ten years ago.

I almost expect to find Vanessa in one of the rooms—maybe naked, maybe standing on her head? Maybe standing on her head naked? I arrive at the door marked EMERGENCY ROOM. She's standing in the middle, photographing it. The lime green paint is peeling. I flip the light switch, but to no avail.

"The National Historic Landmark plaque is in here somewhere," I quip, my voice echoing.

"Eighteen years ago your mother gave birth to you in this room," she says, and strolls about. "You tasted air and cried for the first time in here. You shouldn't pretend it has no significance."

"You know, you're right." I look around as if in wonder. "I probably should give it more thought. It's kind of neat if you really think about it."

She sees right through me, crosses her arms, and narrows her eyes.

"My brother and sister were also born in here. Maybe I should bring them."

"Your mom too."

"She's dead."

"Oh, I'm sorry."

Suddenly I notice the water stains on the ceiling.

"See that stain up there? Just to the left of the light?"

She looks.

"I remember looking at that as a kid and thinking it looked like a giant marshmallow."

"How old were you?"

"I was in the second grade. Doc Hayes, the same guy who delivered me, told me to focus on the stain while he took the glass out of my arms and hands."

"Glass from what?"

"I came home from school and found Mom passed out on the floor, bleeding everywhere. She had accidentally walked through our glass door to the patio. I went to pull her out and fell and cut myself pretty bad. It took Doc Hayes over four hours to get all the shards out. I stared at that marshmallow the entire time."

"What happened to your mom?" she says.

"She lost so much blood she had to have a transfusion. I remember she was lying on a table right over there. They put one of those cloth screens between us, so we couldn't see each other. She spent almost a week in the hospital. I got to go home that night."

"That's awful."

"It doesn't bother me anymore. I'm over it."

She arches an eyebrow that tells me she knows I'm lying, then walks out. This annoys me, her knowing something I don't altogether grasp.

27

When I step out, I see her at the far end of the hallway, near the old nurses' desk.

"There was this chubby nurse, Mrs. Higgles, who always gave me a butterscotch candy whenever I came by to visit Mom."

"Do you remember where your mom's room was?"

"Right there." I point to the open door beside the desk, the one with the big lock on it.

She steps into the room. But I can't. So I just peek inside from where I'm standing. The walls are still that same blue, only fading and peeling. The rusted bed frame, minus the mattress, rests against the wall, right where it was when Mom slept on it. Dad couldn't afford a fancy alcoholic treatment program, so Doc Hayes kept Mom here. Originally she was in another room, down the hallway, but Mom's dad, Grandpa Kohl, a drunk himself who wasn't allowed in the hospital, kept sneaking her booze through the window. Doc Hayes moved Mom to this room, where the windows were nailed shut and the nurses could keep an eye on her.

I head down the hallway and enter the small bathroom off the waiting room. I get on my knees, reach behind the toilet, and pop out a loose piece of drywall around the pipe. A small vodka bottle falls out and clatters on the floor. This was the hiding place Grandpa Kohl made. He'd been a patient here many times himself and was handy with a pocket-knife. He carved this space so his drinking buddies could keep him well supplied.

I pick up the bottle and unscrew the top. God. I see the faint smear of Mom's tangerine lipstick around the opening. Mom told me that if I wanted her to get well, I would bring her the bottles that Grandpa Kohl would sneak me, then put them in this hiding space. It was our special secret.

"I'll meet you outside," Vanessa says from down the hall.

Here I sit on this dusty bathroom floor, holding the vodka bottle I snuck to my mother ten years ago, all because of a beautiful, annoying girl from California. I hurl the bottle against the wall and it shatters.

Outside, I find her reclining and smoking in the passenger seat of the Death Mobile, the door open, her feet resting in the open window.

I fall in. She pulls her door shut. I stick the key in the ignition. On the third try, the engine kicks over.

"There you have it," I say, and tap the steering wheel. "Part one of the Arthur Milton Flood biographical tour."

"You sound pissed off."

I fake a grin and reverse out. "Why would I be?"

"Was it something I said?"

I shift into drive and start down the hill. "It's always a mood lifter to visit where good old Mom was stitched up."

She nods understandingly. "I'm sorry if I upset you by going in there."

"Why do you keep insisting I'm upset? A little annoyed maybe, but not upset."

"Y'know, painful as it can be, sometimes it's a good thing to revisit the past," she says. "It can help you move on."

"Is this Vanessa or Vanessa's shrink talking?" I ask pointedly. "Look, maybe revisiting the past is big at Menninger's, but I'd sooner forget about it, thank you very much. What's done is done. In three weeks I'm outta this burg. No looking back for me."

"You really believe you can just forget about all that's happened to you here?"

"I'm a-gonna try."

I tap my thumb against the steering wheel. She's getting on my nerves big-time.

"Seems to me this is the perfect time for you to make peace with the past," she persists, "and with your family."

"And it seems to me that my family is none of your business."

"You're right," she says, and slaps her knees as if with a gavel.

After a minute I ask, "You always stick your nose into the private lives of people you've just met?"

"Only the interesting ones."

She finds me interesting? In a romantic way? Or in an oddity way? We cruise down Broadway.

"Wanna go for some fries and a shake?" I ask. "I know a good place."

"It's almost six," she says. "Uncle Roger's expecting me home."

"No problem." I turn the radio up loud as we speed past the Frosty, where Geraldine's Chevette is parked next to Barry's Nova.

Five minutes later, as I steer the car around the big lake curve, she turns down the volume. "You still pissed off at me?"

"I'm not anything, but if you keep asking me that I will be."

She turns the radio volume back up and stares silently out the passenger window.

Her uncle's Chevy pickup is parked beside the grain silo when I pull into their driveway. I park, hop out, open the coffin door, take out her bike, and roll it to her.

"Thanks for the lift," she says. "Stop by again soon."

I nod and climb behind the wheel. Part of me wants to gun the engine and kick up a cloud of dust for her to choke on. Part of me wants to run back outside, grab her, and slide my tongue down her throat. I give a little honk as I roll away.

Her footprints remain on the dusty dashboard. I go to wipe them off, but then I don't.

28

I walk into our living room. Shirley motions me to the chapel with an angry jerk of the head.

She closes the accordion doors behind us. "What's this nasty rumor going around about you and Carole Kaye?"

"It's bullshit, Shirley."

I'm pulling open the door when she clasps my wrist. "This reflects poorly on the family and the business."

"I'm telling you, it's a total and complete lie."

I tear my hand free and stride up the stairs two at a time. The bedroom door is locked. I knock.

"Who is it?" Allen says.

Oh, no. The weed makes him paranoid sometimes.

"It's me, Allen. Open up."

The door cracks and he peers out.

"You alone?"

I nod and he lets me in and quickly locks the door. The lights are off and I might as well be inside a bong. He paces in the dark like a caged cougar, his bloodshot eyes darting. I kick off my shoes and crawl up on my bunk.

"Did anyone follow you home?"

"Nuh-uh."

"You sure?"

He opens the blinds and points. I look out. Across the street, in the bank parking lot, Sheriff Bottoms, in his cruiser, faces our house.

"He's been sitting there all evening. I'm telling you, he's staking me out."

"So just get rid of your stash and you won't have anything to worry about."

Allen stares at me with alarm in his eyes. "Bottoms has gotten to you, hasn't he?"

"Yeah, Allen. He told me they're going to make an example out of Allen Flood because he's the most successful, most respected stoner in town. He's coming for you, Allen! Run for your life!" I unlock the door and leave.

As I soak in Mr. Bubble, I feel bad for saying what I did to Allen. People always say it was because Allen watched Mom burn up in the house that he can't get it together, but I disagree. Allen was sixteen when Mom died and he pretty much dealt with it okay, far as I remember. It was when that Renee dumped him, on the day they graduated from high school, that my brother just lost it and never got it back. Looking at Allen makes me glad I've never really fallen hard for a girl.

I yank the white plug on a chain and watch the water swirl down the lime-caked drain. I lie there all pruney and think about Vanessa and finding Mom's vodka bottle, long after the water is gone.

29

"**R**enee's probably gonna want to keep her stewardess job," Allen says. "I'm cool with that. I'm not going to be one of those control-freak boyfriends."

I'm lying on my bunk, staring at the cracks in the ceiling. It's got to be around midnight.

Five minutes later, the phone rings once. Then, a minute later, it rings again. The signal.

A half hour later, at the boneyard, Mrs. Kaye and I lie naked and spent in the back of my coffin cart.

"Who was that looker in the car with you today?" she asks.

"Oh, her. Just a . . . cousin."

"Oh, really?" she says, sitting up and lighting a joint. "Never mentioned her before."

I don't know what to say, so I don't say anything. I push open the back door with my foot to let the smoke out.

"There's a rumor going around about us," she says. "Did you say anything to anyone?"

"Course not."

"Your taking Geraldine to the prom should help things.

Be sure to kiss her a lot in public and give her whatever she wants."

If I don't de-virginize Geraldine Friday night, I know she'll go crying to her daddy that I tried to break her heart. Then Allen will be arrested and sent to prison.

"What if your husband found out?" I ask.

"He'd probably kill us both. Not because he cares about me—he doesn't—but because his manliness would be tarnished." She turns to me and slowly slides her index finger down the center of my chest. "I've been thinking a lot lately about divorcing him."

"Why would you do that?"

"Isn't it obvious? All he's ever cared about is the goddamn army."

"Why'd you marry him in the first place?"

"My sister wanted him, and I couldn't live with the idea of her having something I couldn't. I know that sounds stupid but I *was* stupid, I was seventeen. Besides, I was desperate to get out of my daddy's house."

In all the time we've been doing what we've been doing, Mrs. Kaye and me, we've never discussed her husband unless it was in regard to his schedule. It occurs to me that I don't know of one happy marriage.

"If I were to divorce him," she says as she outlines my right nipple with her fingertip, "then, after you graduate, we won't have to hide like this anymore. You could even move in with me."

"But I'm leaving town."

She arches her eyebrows. "And just where are you going?"

"Australia."

She scoffs. "And on what, may I ask? Don't forget who's paid to get your car repaired twice in the last month."

"I fully intend to pay you back for that."

"Oh, let's not be small." She's now outlining my left nipple. "If we lived together, I could bake you brownies every night."

"Look, Mrs. Kaye, if there's one thing I'm certain of, it's this: I'm leaving one second after graduation. Even if I have to walk out of this stinking town."

She just grins at me. Another woman who thinks she knows something I don't.

30

Friday morning. Prom day. Waking to the scent of Aqua Net and hot curling irons, I pull the sheets over my head but can't escape the smell. The odor seems a harbinger of what the day has in store for me. Asphyxiation?

I head down to the kitchen, where Kristy Lynn Kline is under the cone-shaped hair dryer and Shirley is shampooing Ladonna. At the table, Geraldine, hair in giant rollers, sports a white foam peroxide moustache and flips through *Hair Styles* magazine. Prom day is Shirley's busiest of the year. Her first customer arrives at 6:00 A.M. and they keep coming right up till the promenade at 6:00 P.M.

"Morning, Arty," Geraldine mumbles like a ventriloquist, her upper lip frozen, and hands me a folded note with *For My Man* written on it.

"Uh, thanks," I say. "Bet you'll look great tonight."

On my way to school, in the Death Mobile, I open the note, which is written in her exaggerated curlicue cursive:

Tonight is the night we have waited so long for.
Because you are the man I love and adore.
May we cherish this prom together.

For we both know our love is forever!!!!!!!!!
The Future Mrs. Arthur M. Flood.
P.S.: I trust you'll have the neccessery item.

Prom day is a day off from education, never a big priority at ol' Harker City High, anyway. Girls get their hair and makeup done, boys set up for the banquet in the gym.

After school, I tap on the Stileses' office door.

"Come in," Mr. Stiles says.

He's eating a Zip Burger at his desk. Barbecue sauce drips from his chin. At her desk, Mrs. Stiles, in her sunglasses, nibbles on her left pinky nail.

"I, uh, just wanted to remind you about the money," I say.

"I'll have it for you first thing Monday," he says.

Heard this one before. He damn well better not flake on me.

Later, I fall asleep on one of the design tables. In my nightmare, I'm in the back of the Death Mobile with Geraldine. We're both naked and fooling around when blood starts gushing from her vagina. I scream. The blood keeps pouring, like from a ruptured fire hose. "Take me!" Geraldine yells. "Take me!" I throw open the door only to find Sheriff Bottoms aiming a rifle at me. Should I take her? Is that what Sheriff Bottoms wants too? Oh, God!

I wake in a sweat, look around, and wonder how long I've been sleeping. Mr. and Mrs. Stiles are gone. Outside, people sit in a line of cars parked on Broadway. What's going on? The bank clock says twelve minutes to six. *Shit.*

When I get home, Shirley, sweeping up snippets of per-oxided curls from the kitchen floor, tells me that an irate Geraldine has called for me four times in the past half hour. I change into my funeral suit and throw on one of Dad's hook-in-the-back bow ties. This is it.

31

The Bottomses' front door flies open before I can knock.

"Where've you been?" Geraldine yells.

She's terrifying. Her eyebrows are gone, replaced by two penciled-in St. Louis arches. Under her blue eye shadow, her eyes are puffy from crying and her mascara is streaked down her brilliantly rouged cheeks. She looks like a clown melting. Her lacy, tight-fitting purple sleeveless dress reveals a shocking amount of cleavage.

I force a smile. "Well, look at you . . ."

She grabs my arm and yanks me inside.

Sheriff Bottoms, his red face a mask of loathing, glares at me and holds a Polaroid camera. "She's been waiting for over an hour."

"I'm sorry, sir."

"Don't apologize to me," he growls.

"Geraldine, I'm—"

"Where's my corsage?"

"Uh . . ." is all I get out before Geraldine screams.

Sheriff Bottoms' right cheek quivers. The family Chihuahua rips at my socks.

I consider running out but there's no way Sheriff Bottoms'll let me leave alive. The fucking corsage.

"I'm real sorry," I say, and give the dog a little kick.

Amid the glares, the tears, and the possessed rat biting my feet, I look around the living room at the plastic-covered sofa and the long-departed Mrs. Bottoms' collection of dolls, thimbles, Precious Moments figurines, spoons, lace, and other trinkets. Geraldine's confirmation portrait sits above the upright piano. Her hands are folded and she's looking heavenward. *What am I doing here?*

"Promenade starts in two minutes," Sheriff Bottoms says, and motions Geraldine and me over to the electric fireplace for a picture. I put my arm around her and try to look happy. Geraldine's perfume attacks my eyes and sinuses. She must have bathed in the stuff. The camera flashes just as I sneeze on her dress.

"We better be going," I say, and take Geraldine's hand.

"Flood, I wanna talk to you," Sheriff Bottoms says with a jerk of the head.

I approach cautiously. He stares with lethal, unblinking eyes. "My Geraldine will be home by midnight. And I best not smell alcohol on her breath, y'understand me, Flood?"

I nod vigorously, not trusting my voice.

"I mean it, Flood. Midnight. And no hooch."

The family Chihuahua snarls at my heels on our way out.

"You didn't even wash your car!" Geraldine says when I swing open the passenger door for her.

We're barely out of the Bottomses' driveway when Geraldine takes out a small flask, unscrews the lid, and swigs heftily.

"What're you doing?"

"Getting into a party mood."

I grab the flask from her and sniff the Jim Beam.

"Are you crazy? Your old man'll kill me." I stuff the flask in my pants pocket.

"You better've brought the rubbers."

"I got 'em."

"At least you did one thing right."

32

As I turn into the gravel parking lot of the Bank of Harker City, promgoers mill about in their tuxedoes and crinkly dresses.

"Now that those lovebirds Geraldine and Arty are finally here, we can start," Mrs. Kaye, the senior-class sponsor, yells. "Let the 1988 Harker City High promenade begin!"

The line of couples, headed by glamorous Kristy Lynn and Kevin—the couple at the top of our food chain—start up the sidewalk. We file past the parked cars, where parents, relatives, and no-life locals watch and snap photos. Geraldine, her left arm hitched into mine and cutting off the circulation in my right side, smiles and waves. I feel like a 4-H-er leading his prize heifer into the ring.

She hisses through her smile: "That's not a real tux you're wearing, is it?"

"It's a formal suit."

"The bow tie isn't even the same shade of black as the suit. You're the only guy here without ruffles and a cummerbund."

I am contemplating the many and varied ramifications of telling Geraldine to go to hell when Mr. Windall, the editor of the *Harker City Bugle,* steps in front of us with his ancient camera and says, "Smile for the paper, kids!"

I fake a huge smile as he snaps our picture. When people look at the yearbooks fifty years from now, they'll see me beaming and tethered to Geraldine. Just imagine.

"This is the most important night of my life. And I don't even have a corsage."

Barry and Ladonna are in front of us. Barry, in a gleaming black tuxedo, ruffled shirt, pink bow tie, and matching cummerbund, waves and beams at the crowd like he's practicing for the Academy Awards. He makes a point of never buying his clothes locally so there's no risk of anyone wearing the same "ensemble."

I look up and see Vanessa standing at the curb, camera around her neck, smoking one of her brown cigarettes. She smiles and I look down. Geraldine's feet are squeezed into a pair of pink pumps, and her radar is sharp as ever.

"Who's that girl?" she asks.

"Never seen her before."

"Well, she looks weird."

I'm sure Vanessa's having a grand old time witnessing our hick high school parade.

Back at the bank parking lot, I'm about to close Geraldine's car door when Sheriff Bottoms pulls up in his cruiser. "I mean it, Flood. Midnight. And not a drop."

"Bye, Daddy!"

33

"No matter where we go in life, no matter how far we travel, no matter how great our successes or failures, we will always be a family," Barry, our class president, emotes from the podium, and wipes tears. "Always."

Mrs. Kaye, at the head table, looks corpselike in her pale lipstick, overapplied eye shadow, and black eyeliner. Beside her is her crew-cut husband, Sergeant Kaye, sitting erect in his white military dress uniform. His sword is sheathed, for which I am thankful. My stomach flinches as I wonder what it's like to be lanced.

The yards of orange and maroon (our school colors) crepe paper and the candlelit, cloth-draped tables can't entirely disguise the school lunchroom. It's kind of sweet that my peers have attempted to transform our fluorescent-lit, white cinder-block cafeteria into a place of elegance for a night. But I'm frustrated that we live in a place that can offer us no real escape from our daily grind. The seating pattern is just like school too, with the jocks and cheerleaders seated at tables up front, the B-list losers in the back. The menu—Salisbury steak, instant mashed potatoes, and lime green Jell-O salad with marshmallows—is just slightly dressed-up cafeteria fare, only the portions are bigger and we get cherry cheesecake for dessert. The prom is titled "I've Had the Time of My Life," from the movie *Dirty Dancing.*

"Cherish tonight," Barry says, "for it comes but once in a lifetime. I love you all." Everyone but me leaps to his or her feet and claps. Barry blows kisses. "Thank you. Thank you very much."

After an eternity the applause dies and Barry clears his throat. "Our keynote speaker tonight is a man who knows the meaning of the word *victory*. He's taught us to believe in ourselves, to be the best we can be, and to reach for the stars. Let's hear it for the one and only Coach Hass."

To a standing ovation, Coach Hass lumbers up to the microphone. He's wearing a maroon clip-on tie and orange shirt.

"Thanks a lot, people," he barks into the microphone. "It's a real honor to speak here tonight. A real honor. I'd like to talk to you people about a little thing that makes a big difference. And that is the right positive attitude."

I want to stand and ask, *By the right positive attitude, do you mean like that time my freshman year when you told me I was a faggot for quitting football after a couple of two-hundred-pound seniors tackled me and broke one of my ribs?* Instead, I stand

and start moving. Geraldine gives me a confused look as I walk out.

My dress shoes clop on the buffed green linoleum floor of the empty hallway. Coach Hass's voice echoes off the lockers but, thankfully, I can't make out whatever bullshit he's saying. I'm mere inches from a clean getaway.

I stop at the entrance, where the trophy cases are kept and pictures of the graduating classes hang on the wall. I find Dad, class of '60, in black-framed nerd glasses and possibly the same bow tie I'm presently wearing. Mom's picture isn't here because she got pregnant with Carrie her sophomore year and the school board made her drop out. Vernadell, class of '52. If it wasn't for her name, I wouldn't recognize her. She looks so young and happy here, with long curly hair and sparkling eyes. Sheriff Bottoms, class of '63, has hair, but not much. Am I truly going to pork that smiling kid's daughter tonight? In the class of '54, I find Mitchell "Buddy" Mann, the movie guy who's directing the Centennial pageant. With his thick pompadour and Guy Smiley grin, he certainly looks like Mr. Hollywood. Allen, class of '82 (in the same bow tie). Carrie, class of '78 (in the same hairdo).

Everyone looks so young and hopeful in these pictures that I wonder where all the joyful anticipation went. Will the sparkle go out of my eyes too someday? And if so, when will it happen? Is it a gradual thing, caused by years of bills piling up and too much responsibility? Or is it part of the natural aging process, like graying hair and a drooping face? Or perhaps is it that moment when you realize the most elegant night you'll ever know was when your lunchroom was draped in crepe paper?

34

I'm at the urinal when the bathroom door opens and Mrs. Kaye's husband strides in. I turn and face the wall; my stream retreats to a dribble. Out of the corner of my eye, I see him staring at me. The bronze sheath of his sword gleams under the fluorescent lights.

"You Arty Flood?" His voice rings with command.

I am dead.

"Um, yeah."

"I've been looking for you." His words are clipped, ominous. I have a flash vision of him whipping out his sword and whacking off my pecker.

"Me?"

He steps toward me. I zip up and slide to the sink, where I wash my hands slowly and casually, like I'm not worried about one teeny thing.

In the mirror, he watches me with lethal calmness. Remember, he's a trained killer. Before he kills, he becomes focused.

"There comes a time in every man's life when he can no longer be indecisive," he says.

I think about making a dash for the door.

"When he must act," he says. "Do you know what I'm talking about, Flood?"

"Um, not sure, sir." I move to the paper-towel dispenser and wipe my shaking hands. He turns off the faucet I left running.

"Before a man acts, he must weigh his options," he says to my mirrored reflection. "A man must keep a cool head, know what his plan of action is. Am I making myself clear?"

I nod in vigorous agreement.

"What do you know about me, Flood?"

"You're in the, uh, army."

"Do you know what I'm trained for?"

I shake my head.

"Hand-to-hand combat. If I'm forced to, if I'm called to do it, I will not hesitate to kill. That's my duty as a soldier."

I don't dare breathe. He's between me and the door. No escape!

"Flood, how old are you?"

"Eighteen."

"An adult," he says. "You're responsible for your own actions. Accountable. It's time you woke up to this fact."

I make a pathetic bleating sound.

"Do you know what I see when I look at you?"

Me doing your wife doggie-style in a hearse?

"I see a tank commander, maybe a communications

sergeant. I see major potential. Tell me, have you considered the military after graduation?"

I stare at him, too thrown to speak.

"I want you to give this some serious thought. If you don't mind me saying so, you look like the type of young man who could use some discipline."

I exhale and try to contain my grin. "Thank you, sir!"

"The army can give you the discipline you need."

"I'll certainly think about it, sir!"

"Good." He hands me a brochure, salutes me, spins on his shiny black heels, and leaves.

I collapse against the sink and Geraldine's flask clanks in my pocket. I empty it in three clean swigs.

35

An hour later, I am in the gym, slow-dancing with Geraldine to Lionel Richie's "Say You, Say Me." God, I hate Lionel Richie. Reverend Hanky, who gave the never-ending invocation at dinner, stands on the edge of the dance floor, keeping a close eye on all couples. If a couple is dancing too close, she'll run up and place a Bible between them. "Remember, Bible's-width apart," she'll say.

I see Mrs. Kaye dancing with her G.I. Joe husband. He spots me staring and gives me a manly nod. I nod and give an awkward salute. Ladonna and Barry dance over to us.

"Good luck tonight, you two," Ladonna whispers.

"Thank you," Geraldine gushes.

Barry gives me a thumbs-up and my stomach heaves. Geraldine lifts her head from my shoulder and smiles coyly. "Let's go for a walk, darling."

At the dark far corner of the school parking lot, in the curtained back of the Death Mobile, Geraldine Bottoms French-kisses me. Muffled strains of Madonna's "Like a Virgin" reverberate from the gym.

Geraldine unzips my fly and touches me. "Why ain't you hard?"

"Nervous, I guess." A boozy belch slips out. "I've never done anything like this before."

She huffs bitchily. "Lie back and let me suck on him just a little wittle bit."

She takes me in her mouth. I close my eyes and try to imagine almost any other woman doing what she's doing.

She pulls back and says, "Quick! Get out the rubber."

I take the Trojan out of my inside jacket pocket, unwrap it, and start to slip it on. I haven't worn a rubber before because Mrs. Kaye can't get pregnant.

"It feels too small," I say.

"Don't flatter yourself," she scoffs. "I read rubbers are made to fit any size dick."

She takes off her panties and parts her flabby legs.

"C'mon!" she says.

"I . . ."

She sits up on her elbows and sighs. "Shit, you're all deflated. What's the matter with you anyway?"

She takes me in her hand and strokes me. I try to think about being in a Madonna–Olivia Newton-John sandwich. Geraldine bends down and takes me in her mouth again. Nothing. She spits me out.

"Auh! This is the worst moment of my life!" she says as she wiggles her panties back on. "You're pathetic!"

"I'm sorry, Geraldine."

"No, you're not!"

I put my hand on her shoulder. "No one needs to know about this."

"Damn right they don't! We're going to tell everyone we did it. And it was great. It was great! Do you understand?"

"Of course."

We finish dressing and I go to open the back door when she says, "Not yet! If we go in now, they'll know." Then she breaks down. "You don't love me," she sobs. "You never have. I'm not stupid, Arty."

"Aw, Geraldine."

A half hour later, hand in hand, we walk into the gym. Geraldine does her best to look dreamy.

"I hate you. I really, really hate you," she hisses under her smile.

She gives me a poisoned kiss, then heads over to the gaggle of eagerly waiting Ichthus girls. Mrs. Kaye, standing at the punch bowl and talking with Mr. Richards, the Spanish teacher, looks at me. I give her the slightest of nods.

"I thought, how is that big thing ever going to get inside me?" I hear Geraldine's voice waft over Prince's "Purple Rain." "But the pain went away quick and he was wonderful. I feel so different."

36

At a little past eleven, the dance is over and everyone files out of the gym. Reverend Hanky stands at the exit handing each couple a leaflet: "Celibacy: His Way."

I walk hand in hand with Geraldine to my car, where I tell her that I'm tired and want to call it a night.

"I don't have to be home till midnight," Geraldine says as I open the passenger door for her. "And you are taking me to the keg party, Arthur Flood."

"Yes, dear."

"And don't even try to be funny."

"No, dear."

I roll up to the spillway, where about ten cars are parked in a circle, their headlights shining inward. Promgoers stand around drinking tumblers of beer.

"Just please don't drink anything," I say to Geraldine as I park. "I promised your father."

Geraldine bolts from the car and rushes for the keg, which has been set up in the back of a pickup from where REO Speedwagon is blasting.

I am heading to retrieve Geraldine when a swaying Barry

blocks my path, thrusts a cup of beer in my hand, and says, "Here's our man!" His beer breath could melt fire hydrants.

Allen, who is also drunk, stumbles over and gives me a hug. "Join the party, bro!" Is there anything sadder than a twenty-four-year-old guzzling beer with high schoolers? Hope not. Barry drapes his arm around my shoulders and proceeds to tell Allen how much he's going to miss me next year.

I desperately look around for Geraldine and see her piling into Ladonna's idling Camaro, which then speeds off into the night. *Shit!*

I run to the Death Mobile, but by the time the engine kicks in, Ladonna's car is long gone. I kill the motor and trudge over to Barry.

"Where was Ladonna going?" I ask.

He shrugs, opens his mouth like Pavarotti, and belches for a record amount of time.

Allen holds up an okay-everyone-watch-this index finger, draws in his gut, and rips himself a ten-decibel burp. Barry cracks up and high-fives him.

A half hour later I'm sitting in my car, tapping my thumbs on the steering wheel. On the radio, Mrs. Kleinstadt pleads for Douglas to come home and offers her two-thousand-dollar reward to the radio cosmos. I run through the scenarios of what Sheriff Bottoms will do to me if I don't have Geraldine back by midnight. Nightstick up the pooper?

Bullet through the brain? Uh-uh, that would be too quick and painless. Maybe dragged by a rope behind his cruiser?

My passenger door opens and Barry starts to climb in.

"No beer in my car!"

He places his cup on my hood, then falls into the passenger seat and closes the door. "Why are you hiding in here?"

"Just feel like being alone."

"You always want to be alone. How 'bout having a little fun? It's our senior prom." He undoes his cummerbund.

"What do you want, Barry?"

"I just came by to give you some company." He belches again. "That's what best friends do, you know."

"Best friends also respect their best friends' privacy."

"I'm really going to miss you next year."

"Thanks."

"I've been thinking. Why don't you go to K-State with me? We can room together. It could be a lot of fun. Like high school without parents around. Have a place of our own. You could probably still get in if you really wanted to."

"Told you, I'm getting as far away from here as I can."

"Don't you want to go to college, better yourself? I mean, what is it you want?"

"Since you asked—I gotta swim in the ocean. Hell, I gotta *see* the ocean!" I say. "I gotta meet people who aren't white, who don't believe Jesus died for their sins, who don't live for the big K-State game. I want to eat strange foods with my bare hands. Watching movies and TV shows about other people having adventures—I can't be satisfied with that anymore! Maybe there'll be time for sitting in a classroom and taking tests. But right now I have to get away from everything and everyone I know. If I don't, I'll just . . . I'll just explode!"

I feel *great* at finally letting this out—at finally giving words to how I feel, at finally declaring *my future*. Then I hear the snoring. Barry, his mouth hanging open and his eyes closed, is slumped against the door.

I look at the dashboard clock: ten minutes till midnight.

I nudge Barry, who wakes with a jerk.

"I've gotta locate Geraldine." When I turn the ignition, I see the headlights approaching in my rearview. Ladonna's Camaro. *Thank you, God. I will not forget this.*

I hop out, run to the car, and open the passenger-side door. Geraldine falls out, laughing. Her breath is Munich in October.

"Where the hell have you been?" I ask.

"What do you care?" Geraldine pushes me aside, lowers herself to the ground, and lies in the Kansas dirt in her frilly purple dress.

"C'mon." I grab her arm and pull her up. "I'm taking you home."

She tries to yank her arm free, but I'm madder and stronger and I drag her toward my car. I hear a rip, look down, and see that her dress has torn up the side.

I dust her off as best I can and pour her into the passenger seat. On the drive back to town she blubbers on about not being loved. I turn up the radio. Seven minutes till midnight.

When we get to the Frosty, I dash in and tell Vernadell about my dilemma. She pours coffee into a big Styrofoam cup and grabs a wet dishrag.

"Well, hell." Vernadell peers into the car at passed-out Geraldine. "Sheriff Bottoms might have himself a good old-fashioned lynching party tonight."

"Don't think that hasn't occurred to me."

Vernadell does her best to wipe the dirt from Geraldine's dress and legs while I spoon-feed her coffee, which she spits out onto her dress.

Two minutes till midnight and the coffee has had no effect, but Vernadell has done a terrific job cleaning her off.

"I've got to get her home."

"I'll say a prayer for ya."

37

When I turn onto Arnold Street, Geraldine falls over into my lap. With my free hand, I prop her back up when I see Sheriff Bottoms standing in his yard, smoking a cigarette. His bald head and, at his feet, the Chihuahua's watery eyes reflect in my headlights.

I park and jump out.

"Hello, sir," I say, a little overly friendly, and trot around to the other side of the car.

He tosses his cigarette and mashes it underfoot. His cheek twitches.

I open the passenger door and my hand catches Geraldine's shoulder before she hits the concrete. I push her back in the car and smile at Sheriff Bottoms. "Guess it's past her bedtime."

I have placed her arm around my shoulder and am wedging her out of the car when her left breast falls out of her dress and gleams in the porch light.

"What the hell . . . ," he grumbles.

She comes to and says "Daddy" before hiccuping.

Sheriff Bottoms leans in and sniffs her breath. "She's drunk."

"Not really," I say.

Then she hiccups again and vomits all over his pants. He looks from his legs to me. His eyes are laser beams that cut right through me. I wonder if I can reach for his gun before he does.

Finally I say, "I'll, uh, escort her inside."

I start to drag her up the walk, the damn dog yipping at my heels.

"Your goddamn fly is open," Sheriff Bottoms rasps. "And why is her dress torn?"

I struggle to zip my fly but lose my grip on Geraldine, who drops like a sack of feed. I carefully arrange her soaked, comatose mass on the front porch. Sheriff Bottoms' right cheek quivers like it's about to pop.

"Well, I guess I'll be going, then," I say as I slink toward my car. At any moment, a bullet will hit me in the back and explode out my chest.

I am reversing out of the driveway when there's a yelp and a bump. I throw the car in park, jump out, and see the Chihuahua lying lifeless under my back left tire, his eyes more bugged-out than usual. Blood seeps from his bat ears.

"Chi-Chi!" Sheriff Bottoms yells, and rushes to the dog.

"I'm—it was an accident."

Sheriff Bottoms scoops it up and cradles it in his trembling hands.

"I'm so sorry, sir." My voice sounds like that of a man about to be guillotined. "I really and truly am just so sorry. For the dog. For . . . everything."

He slowly lifts his eyes from the dead pet to me. Can looks kill?

I jump back in my car and reverse out. Sheriff Bottoms, shaking in anger, glares into my headlights. I'll wake Dad, go over the basic arrangements, and have him measure me for the coffin as soon as I get home.

I make it into our driveway without police lights appearing in my rearview. The house is dark and quiet. I shakily pour myself a glass of milk and stand drinking it in the kitchen, wondering how long I have left. Then I see the metal tackle box on the counter. This is Shirley's tackle box, the one she uses as a cash register. I look furtively around; I'm completely alone. I open the tackle box and see the pile of cash. There must be five hundred dollars in here—money from all the prom hairdos. I stare at the cash. How far would this take me?

Who knows, maybe they'd have radio ads and a reward for my whereabouts, begging me to come home, like they do for old Doug Kleinstadt. Maybe they'd even have a candlelight vigil where everyone talked about what a great guy I was and how much they missed me and wanted me back.

A more likely scenario: I steal this money and tomorrow morning Shirley calls Sheriff Bottoms. He issues an all-points bulletin for a fugitive in a 1965 Cadillac hearse. I'm

machine-gunned down, Bonnie and Clyde–style, while speeding toward the Texas/Mexico border. Or I'm apprehended
and carted back to Harker City. The whole town spits and
hisses as I'm dragged into the courthouse, where the good
sheriff and his nightstick await in my basement cell.

I'm about to start upstairs when I see, in the pile of junk
mail on the edge of the kitchen counter, an envelope ad-
dressed to me. I recognize the handwriting as you-know-
who's. I rip open the envelope.

PART TWO

1

Next morning, sometime after ten. The sun is bearing down. Hot, dry winds gust out of the west. The bank thermometer claims it is 85 degrees. I'm heading out of town in the Death Mobile, having picked up Pierre along the way. Sheriff Bottoms hasn't killed me yet. In fact, early this morning Geraldine called. She was crying and saying how sorry she was for last night. That she had convinced her dad that it was her fault she got drunk. I accepted her apology and sincerely thanked her. My new plan is to humor her until I leave on graduation day. But I have a sneaking suspicion that her dad isn't ready to bury the hatchet anywhere except in my ass.

The mailbox marked R. HOLTZ crops up on my left. I slow down and turn up the gravel lane. Sure enough, I see her reclining on the front porch swing, reading. She looks cool there in the shade. I honk. She sits up and waves, and my stomach flutters like the first time I saw her—God, what is it with this chick? Those tan legs step off the porch as I roll to a stop at the gate. White T-shirt, cutoff jeans shorts, bare feet. Pierre barks like crazy at her. The dog has good taste.

"Well, this is a pleasant surprise," she says as she leans in the passenger window and pets Pierre. "Hiya, boy. I missed you, boy."

She's the only girl I know who will allow a dog to lick her face.

"Where's your camera?" I ask.

"Huh?"

"You wanna see the Dog Lady's house or don't ya?"

"So you got my letter," she says as she strokes Pierre's head. "Apology accepted?"

"So long as you don't try to psychoanalyze me ever again."

"Deal."

She bounds across the yard and into the house with gazelle-like grace. Pierre whines; I pet him and assure him she'll be right back.

About a minute later, the front door flies open and she shoots out, this time in black Converse sneakers and with the camera strap slung over her left shoulder. She piles into the passenger seat and pulls the door closed.

"I'm so happy you came," she says, reaching over and giving me a quick hug around the neck. She smells like the great outdoors.

My right foot hits the gas, gravel kicks up under my tires, and we're off.

"This time I get to ask the questions," I say.

"Fair enough." She repositions herself on the seat, as if digging in for an interrogation.

"Why do you want to see the Dog Lady's house?"

"A woman who lived with two hundred dogs and they ate her. It's just too cool. Don't you think, Pierre?"

"You're weird."

"This from a guy who drives a hearse."

Got me there.

"The other day," I say, "you said your parents have a total disregard for who you are and what you want. What'd you mean by that?"

"My whole life they've tried to indoctrinate me into their shellacked Neiman Marcus mind-set."

Who's Neiman Marcus?

"If I don't become an attorney, doctor, or Silicon Valley executive, then I better damn well marry one," she says. "What they refuse to get is that I don't need or want what they have—the Benz, the gated community with a view of the bay, the condo in Aspen."

Actually, a Mercedes and a condo in Aspen sound pretty sweet to me.

"It's inconceivable to them that someone might just want to experience life as opposed to purchasing it." Out of the corner of my eye, I see her lift Pierre's right ear. "They don't get it, Pierre. And they don't want to get it."

"By the way," I say, "don't think for a minute that the girl you saw me with at prom is my girlfriend."

She rubs Pierre's neck. "Who is your girlfriend?"

"Why do you assume I have one?"

"What woman could resist a guy who hangs out with Pierre?"

My pulse ratchets up a notch. This just might be my lucky day.

2

Six miles later, I swerve onto the deep-rutted dirt road that leads to the Dog Lady's house. Weeds and trees have all but swallowed it up. I hardly recognize the place with the front porch caved in at one end. One good gust could knock it over.

The front gate creaks when we open it and a buzzard flies out of a broken upstairs window. She snaps a picture. "Cool."

And I realize it sort of is.

Pierre sniffs along the foundation, picking up the scent of long-dead canine relatives.

Vanessa points at 666 SATIN RULES spray-painted across the side of the house and says, "What do they have against silk?"

It takes me a second to get her non–Harker City joke.

I point to a 1950s pickup with flat tires and a spiderweb crack across the windshield. "That was her truck. Keys still in the ignition."

"You knew her?"

"I'd see her in town from time to time. Mumbled to herself a lot. Wore men's clothes and a flannel Elmer Fudd cap, even in the summer."

"Ever talk to her?"

"Only once. I was in the sixth grade. Came out here with Dad. Our beagle, Preston, had died and Dad thought she could use the bag of leftover dog food. I remember there were what seemed like a gazillion dogs barking like hyenas. She met us at the fence there, took the bag, said thank you, and walked away."

We step onto the porch and the boards groan so loudly I fear they'll snap under our feet. A NO TRESPASSING sign dangles on the front door.

She pushes open the door and slips inside. I glance around before I enter.

A wood-and-wire sofa frame stands alone in the living room, except for rusted Alpo and Husky cans strewn across the sagging floorboards. I find Vanessa in what must have been the kitchen. It's stripped except for an old chipped sink. She takes pictures of a hill of dog food cans.

"How'd she afford to feed two hundred dogs?" she asks.

"She didn't. That's why they ate her."

"Ah, good point."

I follow her upstairs, eyeing her shapely calves. The stairs creak like the front porch.

"What was her name?"

"Joyce Bell," I say. "They say she was married once. To a handsome rottweiler."

Vanessa laughs and shoves my shoulder.

A mouse scurries across the top step. I stifle a yelp.

Vanessa doesn't as much as flinch. In the bedroom, a rotting mattress lies on a carpet of ancient dog poop.

I walk to the broken window and look out at the yellow wheat field. Beyond it, I can see the hangar and the beacon tower at the old air base. Puffy white clouds are assembling in the west. *Click.* I spin and see she has her lens aimed at me.

"Please don't take my picture."

"Why not? You're a good subject."

"Only if I can draw you sometime."

"You're on."

A nude study?

"We should have a séance here sometime and call her spirit," she says as she photographs the peeling blue flower-print wallpaper.

"The spirits of two hundred dogs are liable to come with her."

"*Riiight,*" she says. "I'll just take some more pictures."

3

On the porch, I gulp fresh air. Meadowlarks sing in the nearby trees. Pierre lies in the shade of the Death Mobile. Vanessa comes out behind me, points to the round beacon tower beyond the yellow field, and says, "What's the tower over there?"

"Beacon for the old air base."

"There's an air base out here?"

"There was. During World War Two."

"This place gets better all the time. C'mon, Pierre."

I watch as she pulls up the bottom strand of a low barbed-wire fence so Pierre can slip under. She lowers the wire, lifts her legs over the fence, and heads off across the field. I grab a can of Dr Pepper from my glove compartment and follow.

As I step out of the wheat field, I find her snapping pictures on the edge of the massive runway. Wavelets of heat rise from the buckled concrete.

"Immense," she says.

"The plane that dropped the bomb on Hiroshima started out from here."

"The *Enola Gay*."

"That's right."

We walk down the center of the runway. Pierre sniffs the weeds that poke out of the cracks. I hand her the opened Dr Pepper can.

"Y'got cooties?" she asks.

"The most deadly kind."

"Good." She swigs and hands it back.

I press my lips where hers were on the soda can.

"You're graduating soon."

"Uh-huh."

"Congratulations."

"Thanks, but I mostly slept through twelve years of school. I'm not smart like you."

"I think you're intelligent."

"Hmmm . . . how so?"

"You notice details most people overlook. It shows in your drawings." She snatches my Dr Pepper can and swigs. "Besides, I wouldn't be hanging around you if I didn't think you were interesting and smart."

All right, then.

She slices across the runway and clicks a picture of the old B-29 hangar, a massive Quonset hut covered in a patchwork of tar paper and corroded tin, unhinged and curled—as dilapidated as the Dog Lady's house. The giant rolling doors hang half on, half off their tracks.

"They used to have USO dances in there during the war. My dad says Glenn Miller and his orchestra performed here once. Check this out. . . ."

We cross a field overgrown with sunflowers to a huge rectangular concrete hole in the ground.

"Behold! This, my dear Zelda-Lucia-Vanessa, is an Olympic-sized swimming pool."

"How surreal," she says, and photographs the cottonwood tree that has grown out of the deep end and the rusted lifeguard stands that sit dutifully on both sides of the fissured pool. In this moment it strikes me that the glory days of my hometown are so very far in the past.

"Hand-dug by German prisoners of war," I say as I lean against the lifeguard stand. "At one time, this was the largest pool in the state."

"Any of the Germans escape?"

"Not that I know of, but a lot of them stayed after the war. A few of them are still farming around here."

"This is a trip," she says, and jumps into the shallow end of the pool and wanders around. "How do you know all this, anyway?"

"You're looking at the official Harker City historian."

"See, I knew you were well informed. God, Kansas is the most abandoned place I've ever seen," she says. "It's the state that time's forgotten."

"In a mere two weeks I hope to forget it too."

"I'd probably be frustrated if I grew up here. You never

know, though. Once you move away, you might look back and remember it fondly."

This, I admit, has *never* occurred to me.

"Think what I'll miss most about this place—next to you and Pierre and my uncle, of course—is the sky," she says. "It's so vast."

I continue along the edge of the pool and she walks parallel with me to the deep end. The way she said that I'll move away sounded so matter-of-fact that I am filled with hope.

"You know that World War Two has been over for a long time when a twenty-foot tree has grown up out of this pool." She takes another picture of the tree, then sets down her camera.

I squat on the pool's edge and watch her grab on to a branch. In one fluid movement, she whips her legs over her head, hooks her knees over a limb, and lowers her lithe body until she's upside down. Her T-shirt falls around her face and I gawk at her bare breasts.

She hangs there, her naked chest staring at me, her face covered by her T-shirt. Her breasts are divine. I glance around to see if anyone's watching. Does she want me to touch or, better yet, lick her glorious pink globes? God, they're amazing. I'm just beginning to climb in when she pulls the T-shirt over her head and lets it fall to the ground.

"Am I embarrassing you?"

"Not at all." But my high-pitched, strained voice betrays me. I glance away, up at the clouds piling up in the west.

"I'm just very comfortable with my body."

I want to say, *That's great!*

Head facing the sky, I glance at her chest again. Time to be a man of action, Arty. I grip the rusted ladder. It creaks under my foot, then breaks away from the side of the pool. I tumble into the deep end.

"You okay?"

"Fine!" I jump to my feet to prove it. "I'm *great!*"

The wind blows her shirt along the floor of the pool. I pick it up.

"Thanks, buddy." Hmmm, no hint of seduction in that "buddy."

I'm about to hand her her T-shirt when I realize I'm hard and have to cover my protrusion. "I'll, uh, just hang on to this until you're down."

She flips back over with a gymnast's ease and lowers herself down. I hand her the T-shirt and watch her put it on.

"Hope you didn't misinterpret that."

I laugh a totally fake don't-be-silly guffaw and follow her up the incline to the shallow end.

"Don't you hate how nudity and sex are equated?"

"It's the worst." I kick a loose chunk of concrete, trying to act like I'm not bothered in the least. "The absolute worst."

4

We amble to the beacon tower. Pierre sniffs for an elusive tweeting bird in the waist-high bluestem grass. What did she mean by "I hope you didn't misinterpret that"? That she's not interested in sex with me? But she did say she thinks I'm intelligent and interesting and what woman wouldn't want to date a friend of Pierre's? Is she the type you have to have a long, deep conversation with before the clothes come off?

We stop at the base of the tower and look up at the giant concrete tube. She grabs on to the ladder that runs up the side and climbs.

"I'm not sure this old ladder will hold us," I say, but she keeps ascending. I pull hard on the bottom rung to make sure it's secure. The last time I was on this tower was in the seventh grade. Dad had brought Allen and me out here to show us what he remembered of the base from when he was a boy. I thought this tower was the tallest structure in the world and wondered if I would be able to see the skyscrapers of New York from the top.

We seem to climb forever. About halfway up, I look down and it suddenly scares the shit out of me. Pierre is a fuchsia speck in an ocean of green. I feel freaked out and dizzy, and to keep my balance I concentrate on Vanessa's ass swinging side to side with each step. Just curious, noticing the details because I'm so intelligent. Not trying to "misinterpret" anything.

I make it to the top and my hands are stinging and red from the rust. Vanessa sits Indian-style at the edge, facing west, her back to me as she undoes her ponytail. There is no railing and the wind blows hard up here. I clutch the rusted beacon, with its cracked red glass globes, bolted to the center of this large, flat concrete platform.

She focuses her lens on the land below, an endless quilt of narrow gold rectangles, striped brown squares, and green circles. The hangars and the Dog Lady's house look like they belong with my old Tyco train set. The roads resemble gray lines drawn in the brown dust.

"What are those giant circles in the fields?" she says.

"Pivot irrigation. See that long pipe in the center? It makes a slow circle."

"Like a giant clock?"

"Uh-huh."

She takes pictures of the looming, mountain-high white thunderheads. Lightning veins through the clouds' gray base of rain, a dark backdrop against the tiny white Harker City grain elevator and silver water tower. Beyond it, I can see the lake.

"Looks like Harker City's about to get pounded," I say.

"I'd love to photograph a tornado. Ever been in one?" she asks.

"Several. The biggest was the summer between third and fourth grade." I lean against the beacon. "Hit town around three in the morning. All the windows in our house blew out at once. We ran to the basement. When we came up in the morning, the town looked like an atom bomb had gone off. They found our porch swing in Horace Harker Park."

"Sounds intense."

"Ever been in an earthquake?" I ask.

She nods and takes out a cigarette. "I remember watching our refrigerator dance into the middle of the kitchen and all of Mom's china pouring out of the cupboards. I was twelve."

She cups the lighter in her hands, lights the cigarette. She smokes and stares at the approaching, darkening clouds as if defying them.

We sit here atop the world and listen to distant thunder.

The wind roars harder, blows her hair straight up. I stare at her thin back and long, slender neck. I'm scooting toward her to touch her hair when she says something I can't hear.

"What?"

"I said, I have the biggest urge to jump."

I freeze.

"What do you think it would feel like? Falling, I mean," she asks.

"Good, then suddenly not so good," I reply.

I urgently remind myself she is a psychiatric patient under treatment for attempted suicide.

"But what would it be like," she says, "just for those few seconds of falling, knowing you're going to die? I bet there's a moment of epiphany. Like when people see their lives flash before their eyes."

"You tell me. You're the one who drove into that tree."

"What insight would I suddenly have?"

"That it was a stupid idea," I quip.

She crinkles the corner of her mouth and gives me a "very funny" glance.

"Please don't jump," I say. "I've had a challenging enough week as it is."

"Why don't you jump with me? We can do it holding hands. I bet we'd make the front page of the *Harker City Bugle*."

Truth is, I once seriously considered jumping off this tower. It was my freshman year, when I cared about nothing.

"As I see it, there's two problems with jumping," I say. "One, if I do it, I will have lived my whole life in Harker City. Two, if you do it without me, I'd have to look at your guts splattered everywhere."

"Maybe I have beautiful guts."

"I'm sure you do. But do me a beautiful favor and keep 'em inside yourself."

"We could let Pierre eat 'em." She turns to me and smiles. "You're really afraid I'm going to jump, aren't you?"

She falls on her back and closes her eyes. I want to kiss those full, curved lips. "They say time slows right before you die, that a second can last an eternity," she says. "Maybe we've already jumped and we're just living out the last second before we hit."

The nearing clouds block the sun and the temperature drops a few degrees. The lightning increases in frequency.

"Y'know, this isn't the best place to be when a storm hits," I say.

"I wonder what it feels like to be struck by lightning."

"Jesus, Vanessa!"

She opens her eyes and squints at me. "You afraid of dying?"

"Yes! I mean, I guess I'm afraid of dying before I've really lived. How can I want to croak when I haven't even seen a mountain or the ocean?"

"Well, I'm not afraid to die." She sits up on her elbows and gazes at the western horizon, where electricity strobes through the thunderheads.

"Yeah, well, you've seen a little more of the world than I have."

"I doubt there's a heaven," she says, lost in her thoughts, "and I'm certainly not religious. But why fear death? At worst, it's just nothingness. . . ."

"If it is nothingness," I say, "shouldn't we make the most of our time while we're alive in all the somethingness?"

"Question. How do we make the most of being alive?"

"See as much as you can," I say. "Do as much as you can."

"That would be my mom. Travels everywhere, buys everything she can get her hands on, stays busy at all costs. But is that really living? She's certainly never satisfied. Maybe doing what we're doing right now, sitting here and looking at the clouds and talking, is making the most of life. Maybe it's when we're seemingly doing nothing, inhabiting this very moment, that we're most alive."

Conversations like this are nonexistent in Harker City and I struggle to offer a deep, illuminating response.

"My brother lies in bed all day and smokes pot," I say. "But I hardly think he's making the most of his time here on earth."

"As we speak, my mom is cruising the Greek islands with her aerobics-trainer boy toy," she says. "And I can tell you she's not making the most of life either."

"Seems to me connecting with someone, really connecting, is when I feel most alive." I hope I'm not sounding too obvious in steering this toward sex.

Lightning flashes nearby and thunder cracks. Pierre barks below.

Gripping the beacon, I heave myself up. "Let's make the most of being alive by staying alive. What do you say?"

She takes a final drag off her cigarette and flicks it over the edge. I follow her down the ladder.

5

We're on the highway heading to town when the rain begins beating against the windshield. The farther we drive, the harder it pours. I turn on the wipers but I still can't see much beyond the hood ornament. I pull onto the shoulder, switch on my hazards, and throw it in park. Vanessa calms Pierre, who whimpers beneath the dashboard.

"Maybe you'll get your tornado after all," I say.

She stares out the windshield, mesmerized. The rain. The car. Shut off from the world. This is my chance. I'm reaching over to kiss her when she opens her door, jumps out, and slams the door behind her.

What the . . . ? I can see her only faintly at the front of the car. I turn on the headlights. She's dancing in the middle of the empty highway.

She motions me outside. I feel momentarily frozen. She motions harder.

"What the hell," I say, and hop out. I'm soaked in an instant. The rain is cold but feels good.

She takes my hand. "Dance with me! C'mon!"

I hop around in the rain with her and wonder when an

eighteen-wheeler is going to mow us down. I am laughing harder than I have in far too long. It's just so damn silly, what we're doing. A pickup truck creeps past. The old farmer behind the wheel gawks at us. We wave and blow kisses.

I pull her toward me, but she breaks away and twirls around. I grab her again and press my mouth to hers. Her lips are so soft I'm smashing them. She opens her mouth a little and our tongues touch. A surprise. She's a light, gentle kisser. We kiss for a nice long time. I hold on to her, and our bodies melt together and I can feel her nipples insistently poking against my shirt. Wet breasts. Wet shirt.

She moves back and stares at me as if I just did something wrong. I reach for her again, but she resists. Suddenly something stings my neck and arms. We're being pelted with little chunks of ice. Hail! We take cover in the car and I turn on the heat. The popping of hailstones on the roof is deafening. Her wet hair sticks to her face and her nipples cling to her soaked T-shirt. She hugs Pierre tight.

I throw the car in drive. The wheels slide on the icy highway. We ride in silence when the hail and rain stop.

"I'm leaving here soon," she says, staring out the windshield. "There's no point in starting something."

"A little something is a whole lot better than nothing."

"Look, I like you," she says. "If circumstances were different, maybe something amazing could happen."

She has just ripped open my chest, reached inside, and strangled my heart.

"What happened to 'inhabiting this very moment'?"

She shakes her head. "I just got out of a relationship. To start another one . . . No, I can't right now."

I laugh ludicrously. "You make it sound as if I'm talking marriage."

She's still shaking her head. "I'm sorry."

I should have jumped off that tower. Before we get to town, the sun breaks through the clouds. I roll down the window and breathe the damp, earthy-smelling air.

"You all right?" she asks. "You're awfully quiet."

"I'm okay."

"I really . . . like hanging out with you," she falters.

If she says she still wants to be friends, I'm going to snatch her fancy camera and toss it out the window.

"You look . . . angry," she says.

I want to shout: *I'm furious at* me *for allowing myself to be burned by you for the third time.* Instead, we cruise into town in silence.

"Why can't you be honest with me?" Vanessa says when we're almost to the lake. "If you're angry, which you clearly are, I would appreciate you telling me why."

I turn to her. "Want me to be honest?"

"Please."

"I think you like messing with my head."

"I'm sorry you feel that way," she says. "It was never my intention to mislead you."

I slam on the brakes in the middle of Broadway. "Oh,

Jesus Christ, cut the crap, Vanessa! You take my picture, tell me how intelligent and interesting I am, take your shirt off in front of me, dance with me, kiss me, and then you have the nerve—the fucking nerve!—to tell me you didn't mean to mislead me! Who do you think you're kidding?"

She gives me a long, wet-eyed look and says, "I'm . . . sorry."

A pickup truck honks behind us. I hit the gas, jerking us forward. Not another word is spoken.

6

That night, I'm so desperate to escape my life that I take Barry up on his offer to go to a keg party. When we arrive, I pretend not to see Geraldine talking with Ladonna.

I sit alone, swigging beer after beer. I. Will. Not. Think. About. Vanessa.

Round about the seventh beer, Geraldine saunters over to me. I take her into a golden wheat field, and therein I pop her cherry.

7

It's Monday. The day Mr. Stiles told me he'd have my money. When I get to work, I park between Hal Denton's Benz and the Stileses' Toronado. I open the front door and Pierre runs and jumps on me. "Hey, boy!" I say. He's trembling. I hear muffled shouts from inside the office. Mr. Denton is saying, "I can't give you another day, Harlan. You're six months overdue." There's about five more minutes of shouting, then the office door opens and Denton charges out. He slams the door and stomps right past me out the front door.

Then I hear Mrs. Stiles sobbing.

"This was all your idea," Mr. Stiles yells. "You stupid cunt!"

The sound of hand smacking flesh. I step back. That asshole. He *hit* her.

Pierre goes apeshit, growling and digging at the door.

"Here, boy," I say, tugging on the collar.

"Arty?!" Mr. Stiles shouts.

"Yes?"

"Take Pierre to the lake!"

"Uh, you okay, Mrs. S.?"

"Please, just go, Arty," she says.

I drive around town for half an hour but strenuously avoid the lake. Pierre whimpers and rests his head on my lap and I rub him between his ears. Mr. Stiles never seemed the type to hit his wife, or anyone else. It was such a horrible sound, flesh slapping flesh. Then the even worse sound of Mrs. Stiles choking on her sobs. I bet Mr. Denton's foreclosing. It'll be the end of Stiles' Styles. I'm scared for them. And for me. I have to have that money. I have to launch my life. I'll die if I don't.

I pull into the Frosty, park in the shade, and crack the window for Pierre. Barry is there, playing Ms. Pac-Man.

"Hey, Bar."

"Well, have you met him yet?" Barry asks.

"Who?"

"Mitchell Mann, of course. He got into town last night. Staying right here at the motel. He's . . . he's amazing. I pitched him my ideas for the pageant and he said he's real interested."

For the next ten minutes, Barry gushes about the pageant. I slouch against the Rock-Ola, watch him eat pellets and outrun the ghosts, and worry about the Stileses.

A ghost finally kills him and ends the game. He slaps the machine. "Wanna play doubles?"

Suddenly the front door flies open and Dennis Dickers runs in, breathless. "It's on fire! The whole damn building is in flames."

"What building?"

"Stiles' Styles!"

Holy shit. Outside, a massive column of black smoke rises into the clear blue sky. I climb into the Death Mobile and round the corner onto Broadway and see Stiles' Styles burning out of control. Pierre claws at the dashboard and howls. The 1950s-era Harker City fire engine is there, and volunteer firemen drag hoses, shout orders, and fall over each other like the farmers, shoe salesmen, and insurance agents that they are.

I hit the brakes and leap out, and before I can block him Pierre bolts past the firemen and into the front door of the factory.

"Pierre! Get back here!"

I chase after him until Sheriff Bottoms' massive hand grasps my shoulder.

"I gotta get him!" I yell. "I gotta get Pierre!"

"Can't go in there."

"Someone rescue that dog!" I yell. "Someone!"

The flames leap high into the sky and I feel the scorching heat on my face.

"Pierre! Pierre!"

Sheriff Bottoms shoves me back. "You just get across the street, boy!"

"Please save the dog, sir!"

"Now, boy!"

In the lot across the street, in the gathering crowd, I wipe my eyes with my shirtsleeve. The whole town is watching. People are bringing lawn chairs and coolers of beer. Colonel Sparks drives up with his portable BBQ wagon, the one he takes to rodeos. You'd think this was a goddamn fair by the look on everyone's faces. Dad and Carrie run out of the crowd and sandwich-hug me.

"We were afraid you were inside," Dad says, his voice halting with emotion. "I love you, son."

This is the most feeling I've seen from Dad since Mom died. Carrie sobs on my shoulder and thanks Jesus for saving me. Allen, who smells like beer, pumps my hand.

"Pierre's in there!" I say. "Someone has to do something right now!"

Geraldine skitters up, hugs me, and plants a big wet one on me.

"Oh, Arty!" She's choked with tears. "I'm so glad you're okay!"

"Word has it Mrs. Stiles is trapped inside," Dad says.

I suddenly catch sight of Mr. Stiles sitting on the curb, head in his hands.

He looks like a defeated little boy, bawling into his palms, shoulders moving up and down. A few feet behind him stands Hal Denton, the dancing flames reflecting in his glasses.

The wind kicks up and the fire rages higher. I can feel the

increase in heat on my skin. The firemen aim their hoses at the roof, but their low-pressure arcs don't make a bit of difference. I think about Mrs. Stiles' turban burning her scalp and her skin melting into her sunglasses, like the Nazi's dripping face at the end of *Raiders of the Lost Ark*. My eyes are watering and I swear I hear a bark.

A sudden blast like a bomb shakes the ground and a ball of fire shoots skyward.

Then comes the strong smell of burning plastic. The heat intensifies and everyone steps back. Pierre shoots out the front door. I sprint past the firemen to him. It feels like a thousand degrees as I run toward the building and grab Pierre's collar. The buckle burns my fingers, but I don't let go.

"Everyone get back! The roof's about to give!" yells Dale Clements, the fire chief. I dash across the street with Pierre and the firemen. The front of the building implodes in a blast of smoke and dust, burying the hoses under tons of bricks and smoke.

I remove Pierre's collar and try to calm him. In a nearby lot, the defeated firemen throw off their helmets and collapse on the grass.

"Did you see that, folks? Oh, the humanity!" I hear Barry say. God, he's *always* on.

Barry holds a microphone and speaks to a video camera, which is being held by Danny Carlson.

"Right over here, folks, we have Arthur Flood, an employee

at Stiles' Styles. Arthur, what do you have to say to the people watching?"

He sticks the microphone in my face and I just stare at him.

"Tell us what's going through your mind, knowing that your boss, Mrs. Stiles, is trapped inside the raging inferno."

Barry covers the microphone with his hand and whispers, "I'm hoping to sell this to the TV stations in Wichita."

I feel acid rising into my throat. I pick up Pierre and resolutely carry him to my car.

"Where you going?" Barry yells. "Don't you want to be here when they pull her body out? Folks, Arty's obviously very upset. . . ."

I climb in the Death Mobile with Pierre and hug him tight. We're both hypnotized by the smoke and flames. Mrs. Stiles was barely five feet tall. She wore rhinestone earrings to match Pierre's collar. Towering wigs. Pink two-inch fingernails. She called me "sugah" in her Arkansas twang. She believed I had talent. Taught me about color and perspective. Said I had a future as an illustrator or designer, while everyone else in town I dared to ask said it was an impractical dream. Mrs. S. up in smoke. Literally. A lump rises in my throat that I can't swallow.

I want to go far away. But I'm low on gas and broke, so I just drive home. I put Pierre in the backyard, where we kept our beagle, Preston, who died six years ago, the day Shirley moved in. Preston always was a good judge of character. I give Pierre a light hosing off, a bowl of water, and some raw hamburger.

Everyone else is still at the fire. I trudge upstairs to my bed. If I was a believer, this would be the time to pray. Instead, I do something else I never do. I go to Allen's little refrigerator, take out a six-pack of Coors, and drink till it all goes away.

8

I step through the patio door at the lake cabin. Mom and Mrs. Stiles are seated at our old round kitchen table with the red and white checkered tablecloth, having coffee and chatting. They turn and smile at me.

"Why, sugah," Mrs. Stiles says, "we were just talking about you."

"I'm happy you two finally met," I say.

"Mrs. Stiles was just telling me what a good artist you are," Mom says. "That makes me very proud."

"We must go now, Carla." Mrs. Stiles gets to her feet.

Mom nods, stands, and carries the coffee mugs to the sink.

"Mrs. S.," I say, "what am I going to do now? I have no money."

She says nothing as she walks to the back door.

"Where are you going?" I ask. "Can't we talk awhile? I'm scared."

"You'll figure it out," Mrs. S. says as Mom hangs her apron on the hook on the wall beside the refrigerator. Mrs. S. opens the back door. Dad's hearse, the coffin door wide open, idles in the driveway.

"Please don't get in there!" I shout.

Mom and Mrs. Stiles crawl into the back of the hearse, and Mom pulls the door shut behind them. Instead of going forward, the hearse shoots backward toward the lake. I see Grandpa Flood, not Dad, behind the wheel.

"You're going the wrong way!" I yell, and wave my arms. "Grandpa!"

The car splashes into the water. I run after it, but it's sinking fast. Grandpa just smiles his white dentured smile at me as the lake swallows the vehicle. Within seconds, the car is gone. And I . . . and I . . . and I try to . . .

9

With a pulsating headache and churning stomach, I stumble into school two hours late. I would've skipped, but I've skipped too many days as it is, and Principal Swedeson will slap me with detentions till I'm eligible for Social Security. I enter the front office and ask for a late pass. Mrs. Krause, the school secretary, looks up from her typewriter. "Arty. Principal Swedeson is looking for you. You're to go straight to his office."

I brace myself for the lecture about adult responsibility and real-world punctuality I'm about to hear. But when I arrive at his office, Principal Swedeson is conversing with Sheriff Bottoms and a tall, thin, gray-bearded man who's wearing a tie with a painting of a fire extinguisher on it.

"Arthur, you know Sheriff Bottoms, and this here is Mr. Fry," Principal Swedeson says. "He's an investigator with the state fire marshal's office."

Sheriff Bottoms eyes me like I'm a zit on the end of his nose.

"Stan Fry." He pumps my hand. "Good to meet you."

"Why don't we use my office," Principal Swedeson says.

He rolls in an extra chair for me and closes the door behind him.

"I'm here to investigate the Stiles' Styles fire," Mr. Fry says. "I assure you that you're not a suspect in the fire or the death of Mrs. Stiles." Hearing this hits me in the pit of my stomach.

"But because of your closeness to the Stileses," he continues, "I have some questions for you." He takes out a thick notebook and a pen from his briefcase.

Sheriff Bottoms pushes a button on his handheld tape recorder. For the next two hours Mr. Fry drills me about my job. What was my relationship with the Stileses? Did I ever smoke at work? Did Mrs. Stiles ever make sexual advances toward me? Did I ever hear or see Mr. Stiles threaten his wife? Never once does Mr. Fry ask my opinion about what I think happened. I don't doubt that Mr. Stiles was capable of arson, but I don't think he was capable of murdering his wife. Mr. Fry has me diagram the factory right down to the piles of fabric, the electrical outlets, and the placement of cleaning supplies. Sheriff Bottoms doesn't say one word, just gazes at me with those vulture eyes.

They give me one ten-minute break; I get a Dr Pepper from the hall machine. When I return, Mr. Fry asks me the exact same questions all over again, only slightly rewording them.

Then Sheriff Bottoms takes out a large plastic bag. "Found this in the rubble."

He hands me the charred remnants of my caricature notebook, which I kept hidden between two bolts of fabric. There are dozens of pictures of Sheriff Bottoms with an exaggerated honker and elephant ears; one with his bare fanny sticking up in the air is entitled "Sheriff I-Like-It-in-the-Bottoms." Stuck between the singed pages is my copy of *Juggs* magazine.

"These yours?"

I nod but keep my eyes down. Mr. Fry thanks me for my time, gives me his card, and asks me not to speak to anyone about this.

10

In Spanish class, Barry updates me on the latest rumors, which have grown to astonishing proportions. My favorite? I was having a steamy affair with Mrs. Stiles, and when she wouldn't leave her husband for me I killed her and torched the factory to exact my heartbroken revenge.

My persona is now that of a notorious murder suspect and thus I'm suddenly popular. At lunch, I'm invited by the quarterback of the football team, Kenneth Ray Schneider, to sit at the jocks' table. I graciously decline and instead sit with the shop rats and stoners, who each high-five me and call me "bro" when I'm barraged with questions. I lower my voice to a hammy whisper and tell my rapt listeners that if I breathe a word of "what I know," I could be arrested on the spot. This takes my reputation to even greater mythical heights. Geraldine, thrilled to play the devoted girlfriend of a celebrity, hangs on me and vigorously shields me from questions like she's my nervous lawyer. "The FBI simply won't allow him to speak," she says.

At noon, Principal Swedeson orders all seniors to the cafeteria to watch Barry's video report of the fire on the Wichita news. But the TV news only shows about ten seconds of the video, none of which features Barry's play-by-play reporting. In fact, all you can see of him is a brief shot of the back of his head. Red-faced and humiliated, Barry charges out.

"Way to go, Geraldo!" someone shouts after him.

Between fourth and fifth hours, Ginger Murphy, a very blond cheerleader, saunters up to my locker to inform me she's no longer going steady with her fullback boyfriend. By sixth hour, Barry climbs aboard my popularity train. In class, he tells everyone that, as my best friend, he's concerned about all the stress I'm under: "Give him space. He's their star witness and he's under tremendous emotional strain."

During forensics class, Mrs. Kaye reads "Ode on a Grecian Urn" and tugs on her right earring twice—a signal for me to meet her in the auditorium dressing rooms during study hall. I don't.

May 7, 1988, the day Arty Flood became, oh so briefly, the most popular person at Harker City High School.

11

After school, I drive past the Stileses' beige double-wide trailer. The Toronado is parked in the drive. At home, Dad is watering the Bermuda grass while smoking his pipe. He motions me over.

"Son, I haven't had a chance to tell you how sorry I am about your boss," he says, with his pipe still in his mouth. "I know you were real fond of her."

"Thanks, Dad. She was . . . a real nice lady."

"Been doing some thinking. I realize Mr. Stiles can't afford it, but it seems we ought to have some kind of memorial service."

"That'd be good."

"I'll put something together. Arty, one more thing."

"Yeah?"

" 'Bout the dog. Shirley is—"

"Unhappy, I know. I'll find him a home."

"If it was up to me, you could keep him," Dad volunteers. "He's a good dog."

I nod. Dad blows smoke and turns the hose back on the Bermuda grass.

"What's that dog doing in our backyard?" Shirley says when I enter the kitchen. She violently backcombs Mrs. Fudge, making the old woman's head jerk with each insistent stroke. "I don't have the time to take care of that mutt."

"How about some of your famous Christian charity?" I ask. "Pierre's an orphan."

"That dog has upset my Kitty Boo."

Kitty Boo, Shirley's bitchy Siamese, lives in the house and Pierre is outside. Shirley is immune to this sort of common sense.

"You have two days to find that dog a home," Shirley yells, and points the hairbrush at me. "Else I'm calling the pound!"

I load Pierre in the car and drive past the smoldering ruins of Stiles' Styles, where Stan Fry, dressed in what looks like hip waders, is rifling through the rubble with a long metal pole of some sort. Same thing they did when our lake house burned.

On Walnut, I head west. I was insane to depend on the Stileses for the money to start my real life, to think that the Doggie Joggie order would ever come in and get me to California and onboard that freighter. Will the insurance company pay me my back wages? At Walt's Full-Service Conoco, I charge ten dollars on Dad's account and get a Dr Pepper from the machine. I don't know how I'll pay Dad back, but I've got to get away for a while.

I drive to Junction City, grab a Frosty at Wendy's, and let Pierre pee on the old army tank in Pershing Park.

12

Two hours later, when I swing into our driveway, I almost hit Carrie's red Toyota station wagon. I go to back out but then I see Carrie in the chapel window, waving me inside. Dad pops up behind her, raises his eyebrows, and jerks his head in a get-in-here-now way. I sigh and kill the engine. In the chapel, I take a seat beside Allen and Dad, facing Carrie.

"I'm glad you three are sitting down because I have some thrilling news," Carrie says with breathless excitement. "You ready for this? You ready? There's going to be a Flood family reunion!"

No response from the male Floods. I rub my aching temples.

"Isn't that fantastic?" Carrie exclaims, beaming. "I called Aunt Sandy and she thought it was a great idea. Guess when was the last time all of us Floods got together? Go on, guess."

The silence stretches on.

"Almost seven years ago! At Grandpa Flood's funeral. Can you believe that?"

I bug my eyes out and shake my head at this earth-shattering news. Dad jabs me in the side.

"We're going to have it the weekend of the Centennial." The inevitable Carrie tears spill over her blue eyeliner. "Imagine all of us Floods together again."

Shirley, not being a "real Flood," wasn't invited to this top-level closed-door meeting.

"Listen up. The reunion is only a week away and we all have our parts to play," Carrie says, wiping her eyes. "Dad, I expect you to make your special homemade ice cream and get the boat working so you can take us all water-skiing. Allen, you're to give our little cousins free rides on the kiddy train."

Allen even has a striped engineer's hat and overalls he wears each year at the 4-H fair.

"Arty, you're responsible for making sure everyone gets front-row seats at the pageant."

This is how it works in my family: Carrie makes up her mind about something and assumes the rest of us will go along with it.

"And just what is your role, Carrie?" I ask.

"I'm in charge of making all the arrangements, and of arts and crafts. I'm also making T-shirts for everyone. Now, here's the schedule: on Saturday after the parade everyone's coming here to the house for a big lunch in the family dining room—"

"Well," Dad cuts her off, "that sounds real nice, hon." He gets up to leave.

"There's one more thing, Daddy."

He stops in the doorway.

"I have another surprise for all of you."

Oh, God, no. She's going to spawn.

She reaches into her macramé purse and removes three pieces of green paper. "What I have in my hand is a ticket for each of you to attend Pat Powers' Pep Rally for the Heart. It's this Friday in Topeka! Isn't that exciting?"

She hands us each a ticket. It looks like an oversized dollar bill with Pat Powers' Guy Smiley face where George Washington's ought to be. IN ME I TRUST! is printed on the bottom.

Dad looks at Carrie, puzzled.

"We all need a little redirection from time to time," she says to Dad. "And Pat Powers shows people how to be the very best they can be. Now, I'm going to be very upset if you three don't go. The tickets're all paid for and everything."

"That's real nice of ya, hon." Dad pecks her on the forehead and walks out.

Carrie closes the accordion doors behind him and whispers, "I expect you two to take him."

"How'd you afford those tickets?" I ask.

"Never you mind that. Just promise me you'll take Daddy."

"I promise," Allen says, and slinks out. I remain. I smell a rat.

"Why all three of us?" I ask. "I thought Dad was the one you were worried about."

"To be honest, I think all of you could use a little inspiration."

"Where'd you get the money to buy these tickets, Carrie?"

"That's none of your—"

I stuff the ticket in her purse and make to leave.

"All right," she sighs in defeat. "Aunt Sandy."

"What'd you tell her?"

"The truth. That Daddy's business has been slow lately."

"What else?"

"Only that he was a little discouraged. She was more than happy to send the money."

"And what'd you tell her about Allen and me?"

"Nothing."

"C'mon, Carrie, how'd you justify three tickets?"

"Calm down. I just said I thought it would be good for you two also."

I cross my arms, tap my foot.

"Oh, and I said that, well . . . that you were both a little lost right now and that this seminar might help."

"For your information, sister dearest, I am not lost."

"I only called Aunt Sandy because I care about you."

"Bullshit! You're just trying to make us look bad to her—"

"That's a lie!"

"—because she's rich."

"That's a horrible thing to say!"

"It's the truth. You always suck up to her."

"You want the truth? Huh? I mean, look at the three of you. Dad in a trance, staring into that TV day and night. Allen frying his brain on pot and beer. And you, Mr. Smart

Aleck, here you are graduating from high school in a week and you've got no plans."

"I most certainly do."

"Yeah, well, then what are they?"

"Why should I tell you?"

"Mark my words, you're going to end up living at home forever, just like Allen. I'm just trying to help—"

"Praise the Lord! Sister Carrie is here to show me the way!"

"You're a bitter, disturbed young man—"

"Lay your hands on me, Sister Carrie! Drive out the cursed demons!"

Smack! I feel the hot sting across my left cheek and nose. I clench my vibrating fists. It takes the energy of every cell in my body not to smack her back. I spin on my heels, fling open the accordion doors, and see Vanessa seated on the sofa beside Allen.

13

"**V**anessa?"

"Hi."

"What're you doing here?"

"I hoped that maybe we could talk."

Dad, in his La-Z-Boy, seems curious and a bit amused while Allen gawks at her as if he's never seen a female before. I'm still feeling the sting of the slap.

Carrie runs out of the chapel bawling. "You're a monster, Arty! A hateful, heartless monster!" She throws up her hands and disappears out the front door.

"Meet my sister, Carrie," I say to Vanessa. "Now, perhaps we should go someplace else?"

"Would your guest like some lemonade?" Dad asks.

"I'd love some."

Thanks a lot, Dad.

In the kitchen, we all sit at the table and sip Country Time while Allen regales us with stories and theories about his "girlfriend," Renee. I am anxious and embarrassed for Allen, but Vanessa nods and acts interested. How could she possibly care about my brother's mythical girlfriend? Dad sits at the end of the table and stares dreamily at her. Have I ever seen Dad stare dreamily at anyone? Didn't know he was capable of it. Vanessa does look like a million dollars in her low-cut T-shirt, with her hair pulled back in a ponytail. I love how she doesn't wear makeup or gel her hair. It's all just Vanessa. All natural. Awesome. I'm suddenly not so mad at her anymore.

Shirley, on the other hand, is pointedly avoiding Vanessa. When I introduce her, she barely says hello and gives her a pursed-lip once-over and the fakest smile in town.

When Allen stops talking long enough to sip lemonade, I stand. "Well, we should probably be going."

"I've never been in a funeral home before," Vanessa says to Dad.

"Would you care for a tour?"

"I'd love one."

Shit.

Dad gives Vanessa the ultra-deluxe tour, including the embalming room (which he never shows anyone). Allen follows and can't keep his eyes off her, no doubt building up a mental account of jerking-off material for the next five years. Vanessa asks a million questions, which Dad patiently answers in great detail. I'm not sure what to make of her interest in my family. Is she making fun of us? Psychoanalyzing us?

We're in the chapel when Dad tells Vanessa that what he really wanted to be was a doctor. Geez, Dad never talks about that. Not to me, not to Shirley, not to anyone.

"But the funeral home business can be rewarding," Dad says to her. "You know you've succeeded when the family members look at the body for the first time and say, 'He looks so peaceful, like he's asleep.' That's when I'm glad I'm a mortician."

Shirley, in a red and blue checkered hoop dress, rushes in. "Oh, Milton, sweetheart, it's time for us to go to our audition."

She gives Vanessa another frosty assessment and flounces out.

Dad smiles at Vanessa and shakes her hand. "Please come back anytime, hon."

"Not as a client, I hope," she says.

Dad chuckles and reluctantly releases her hand. Allen offers to give Vanessa a ride to wherever she needs to go.

"Thanks, but I'm going to the audition too," she says. "I'd like to walk."

"You're going to audition for the pageant?" I say.

She hooks her arm in mine. "Escort me?"

14

We're strolling south on Broadway, in the direction of the fairgrounds. Cottonwoods and elms form a green canopy over the street, shielding us from the evening sun. Locusts rattle in the trees.

"Sorry my brother and dad talked your head off."

"They're really sweet."

"You don't have to say that."

"And I wouldn't if I didn't mean it. I told you I'd never lie to you again." She grabs the stop-sign pole at the corner of Walnut and Broadway and swings around like an eight-year-old. "I do feel bad for your brother. He seems so depressed."

"You think so?"

"All the people I know who are obsessed with the past are depressed."

"I've never known him to open up to a stranger like he did with you."

"Don't know if you realize it, but you're his only friend," she says.

"I am *not* his only friend!"

"You are. He looks up to you."

Is she right? Am I Allen's only friend? Is he depressed? I'm suddenly worried about what'll become of him when I leave. We walk in silence, the chattering locusts the only sounds.

"By the way," I say, "isn't our Shirley a charmer?"

She raises her shoulders. "She's dealing with a lot."

"What d'you mean?"

"From what I saw, she's the one putting the food on the table. She's probably really worried about your dad."

Soon we pass Mrs. Kaye's house. The blinds are closed but I can hear the trumpety *Entertainment Tonight* theme on her TV.

"So," I say. "You wanted to talk."

"I want to apologize about my reaction to when you kissed me the other day," she says. "I should say my overreaction."

O-kay. Say nothing, Arty. Let her do all the talking.

"The whole point of my coming to Kansas was to take a break from my life as it is and try to figure out why I do the things I do. And then, suddenly, the other day, I find myself falling for you, and, well, it freaked me out—the last thing in the world I was expecting was to meet someone here. Seemed to go against the very reason I was here, which was to get to know *me*. Does this make any sense?"

I tear a low-lying leaf from a tree and keep walking.

"I've missed you a lot these past couple of days," she says.

"And, well, I guess what I'm saying is that I know we have only a little over a week together, but I'd rather spend it with you than without you. That is, if you're still interested."

My pulse accelerates. Did I hear her right? She wants me?

"What happened to 'There's no point in starting something'?"

"I was wrong, you were right," she says. "Something *is* better than nothing."

Yes! Oh, God, yes! I want to throw my arms around her and kiss her adorable face all over. Instead, I clear my throat and say, very calmly, very slowly, in a regular tone of voice, "I guess that would be . . . all right."

She beams and takes my right hand in hers, our fingers interlacing, and we stroll along. I feel light-headed until Sheriff Bottoms drives by in his cruiser and scowls at us like we're a couple of Democrats.

"I do have a favor to ask," she says. "My meeting with my shrink is Friday morning in Topeka and my uncle can't take me. I'll pay for gas and lunch if you'll drive me."

"No problem."

"Just promise you'll bring Pierre."

An uninvited smile curls my lips. "Will do."

We turn left on Arnold Street and see a long line of people outside the community building. Several folks are tuning their instruments and the result sounds like musical indigestion. At the front of the line, Barry, dressed as Mr. Harker in a fake goatee (the real one he's been trying to grow for weeks having not materialized), round spectacles, and a stovepipe hat, waves his arms and recites something profound in a forced, deep voice. The Larsons practice some kind of chest-out-stomach-in vocal exercises. Dad and Shirley rehearse with their cloggers' group, the men in plaid shirts, the women in hoop skirts. Then I see Geraldine in her red, white, and blue leotard and leg warmers, twirling her baton. I duck back around the corner, pulling Vanessa with me.

"This's as far as I go," I say.

"Looks like the whole town's trying out," she says. "Who's going to be in the audience?" She tugs on my arm. "C'mon, Arty, try out with me. We'll laugh at it together."

"No, ma'am. By the way, what's your talent?"

She smiles and arches a devious eyebrow. "See you at seven Friday morning." She pecks me on the mouth and joins the line.

I want to jump and shout! I, Arty Flood, am officially dating the Girl in the Lake!

15

I'm in my funeral suit, in the front pew of the chapel in our house, facing the closed coffin wherein lie the charred bones of Mrs. Stiles. Dad picked her up from the state medical examiner in Topeka yesterday.

The funeral starts in less than ten minutes and I'm the only mourner. Her pine coffin is an old throwaway that's been in our basement since the Eisenhower administration. Mrs. Gladys Burhoop, all four feet of her, plays "Come, Redeemer of Mankind" on the Kimball electric organ, her blue bouffant bobbing up and down, her feet barely touching the pedals. Mrs. Burhoop has been a fixture here since before I was born. She was my piano teacher, and whenever I see her I still feel guilty for not practicing.

At the foot of the coffin, a stoned Allen, as usher, rocks ever so slightly on his heels. His bloodshot eyes stare at the ceiling; he's no doubt imagining his impending reunion date with the fabled Renee. At the head of the casket, behind the small pulpit, Reverend Hanky reads her Bible silently, her lips moving. Behind her, along the wall, is the mural Mom painted of the Italian countryside. A florid fresco, with undulating hills and a village with a church. Dad claims I inherited my ability to draw from Mom, and he's probably right.

Dad adjusts a crocheted Kleenex holder on the entry table. Although he's not making any money on this funeral, it's good to see him shaved and squeezed into his suit.

I think about when the town had a big rally for Mr. and Mrs. Stiles at the community building just a little over a year ago. Selling their Doggie Joggies to big retail chain stores around the country was going to put Harker City on the map. The high school band played. Mayor Fudge and Hal Denton gave speeches. Now, at this final send-off, so far no one has shown up. Not even Mr. Stiles. It's a painful thing.

Suddenly, the front door opens. I see a short, round woman in a black dress and veil come in. She comes closer and I peer through the veil at the face. Geraldine. She plops down beside me and whispers, "I wanted to be here for you, honey-bunch." She takes my hand. Geraldine didn't even know Mrs. Stiles. Truth is, she didn't have to come and it's damn nice that she did.

The front door opens again and a bald man walks in and greets Dad. At first I don't recognize him. Then it dawns on me—it's Mr. Stiles without his toupee. He has deep dark bags under his eyes and he looks twenty years older. He nods hello to me and sits on the back bench. A minute later, Hal Denton ambles in and sits. Dad steps into the chapel and closes the doors. Mrs. Burhoop stops playing and Reverend Hanky says, "Let us bow our heads in prayer."

During the service, women's chattering wafts in from the kitchen. Shirley usually closes the beauty shop for a funeral, but not today. If you asked her why, she'd give you some excuse like, "Edith Barnes needed a color job before leaving on her Alaskan cruise." The truth? Shirley, like most everyone in town, doesn't think Mrs. Stiles is worth closing up for. It dawns on me that when you fail in the eyes of the citizens of Harker City, this becomes a very cold town.

16

Dad, Allen, Hal Denton, and I lift the coffin, which is so light that Allen and I could've done it ourselves. At the cemetery, Mr. Stiles sits on a folding metal chair in front of the coffin. He hasn't shed a tear. To me, he doesn't even look at all sad. Must still be in shock. When Reverend Hanky finishes, we file past Mr. Stiles and tell him how sorry we are and that we know she's in a better place and all those funeral clichés you're supposed to say.

Mr. Stiles says to me, "Arty, will you meet me at the Frosty Queen in an hour?"

"Sure, Mr. S."

What could he possibly want?

Back at the house, I thank Geraldine, tell her I'll see her at the Ichthus party tonight, and give her a peck on the cheek.

"Don't be sad, sweetie," she says, and cups her right hand on my crotch. "I'll cheer you up tonight, baby."

God, how am I going to wiggle out of this one?

When I come outside, I find Shirley has chained Pierre to the door of my car.

At the Frosty, Mr. Stiles' Toronado has a U-Haul trailer

hitched to it. I park in the shade, crack the window, and tell Pierre I'll be back soon.

"Thanks for coming," Mr. Stiles says as I slide into the booth. His bald head and aged face still throw me.

Within seconds, Barry is at the table with my Dr Pepper.

"Anything else you'd like?" Mr. Stiles asks. His voice is inappropriately chipper.

"I'm fine with Dr Pepper."

He looks at Barry. "I'm good with my iced tea."

Barry nods and sashays off.

"First off, I want to say how grateful I am to you and your dad for having that lovely service for Bernice. Means a lot."

I can't help but notice Barry "cleaning" the spotless neighboring table.

"My attorney says the fire investigation could drag on for years," Mr. Stiles says. "The good news—if there's any good news in all of this—is that when we bought the factory, we had an electrician come in to do some work. He said back then that the wiring was shot and needed to be replaced. I guess he's our ace in the hole if the investigation ever goes to trial." He is saying this with *definite gloating*. "But my attorney doesn't think it'll get to that." A *definite smirk*.

And in the gleam in his dark brown eyes, I see it, know it. He killed her. And doesn't regret it. I think I'm going to puke.

"I'm moving to Little Rock." Mr. Stiles squeezes the last bit of juice from the slice of lemon in his glass. "My brother owns a box factory there and he's offered me a position. I'm heading out today."

This asshole takes a long sip of iced tea. This motherfucking murderer.

"Bernice and me, we gave it our best shot," he says. "If that fire hadn't taken place, we probably could've made a real go of things."

I start to get up.

"Wait, the reason I asked you here—aside from sayin' goodbye, of course—is that the apartment I'm moving to in Little Rock, well, they don't allow pets, see. And my brother's wife is allergic to dogs. Now, your stepmother, she told me that you-all couldn't keep Pierre. But, you see, I can't take him back. And I know how much he likes you, so I was wondering if you could work something out with your folks. I know you'll come through, Arty, you always did. And if you can't, well, I'll have to put him down." He empties his glass and sets it on the table with another definite smirk. "I'm counting on you, Arty."

Un-fucking-believable. I want to kick his ass into next month.

He slaps down a five. "Well, it's getting late and Little Rock's a solid six-hour drive. I should probably be on my way."

I follow Mr. Stiles to his car, where he gives me Pierre's leash, his brush, and a Doggie Joggie. "Well, that's that, I guess."

"No, there is one more thing," I say. "What about the thousand dollars you owe me?"

"Now, that's out of my hands, see. You need to talk to Hal Denton 'bout that. The bank's assumed all of my debts. You don't know how bad I feel about taking out bankruptcy, but I had no choice with the fire. I just know that Hal will be glad to help you."

And I just know that I'll never see a goddamn cent of that money.

I can tell my glaring makes Mr. Stiles uncomfortable. He opens the door to his car.

"Now, you take good care of yourself and Pierre, you hear?"

He starts the engine. I tap on his window. He rolls it down and looks at me, his lying face all knotted up in a grin. I spit. It just flies out of me and smacks him between his eyes.

He wipes it off with his sleeve.

"Don't even pretend. We *both* know what you did, you fucking murderer—"

He peels out, kicking up a miniature dust storm. I watch the car disappear down Walnut Street.

Shirley will shit a brick when I tell her about Pierre. Dad is too henpecked to stand up to her, but I'll fight if I have to. No one's taking Pierre Stiles to the pound.

17

Friday morning. Today I drive Vanessa to Topeka. Last night I persuaded Allen to call me in sick at school today (Allen is excellent at impersonating Dad's voice). I'm up at five. Shower, jack off, shave, mousse my 'do, clip my nose hairs, iron my white dress shirt (the one I had to buy for choir) and pleated khaki pants. When I open the backyard gate, Pierre happily jumps up on me, pressing his muddy paws against my clean pressed pants.

It's ten of seven when I pull up to the Holtz farmhouse. I knock on the front screen door. "It's open," Mr. Holtz yells from somewhere inside.

I follow the rich smell of brewing coffee into the kitchen. Her uncle, in his bib overalls and creased leather slippers, leans over the table reading the *Junction City Dispatch*.

"Morning," he says into the newspaper.

"Morning."

"She'll be down in a minute. Help yourself to some coffee."

"Okay if I help myself to some paper towels?" I point at the paw prints on my pants.

"Under the sink."

I tear off a piece of paper towel, wet it, and try to rub the mud off.

He folds his paper, removes his bifocals, sets them on the table, sips his coffee, and says in a rather conspiratorial tone, "Thanks for taking her today. I got jury duty."

"No problem."

"I'm glad she met you. She was keeping to herself too much before you came along."

I nod, unsure how to respond.

"She's been through a lot, you know."

"I know."

"Her mother warned me she'd be a handful to live with but it's turned out to be the opposite. She cleans the place, helps out with chores, cooks. Hasn't been a lick of trouble. I don't know what I'll do without her."

The thump of feet coming down the stairs.

He whispers: "Trouble is, her and her mother are both too damn much alike. That's why they don't get along. . . ."

She bounds into the kitchen in blue jeans and an over-sized black T-shirt. I suddenly feel overdressed and a bit self-conscious.

"Sorry I'm running late," she says, and slips into her flip-flops by the back door. "Bye, Uncle Roger." She pecks him on the forehead.

"You kids drive safely now, y'hear."

Outside, I slide behind the wheel while she walks around, opens the coffin door, and lets Pierre in the back.

I watch through the little window that looks into the back as she spreads out the crusty sheet I have had countless acts of sex on with Mrs. Kaye, and stretches out.

"What're you doing back there?"

She pulls the door shut. "Going to sleep."

"You don't want to do that, it's . . . sticky back there."

She folds her hands beneath her head like a pillow and closes her eyes. Pierre settles beside her.

"Besides, it's going to be too hot. . . ."

"We going or not?"

18

I pass the high school on the way out of town. I feel good that I'm not going to waste this cloudless, sunshiny day under buzzing fluorescent lights. I'm going to Topeka with Vanessa, over two hours away from here, away from Geraldine and Mrs. Kaye and Coach Hass and the smoking remains of Stiles' Styles. What will people say when I'm not in school today? Pulled out for an FBI interrogation? I enjoy this thought as I turn on the radio.

Twenty-five miles later, I speed up the on-ramp and merge into the eastbound traffic on Interstate 70. The bright red Honda Accord in front of me has Washington State tags and a REAGAN SUCKS! bumper sticker. A dark blue Volvo, with Illinois plates and a ten-speed bike fixed to its roof, passes me on the left. A road sign: TOPEKA—70 MILES. KANSAS CITY— 122 MILES. ST. LOUIS—298 MILES. For the first time in a very long while, I feel that I am among the living. These people on the interstate, they're going *someplace*. Maybe Kansas City, maybe Chicago, maybe even New York. Probably never even heard of Harker City. I bet most of them are just passing through Kansas on their way to someplace way better.

An hour later. Still on I-70, driving over the treeless shoulders of the Flint Hills and listening to crackly voices of truckers on the CB. The dashboard clock shows 8:27. The sun blasts through the windshield and it's heating up in here. I hear a yawn and groan from the back. Vanessa pokes her head through the little window. "How far till Topeka?"

"'Bout twenty miles."

She climbs through the tiny window and falls into the passenger seat. No one's ever crawled through that window before. She leans over and kisses me on the cheek—a kiss, I must add, that isn't any more romantic than the one she gave her uncle.

She rolls down the passenger-side window.

"Sorry my air-conditioning doesn't work."

"I prefer heat. Pull off at the next exit," she says. "Have to pee and get some coffee."

There are no gas stations in sight.

"Up late last night?" I ask.

"I'm up late every night. But last night was especially late. I wanted to finish this novel I was reading. Have you read *Sister Carrie*?"

"No, but I *have* a sister named Carrie."

"It's a beautiful novel. You might like it. After that, I felt like a swim, so I biked to the lake and took a dip. I like to swim late at night 'cause I can skinny-dip."

At this image, I feel a distinct bulge in my khakis.

"Aha," she says, and my pulse quickens. Has she spotted

my hard-on? I turn to her and she points to a sign on stilts: STUCKEY'S! HOME OF THE PECAN LOG ROLL. NEXT EXIT.

"Coffee!" she says.

I take the off-ramp and park in front of a gas station/café with a tall orange roof and glass walls.

"Need anything?" she asks.

"A Dr Pepper'd be nice."

"You got it."

I walk Pierre around the parking lot. He sniffs and pees on tires. This place looks familiar. I think I once stopped here with Dad when I rode with him to pick up a stiff in Kansas City. On the back of a Winnebago, a sticker with a smiling red face reads THE GOOD SAM CLUB and I wonder what this means.

"My appointment's in twenty minutes," I hear Vanessa say. She holds a giant steaming Styrofoam cup and a Dr Pepper can.

Back on I-70, Vanessa sips coffee. "God, this is awful!" She rolls down her window and hurls the entire cup into the wind.

I look in the rearview for the highway patrol while she lights a cigarette.

"What book're you going to read next?" I ask, to jump-start conversation.

"No offense, but I can't make chitchat without caffeine. Not this early."

I hand her my Dr Pepper and she slurps. Traffic picks up

and a Denny's sign peeks over the horizon, followed by one for Texaco and another for Hypermart. We're in Topeka.

"Take the next exit and turn left," she says.

An oversized billboard featuring a familiar clean-scrubbed, grinning face rises into view. Pat Powers. His teeth must be ten feet high. SOLD OUT! is bannered across his gleaming forehead.

"Oh, God," I say.

"What?"

I point to the billboard. "I was supposed to go to that with my dad and brother."

"Yikes."

"My thoughts exactly."

19

At Topeka, I take the exit that snakes over the interstate. I've never seen Vanessa so closed off, and wonder if I didn't make her angry somehow. Maybe she's having second thoughts—about me? Or maybe she's just preoccupied with coming to see her shrink? Soon we're heading up a hill into a wooded area, then onto a brick driveway. The Menninger's campus of manicured grass, pruned trees, and substantial-looking two- and three-story brick buildings sprawls for acres.

Vanessa points to the side of a tall colonial building with white columns and a clock tower. "Park in the visitors' lot over there."

I pull in a spot surrounded by Mercedes, Cadillacs, and Saabs, and turn off the motor. Except for the few barred windows on the upper floors of the main building, there's no indication this is a funny farm. In fact, this is how I would imagine Harvard or Oxford might look.

"Meet you back here in an hour." She climbs out.

As Pierre sticks his head out the window to look around, I notice a group of people on lawn chairs under a nearby clump of trees. They look like a family: a bald middle-aged man who I would guess is the father, two teenage daughters (not bad-looking—one blond, the other strawberry blond), and a middle-aged woman, probably the mother. Her salt-and-pepper hair is kind of messy and she's wearing a tan robe. She must be the lunatic. There is a dark-haired Indian-looking woman in a white jacket. The shrink, no doubt. Over the wind and the rustling of the trees, I hear her say, "Perhaps it would be beneficial for you to try to separate your mother from her depression."

The blond daughter nods and smudges tears with a Kleenex.

This brings back cozy memories of our alcoholic family counseling. Dad couldn't afford a swanky place like this, so we went to St. John's Hospital in Salina. I was in the fifth grade. For one of the sessions, the shrink, a white-bearded man with a lisp, asked to meet with Allen, Carrie, and me, without Mom and Dad. He told us that children of alcoholics often play roles. He said Allen was the rebel and scapegoat for all of the family's problems, and that it was his way of taking attention away from Mom's drinking. It's true that when Mom was around Allen would mouth off to Dad a lot. Carrie was the surrogate mother. I remember that term because I was too embarrassed to ask what *surrogate* meant. He said Carrie took maternal responsibility when Mom was drunk. A week after Mom died, Carrie ran away from home.

He pegged me as the clown of the family. Said I masked

pain with jokes and sarcasm. At the time, I didn't feel funny at all, but I knew that he had nailed something about all of us. He told us we were not responsible for Mom's drinking, that she was a deeply unhappy person, but he never told us why.

What was Mom so unhappy about? She must've had some dreams for her life. Maybe she wanted to go study at an art institute? Maybe she didn't love Dad? Once I heard that Grandma Flood blamed her for trapping Dad into marriage by getting pregnant. Maybe she felt guilty for getting pregnant and ruining Dad's plans of becoming a doctor? When I was a freshman, Carrie wanted Allen and me to go to Reverend Hanky for counseling. She said that we were carrying around Mom's ghost and that it was affecting us negatively. I told Carrie that her church was to her what booze was to Mom. It wasn't a nice thing to say but I still believe it.

Pierre barks at the group under the tree and I shush him. The bald man brushes away tears, his body jiggling. The strawberry blond daughter hugs him. I feel real nervous whenever grown men cry.

If my family were to go to counseling now, what would a shrink say about us? That Carrie uses church, Allen pot, Dad TV, and me sex to distract ourselves?

I stretch out across the seat and close my eyes. Pierre licks my face, then settles down with his head on my chest. The rustling of the oak trees lulls me.

20

I step onto our front porch and the sky is a blinding red-orange, like it's been set on fire. There is no sound. I see a copy of the *Harker City Bugle* lying on the top step. "ARTY FLOOD, 32, HARKER CITY'S ONLY INHABITANT!" is bannered across the front page, which is dated 2002.

I jump off the porch. Our lawn is a weed jungle. Downtown is deserted; business fronts are boarded up and grass has sprouted in the middle of Broadway. The digital bank clock is dark. The town pool looks like the air base pool, with a tree growing in the middle. The roof of the Frosty has fallen in. I see a light on at the high school, in Principal Swedeson's office. Inside, I push away cobwebs. The classrooms are empty and dusty.

Principal Swedeson, in his tan suit and clip-on tie, sits with his hands folded neatly on his clean desk.

"Where did everyone go?" I ask.

"Hello there, Arty-farty-bird-turd. Everyone graduated and moved away years ago," he says, and smiles. "I'm afraid you're the only one left in the whole dang town."

"Is it too late for me to get into college?"

He laughs. "You want to go to college now? I tried to help you, but oh no—you made fun of me. You had all the answers, Arty-farty-bird-turd."

"I'm sorry, sir."

"You're too old, Arty-farty-bird-turd. Face it, you're stuck in Harker City till you croak."

He takes a hand mirror from his desk and shoves it at me.

"Take a look," he says with a devilish grin.

In the mirror's reflection, my cheeks droop like a basset hound's and I have big dark bags under my eyes. What little hair I have is goose white. I touch my face and he laughs maniacally. I drop to my knees and sob. Suddenly I hear Vanessa's voice: "Arty. Ar-tee. Wake up."

I open my eyes and see an upside-down Vanessa peering through the open car window at me. Her eyes are puffy and red. I straighten up and wipe the drool off my chin. She opens the door and slides in.

"Let's go to lunch," she says, and lights a cigarette.

We drive past the green-domed capitol building, the Jayhawk Hotel with its neon jayhawk on the roof, and the sleek white Santa Fe office building. So many people out, so many stores. I'm finally somewhere. Vanessa smokes and absently pets Pierre.

She points across the street. "There's the restaurant."

I drive around the block twice before finding a parking space—something I've *never* had to do in Harker City. I've only been to Topeka twice. Once on an eighth-grade field trip to the capitol. And a few years ago I came with Dad and Allen to pick up a body at the morgue, but we never came downtown. We ate our packed lunch in the hearse, with a dead geezer in the back, right in the morgue parking lot. Why doesn't Dad ever want to go anywhere? What is he so afraid of?

Vanessa leaps out with Pierre.

"We can't take him in," I say.

"It'll be okay."

I follow her across the street to a squat gray stucco building with CAFÉ KASBAH painted on the door. Inside, it's so dark it takes me a minute before I can see anything. High-pitched bee-sounding music plays on a stereo. The smell of spicy fried food makes my mouth water. Vanessa sits at a table near the kitchen and Pierre settles on the floor beside her. Not only is this the darkest restaurant I've ever been to, it's also the smallest. It makes the Frosty look gigantic.

"Interesting place," I say, and sit across from her. "How'd you find it?"

"My shrink told me about it after I complained about the bland food in Kansas."

The floors are hardwood, the walls bare brick—another sign I'm not in Harker City, where floors are carpet or linoleum, walls are plywood-paneled, and lights tend toward the fluorescent. The only other people here are two college-age guys at a nearby table. The brown curly-headed one is wearing a T-shirt that says THE CURE on it, torn blue jeans, and combat boots. The other one, with a ponytail, is dressed entirely in black and wearing thick-soled, pointy shoes. I suddenly feel like a Lawrence Welk singer in my white button-down choir shirt, pleated khakis, and white Nikes.

Vanessa hands me the tiny menu and I scan it, recognizing none of the food. An older, bearded, Arab-looking man comes out of the kitchen wearing a red apron. He looks at Pierre and I expect him to shoo him out, but instead he pats him on the head and says hello to Vanessa.

"Hello, Ali. This is Arty."

We shake hands.

"Uh, hello, sir," I say, sounding stiffer, hicker, and more khaki-clad than ever.

"Ali'll do," he says with a crinkly smile.

"And that's Pierre. I'll have the usual," Vanessa says, and returns the menu behind the candle where she got it.

Ali looks at me, waiting. I look at the menu, then to Vanessa for help.

"The falafel platter is good," she says. "That's what I usually get."

I have no idea what that is. "Sounds great!" *Shit, too much enthusiasm.*

"Turkish coffee?" Ali says.

"First thing."

The man disappears into the kitchen.

"I like this place," I say. "Has character."

"You know, my dad's of Egyptian descent. I didn't realize

how accustomed I was to spices until I came to Kansas. Excuse me. Gotta pee."

I watch her walk to the back. The college guys watch her too. I surreptitiously unbutton my shirt a notch, to look less uptight, less like a small-town dork. Is my hair too short? I decide I'm going to start wearing it longer, like these college guys.

Vanessa comes back, smiles, and lights a cigarette.

"Sorry I was out of it on the ride here this morning," she says.

"No problem."

She leans forward and places her right hand on mine. "I'm not much of a morning person. Plus, my mom called late last night to tell me she's coming here with my sister for my lunatic graduation."

Ali materializes and sets two tiny blue ceramic coffee cups, along with a small, steaming pot with a long handle, in front of us. I've never seen coffee so black. It smells like burnt almonds.

"Why don't you like San Francisco?" I say.

"Oh, I love the city but not the suburbs." She fills the cups and blows on her thimble of sludge. "You should visit. I think you'd like it."

"You don't know where you're going after Memorial Day?"

"I don't like to plan things in advance," she says. "It takes the spontaneity out of life."

"Sounds like bullshit," I say.

"Maybe," she admits.

She drains her coffee in one swig. I do the same. It gets stuck in my throat and I gag. Bitter as vinegar, the most vile stuff I've ever tasted. Like drinking from the bottom of an ashtray.

"Ali!" she says. "Can we get some water, please?"

I'm coughing like crazy, spewing black coffee all over my dork shirt. The cool guys stare at me and snicker. Ali runs out of the kitchen with a glass of water, which I empty in two gulps. But I can't get rid of the bitter flavor.

"Not a Turkish coffee fan, huh?" she says.

"Oh, no," I say, hoarse. "It's just that I haven't had one in a while."

I smile and blink at Ali in a way that says, *I'm fine, now please stop staring at me*. He must get it because he nods and vanishes to the kitchen.

Vanessa smiles at me.

"What?" I say.

"You're funny."

"I am? How so?"

"You just are. You're cute."

Whenever someone tells me I'm cute, I can't help thinking it means that I'm dismissable. A corn-fed boy choking on spicy Turkish coffee. So very cute. The food looks like three little sausage patties covered with a white gravy. They're spicy and taste good. The patties turn out, in fact, to be made from some green vegetable substance.

We eat and Vanessa tells me about all the foods she likes to make, half of which I've never heard of. I don't grasp much of what she's saying because I'm distracted by the two hipsters at the nearby table. They've been eyeing Vanessa since we got here. I want to turn to them and say, *That's right. Arty Flood, from the corner of Nowhere and Nowhere, is with this hot babe. She's mine. Back off, daddy-o.*

Suddenly I feel nervous and heated. My heart kicks inside my chest and my palms and face break out in a sweat. I've been on Dr Pepper highs before but nothing like this. My stomach quivers and my bowels feel shaky.

"Uh, excuse me." I bolt to the bathroom.

I barely have a chance to lock the bathroom door and drop my pants before the explosion.

21

After lunch, we walk around downtown in the blinding white midday light. I'm still vibrating from the Turkish coffee and feel like I could run all the way back to Harker City. Now I know where she gets her energy. She dashes into a store with PHIL'S BOOK NOOK stenciled on the window. Pierre and I stand in the shade of an awning and watch the cars and people pass. I think about how nice it would be to have a job downtown here and to hang out at the Café Kasbah. Maybe I could even learn to like Turkish coffee. If I can't scrape together enough money to make it to Long Beach, maybe I can at least move here.

I daydream for the next fifteen minutes or so, until she emerges from the bookstore with a large shopping bag.

"One more stop," she says, and motions me and Pierre into a store, Jayhawk Art Supply. Countless types of pencils, every color and size of paper, more pens and markers than I knew existed. I spot the most amazing drafting table.

"Pick out a sketchbook and some pencils," she says.

"I'm not in the market—"

"Well, I'm buying it."

"I won't let you—"

"It's your graduation gift. I insist."

"Okay!"

God, I am in heaven. It takes me over a half hour just to pick out a sketch tablet. I ask a cute redhead, whose name tag says JENNA, which pencils she recommends.

"Whose class is this for?"

"What do you mean?"

"You're an art student, right?"

"No, I just want a good pencil for drawing."

She nods and shows me a line of German-made ones. It heightens my mood that she thought I was an art student.

"Now draw me something great with these," Vanessa says at the cash register as she hands me the sack. "Come on, let's go home and swim."

It's an hour later. We're somewhere between Topeka and Junction City on I-70 when Vanessa lifts her head from my shoulder and says, "Hey, Arty, let's get off at the next exit."

"Why?"

"I'm sick of the same old interstate. Let's find our way back some other way."

"I don't know these roads. We might get lost." God, I sound like Mr. Practical.

"So we get lost," she says. "Is that so bad?"

"I'm lost every day," I say, to make up for being a stick-in-the-mud.

I head south on an empty, potholed two-lane highway. I know we're heading south because a million years ago, when Grandpa bought this hearse, he installed a compass on the dashboard.

We pass several abandoned farmhouses.

"This is better," she says. "The real America."

"You think so?"

"What's the matter?"

"Nothing, really."

She rests her bare feet on the dashboard and says, "C'mon, talk to me."

"I don't know. I guess . . . I just don't want to go home and face my life."

"But you graduate in a week."

"Big fuckin' deal. I mean, I'm broke. Which means I'm stuck."

"You're done with high school," she says. "Your life is just starting, in a way."

"Easy for you to say. You've got your rich parents and your ticket to San Francisco."

We drive through a tiny, nearly empty town where a brown and white mangy mutt sleeps in the middle of the bricked main street.

"Can I come to your graduation next weekend?"

"No way."

"But I bought you a gift."

"Thank you and no."

"You can come to my little lunatic graduation."

"I'll mark my calendar."

"It'll be a chance to meet and mock my borderline sister and narcissistic mother."

I don't want to sound stupid and ask what *borderline* means.

"Your dad coming?" I ask.

"Hope not. Whenever I'm in the same room with my mom and dad and sister, it's World War Three."

Her dad has been cheating on her mother for years, she informs me. "Dad fucks around and Mom spends his money."

"Think they'll get a divorce?"

"Never. They enjoy making each other miserable."

"When'd you graduate from high school?"

"I didn't. I dropped out. But I got my GED."

"How old're you anyway?"

"Guess."

"Twenty."

"Seventeen."

"Get out of here."

"Wanna see my driver's license? Never mind, it's revoked."

"You seem older."

"Is that good or bad?"

"Definitely good."

I can't believe I'm older than her.

"I dropped out of school last year and moved in with my boyfriend, Skinny."

"Great name." I try not to sound jealous but know I do.

"Yeah. Skinny's a thirty-four-year-old coke dealer."

My first thought is that he drives a Coca-Cola truck, but then I realize what she means.

"Skinny sounds like quite a prize."

She nods. "Course, my parents shit a brick when I moved in with him. I told them that he was an orthodontist—which he used to be—but they still hated him, which made me go for him all the more. I know, it's totally fucked up."

"Not really. Everything my stepmom tells me not to do, I do it. You and Skinny still together?"

"No, we broke up."

"Sad."

I want to ask her why but don't because I don't want to sound too interested.

"He dumped me the moment I showed him the positive results of the home pregnancy test."

Is she joking?

"So I had to move back home. My parents insisted I get an abortion but I refused. I was going to raise the baby on my own. Well, you can imagine the fights we had. It's when I went to my first OB appointment that I discovered—get this!—I wasn't pregnant. I'd miscarried. That night I got hammered, told my parents I hoped they were happy, and proceeded to wrap my jeep around that redwood."

"That's awful."

"Not entirely. It taught me a lot about the people in my life."

We are silent as we cruise through the ghost town of Latimer (population twelve). All that's left is a peeling white Lutheran church and a rusting grain elevator beside the overgrown railroad tracks. Vanessa looks so sad. No wonder she was so reluctant to enter into a relationship with me. I wish I could think of something to say.

She slides over beside me and rests her head on my shoulder. "Thanks for listening."

I put my arm around her.

22

When we approach the outskirts of Harker City, she turns to me, all intensity and boldness behind those blue eyes. "Let's go up to the beacon and watch the sun set."

Something tings in the pit of my stomach. "You got it."

So I turn the car around, drive out to the old air base, and park beside the tower. Pierre spots a jackrabbit, leaps out of the car, and tears through the weeds after it.

Vanessa takes my hand and leads me to the tower. I follow her up the ladder. I have this feeling like a big event is about to take place. Vanessa moves with a silent urgency and expectation I've never seen in her, like she's made up her mind about something. My heart jolts at the thought of what that something might be. I am propelled up the rungs.

There she is, seated at the edge of the tower, when I climb off the ladder. I drop down beside her, so close that I can feel the heat from her body. I place my arm on her shoulder and pull her snugly to me, and she drapes her left arm around my lower back. We watch the western horizon, where orange sunbeams splay through the broken clouds.

After a few minutes, she turns and looks at me as if she

were photographing me with her eyes. God, she's so fucking beautiful. Her face is so close to mine my breath catches in my throat. She closes her eyes and her lips barely part. I take her chin in my hand, tilt it upward a little, and place my mouth on hers: first just lips, then our tongues touch. She wraps her arms around my neck and our kissing intensifies. After a minute, she pulls back a little and lifts off her T-shirt, her long hair falling around her bare chest and shoulders. I cup her small, warm breasts in my hands and brush my tongue across her nipples. *Am I dreaming? Is this really happening?*

After a while, she unbuttons my shirt and undoes my belt. I help her out and toss off my khakis and BVDs.

We're naked. I ease her onto her back. Skin against skin. Our legs intertwine, our arms snug around each other, our tongues touching lightly. I take my time, touching and kissing her everywhere.

She wiggles out from beneath me and I roll onto my back. Then she crawls on top of me—she seems almost weightless—and kisses me some more.

It's as if she's suspended above me when she takes my dick in her hand and slips me inside of her—she's sooo wet. Eyes wide open, I see her arching over me, feel her hair draping down around my face and her chest pressed against mine. My hands caress her back and hips. She moans softly in my right ear as we make love, slow and sensual. It is, truly, my first time.

Warm winds gust around us. I can't tell where she begins and I end. We are on our own floating island, hovering fifty feet above the earth. Nothing else matters. And I never, never, never want to come down.

I stare into those blue eyes and before I know it—too soon?—I'm in the throes of an awesome orgasm. Shuddering and breathing fast, exhaling and sighing in exhaustion, she collapses onto my chest, burying her face in the crook of my neck. I put my arms around her and hold her tight. Her hair smells sweaty and real. I stare up at the swift-moving puffy clouds and, for the first time in my life, know that I am completely, utterly, unironically in love.

23

When I wake, the sun is completely gone and the sky blinks with stars. Vanessa lies close beside me, on her stomach, her head propped up on her hands, watching me. It seems wrong to say anything. She smiles and I smile back while running my fingers along her bare back. We look at each other for the longest time. She kisses me.

"Sometimes I think I dreamed you up," I say. "I mean, for the last eighteen years I've been staring at the same faces. Then, suddenly, out of the blue, you swim up to me and here we are. It's unreal."

She grins. "You're sweet. Believe me, it's pretty weird for me too. Two months ago, if you had told me that I'd be living in the middle of Kansas and involved with a guy named Arty, I would have thought you were high."

She flips onto her back and stares at the stars. "Randomness, like our meeting, is what makes life interesting, don't you think?"

"Absolutely."

"And yet it's so hard for people to accept randomness," she says. "I admit, at first I even fought the idea of hooking up with you because it didn't fit into my 'planned random-ness.' " She laughs. "But I have to make *some* choices. Soon. I don't know where I'm going after here."

"You're not returning to California?"

She shakes her head. "Too much emotional baggage back there. I'm thinking maybe New York."

"Why New York?"

"If I'm serious about photography, it's the place to be. More importantly, my parents aren't there."

I nod. "Understand that."

"How 'bout you?" she says. "Think you want to be an il-lustrator?"

This makes me feel suddenly tense. "I love drawing. Don't know if I have what it takes to make it a profession, though."

"Ever heard of Cal Arts?"

I shake my head.

"It's in the mountains outside L.A. I had a good friend who went there for graphic design. She loved it. You should check it out."

"How can I know if I'm good enough to get in?"

"Do you think you're good?"

"My boss thought so. My mom too. I think."

"But do you?"

"Yeah . . . yeah, maybe I do. In a way, I hate to even hope so. And there's the expense. . . ."

She lifts her shoulders. "Arty, there are student loans, or

maybe you could work part time." She plugs her index finger into my belly button and slowly draws her finger up the center of my chest. "All else fails, you can draw caricatures for tourists at Venice Beach for twenty dollars a pop."

"Doesn't sound so bad."

She climbs to her feet. "C'mon, let's go for a swim."

24

Vanessa and I spend every minute of the weekend together. We swim in the lake a lot and both get sunburned to a crisp. She takes countless pictures of me and Pierre, and I do some drawings of her and Pierre. We stay up all night talking about our families and our pasts. She confesses that she once had sex with a girl, Julie, from her private high school. I press her hard for more details. But I can't quite bring myself to tell her about Mrs. Kaye.

We make love on the dock (I've got splinters in weird places), and on the beacon tower again, and in her uncle's hayloft (scratchy). On Saturday night, we go to see *Fatal Attraction* at the Kanopolis drive-in and have our first argument as a couple.

"That misogynistic asshole deserved worse than he got," she says of the Michael Douglas character on the drive home.

"Are you kidding?" I say. "She was a complete wacko! She knew he was married going into it."

"I suppose you think he was an innocent bystander."

"No," I concede. "But she had totally unrealistic expectations."

"*She* had totally unrealistic expectations?" She crosses her arms over her chest. "To think he could just bed this woman, lead her on like he did, and then go back to his wife and kid as if nothing happened—talk about unrealistic expectations. And I love that one line of hers: 'I'm not going to be ignored.' Good for her!"

It suddenly hits me that with Vanessa and Mrs. Kaye and Geraldine, my love life is a lot more complicated than even the guy's in the movie.

"And what a cop-out ending!" she says.

"I don't agree."

"That's because you're a man!"

Pierre barks and leaps on her lap.

"We shouldn't fight in front of the kid," I say.

Vanessa breaks into a smile.

Sunday morning, she makes a pancake feast for her uncle and me. Later in the day, we hold a marathon Ms. Pac-Man competition at the Frosty. She beats me by two games. Vernadell loves her.

Sunday evening. Vanessa asks me to drive her to the football field for the pageant rehearsal. It's not until we swerve onto Broadway that I feel a pang of sadness that our weekend is ending.

"Did I tell you? I landed the role of Dorothy."

"Congrats, I guess."

"Your gay friend—what's his name . . . ?"

"He's not gay!"

She rolls her eyes. "His name?"

"Barry."

"Right. He's playing Mr. Harker. You should see him—so campy!"

The bank clock shows 8:10 P.M. We're the only car on Broadway. Vanessa reaches into her back jeans pocket and pulls out two twenties. "For my share of the gas," she says. I desperately want to refuse the money but can't afford to, so I thank her and slip it in my shirt pocket.

I park at the entrance to the football field. It looks like half the town is milling about the field while Mitchell Mann barks orders over a bullhorn, a beaming Barry at his side.

Vanessa leans over and kisses me deeply.

"This weekend was wonderful," she says.

"For me too."

"I have a favor to ask you," I say. "Shirley's threatening to take Pierre to the pound unless I find him a home. . . ."

"I'd be happy to keep him until I leave town," she says. "I don't think Uncle Roger would mind."

"Thanks."

I pat Pierre on the head. She leans over and we kiss again.

"Come on, Pierre," she says, and opens the door. I watch them hop out.

25

I'm pulling into our drive when I notice something new on the back of Allen's Charger, a bumper sticker: PAT POWERS WILL SEE YOU AT THE SUMMIT! I can't believe Allen would mar his lovingly restored Dodge Charger with this stupid sticker.

I make a baloney sandwich and pass through the living room, where Dad snores in his recliner and Shirley watches the ten o'clock news out of Wichita.

"Hiya, Shirley baby!" I say, and she looks at me askance.

I open my bedroom door and enter an alien environment. For the first time ever, the place is spotless: no empty beer cans, no crunchy porno mags, no dirty socks. The beds are stripped. The shades are up, the windows open. The aroma of pot has been replaced by the scent of Lysol. A portrait of a thumbs-up Pat Powers, autographed and with the words YOU'RE ON YOUR WAY, graces the wall where the black-light poster of skeletons having sex used to hang. Allen, on his knees, is scrubbing the refrigerator.

"What the fuck?" I ask.

"The first step in achieving your goals is to be active," Pat Powers says in a rich, commanding voice over the stereo. "You must act and act now. You are the master of your own destiny. I repeat, you are the master of your own destiny."

Allen switches off the stereo. "Take off your shoes, I just vacuumed. Oh, and don't eat that in here."

An unopened six-pack of Coors sticks out of the trash can along with his prized bong, the one he made from embalming tubes.

"Why are you throwing out beer?"

"Too many calories."

Again I ask, "What the fuck?"

Allen leaps up and waves his hands in the air. "I had the most amazing day. Pat was unbelievable, incredible. You should've seen him. You know what he did? He held a mirror up to my face. He made me take inventory of my life, and do you know what I saw? A flabby twenty-four-year-old underachiever. I saw myself for what I really was. I've vowed to change, Arty. And here's the best part: Pat Powers has given me the tools to make that change."

This is not my brother. Can't be.

Allen tells me how he now has direction and how with the "right positive attitude" he will achieve his "life goals." He shows me the chalkboard on the back of the door, *My Goals Are* scratched across it. Beneath these words, a list: *lose twenty pounds, get business going, win Renee back.* Amazing.

I lie on the bottom bunk. "I'm almost sorry I missed it."

"Oh, don't worry, I bought all his tapes. We'll listen together."

"Where are the sheets and blankets?"

"In the laundry. Along with all our dirty clothes."

"You're doing laundry?"

"Well, yeah." He looks at me as if this were the dumbest question ever asked. But I couldn't be more surprised if he told me he was having a sex change.

"I know that you will really benefit from these tapes," he says. "No offense, but you could stand to take a little personal inventory yourself."

"What is that supposed to mean?"

Allen shrugs. "You graduate soon and, frankly, we're all wondering what you plan to do with your life."

"While you're wondering, you can continue doing my laundry."

How can I exploit this? What's next? Breakfast in bed? Loaning me his car? Pat Powers just might end up being my most special best friend.

"Pat says that we must have a big, overarching goal and then little daily goals that will lead to the big goal—he says you get to the top of Mount Everest one step at a time."

"Or you could take a helicopter," I say.

A few years back Carrie invited Allen to one of Reverend Hanky's revivals. There, Allen "felt Jesus" and swore off pot and porn. Within a month, he got bored with religion and was back to weed and whacking off. What will be the expiration date for the Pat Powers Effect?

He reaches into the fridge and hands me the Snickers

with Vanessa's teeth marks in it. "Pat says, 'Junk food leads to a junk attitude.' "

I pop the Snickers in my mouth.

He switches the tape back on. "Let me repeat," Pat Powers says. "You are the master of your own destiny."

I turn it off. "What if you can't land Renee? Then what?"

"That, bro, is what Pat calls stinkin' thinkin'. *Can't* isn't in my vocabulary. And it shouldn't be in yours either."

"Okay. Let's say you win her back but she's changed. I mean, it's been six years. She may not be the same sweet high school cheerleader you once knew. She might be . . . a complete bitch."

"Excuse me," Allen says. He points to a sticker on the mirror: YOU HAVE ENTERED A NEGATIVE-ATTITUDE-FREE ZONE! "I would appreciate it if you'd take your stinkin' thinkin' outside."

26

Around midnight, the phone rings once. Then, a minute later, it rings again. It's the signal. But I can't go to the boneyard to see Mrs. Kaye. Not tonight. Vanessa's essence still swims in my veins.

27

Monday. Senior English class. Mrs. Kaye hands back our graded essays, "My Life After Graduation." Mine has a big red F scribbled on it, and the pages are covered with so much red ink that I can't read most of the bullshit I wrote. Yesterday, when Vanessa and I walked hand in hand out of the Frosty, I spotted Mrs. Kaye parked across the street, watching us. Am I living *Fatal Attraction*? I should just end our affair, or whatever the hell it is, except I have to pass senior English to graduate. Besides, I wouldn't put it past her to tell Vanessa about what we do.

An hour later, I'm doodling in American history class while Coach Hass explains why Eisenhower was our greatest president when the intercom speaker clicks on.

"Coach," Principal Swedeson's voice echoes.

Coach Hass looks up from his rod and reel. "Yeah?"

"Please send Arthur Flood to my office."

What now?

When I arrive at the principal's office, I stare into the solemn face of Mr. Fry, the fire inspector, who sits on a folding chair. Sheriff Bottoms, a toothpick tucked in the corner of his mouth, leans against the back wall. Behind Principal Swedeson's desk sits Mr. Elden, the hedgehog-faced county attorney, in an ill-fitting blue pinstriped suit and green tie. My pulse quickens.

"Arty, you know Mr. Fry and Sheriff Bottoms," Principal Swedeson says. "This here is Mr. Elden. He works for the county."

"What's this about?" I ask.

"Why don't you have a seat, Arty," Mr. Fry says.

Mr. Swedeson steps out and closes the door behind him.

"I can assure you there's nothing to be worried about." Mr. Elden smiles. "We just need for you to clarify a few details regarding the Stiles' Styles fire, is all." He motions to an empty chair. I sit.

Mr. Elden presses the red button on the tape recorder on the desk and smiles his narrow, rodenty smile. "Arty, if you would, please tell us again what happened when you arrived at work on the day of the fire."

I clear my throat. "Well, when I got to work, the Stileses were in a meeting with Mr. Denton. There was a lot of arguing. . . ."

"How long did this go on?" Mr. Elden asks.

"Maybe five minutes. Then Mr. Denton ran out. Mr. and Mrs. Stiles got into it. Mainly it was Mr. Stiles yelling. He said some pretty nasty things. . . ."

"Do you remember what he said?"

"Something about 'This stupid business was all your idea.' Then he called her a . . . well, it was a pretty bad word."

"What was the word?" Mr. Fry inquires.

"It was *cunt*. Then he hit her."

Mr. Elden writes something on the long yellow pad in front of him.

"Did you see him hit her?" Mr. Elden asks.

"No, but I heard it."

"Then what happened?"

"Mr. Stiles told me to take Pierre, their dog, who was barking like crazy, out to the lake. So I left."

Mr. Elden writes some more. "Did you see anyone while you were at the lake?"

"I didn't go to the lake. I drove around town for a while, then I went to the Frosty Queen."

"Were you alone before you went to the Frosty Queen?"

My stomach clenches. Do I need an alibi? "Yes, I was." I sound stupidly frightened, weak.

"How long would you say you were alone for, after leaving the Stileses?"

I shrug. "Maybe twenty minutes."

"Thank you for your time." He switches off the tape recorder.

"That's all?" I ask.

"Yes, that's all."

"I had nothing to do with that fire."

"Thank you, Arty."

"But—"

"That'll be all."

Sheriff Bottoms opens the door for me. His gray eyes shoot straight through me and the corners of his yellow tobacco-tinged lips crinkle into the slightest of smirks. It's in this moment that I realize he knows exactly how he's going to take his revenge on me.

On the walk back to class, terror like I've never known wells in my throat. Did Sheriff Bottoms plant evidence against me? Why would Mr. Elden ask me if I was alone if I wasn't a suspect? Or did that bastard Mr. Stiles tell them some lie about me?

After school, at the Frosty, I find Vernadell leaning over a sink full of dishes in the back.

"You look half dead," she says as she scrubs gunk off a plate. "What's the matter?"

I tell her my fear that Sheriff Bottoms or Mr. Stiles is trying to pin the fire on me.

"Oh, hell, I wouldn't worry about it," she says, and fishes the spoons and forks out of the sudsy waters. "Just look at the facts: Stiles owed half a million dollars. The factory was heavily insured. You got no motive and he does. The man'll say anything to save his ass and old Elden damn well knows it. He's no fool, that one."

"Then why'd Elden ask me if I was alone at the lake?"

"It's his job. Believe me, kiddo, you got nothing to worry about."

"Guess you're right."

My mood suddenly lifts. Good ol' Vernadell.

She smiles. "Got one slice of coconut cream pie left."

"Thanks."

I eat the delicious slice and play a vigorous game of Ms. Pac-Man—but I'm still unable to top Vanessa's score.

28

That night, around eleven o'clock, I'm sitting on the sofa watching the conclusion of *Star Search* when the phone rings. A moment later, it rings again. Dad, in his La-Z-Boy, picks up the receiver. "Hello?"

He slams the phone into its cradle. "Who the hell keeps calling here and hanging up?"

Twenty minutes later, I'm driving to the stiff orchard. I must do the right thing. Tonight. It's only fair. And besides, I want things with Vanessa to be . . . clean.

There's no moon out tonight and the cemetery is pitch-black. I can see the glowing tip of her cigarette in the darkness of her VW, parked beneath the oak tree.

I park beside her, kill the engine and lights, and wait. She doesn't get out of her car, so I get into hers. She's buck naked. In the dim dome light, I notice that she's shaved off all of her pubic hair. What's this about?

She tosses her cigarette out the window and turns to me. "She can't give you what I can."

"Mrs. Kaye, we have to—"

She mashes her mouth to mine, then she reaches over and massages my crotch.

I remove her hand. "Mrs. Kaye, please . . ."

She grabs on to the steering wheel and hoists herself out of her seat, then climbs over the gearshift and onto me. "She might be young and pretty," she says, breathing heavily, "but she can't make you happy."

Her car is way too cramped for this. Her knees jab me in the side and her head is pressed against the roof.

"Please, Mrs. Kaye . . ."

Her boobs jiggle in my face. As she struggles to get situated, a bright light shines in on us. Startled, we both whirl and stare into it. The door flies open and we spill out onto the ground. Mrs. Kaye screams. A massive arm hooks around my neck, and my throat constricts. I struggle to wrench free but I'm hurled to the dirt. I sit up, and *whack*—a boot kicks me in the middle of the chest, knocking the air out of me and sending me back to the dirt. I cough and see stars floating everywhere.

"Gotcha!" hisses Sheriff Bottoms.

The dancing stars soon fade and I catch my breath.

"You're under arrest for having sex on public property!"

I crawl onto my knees, trembling like a newborn calf. Mrs. Kaye is staring expressionlessly into the flashlight beam, her bare, dangling breasts looking so vulnerable and exposed in the cruiser's harsh light. Sheriff Bottoms shoves her onto her stomach and handcuffs her behind her back. Sadistic bastard.

Red and blue flashing lights come on from behind a nearby clump of shrubbery and the sheriff's cruiser pulls around. *Crap!* Deputy Clarkson climbs out, runs around back, and opens the door while Sheriff Bottoms pulls Mrs. Kaye to her feet and pushes her into the backseat.

"Book her!" Bottoms slams the door. He turns and looks at me. "Flood's mine."

The cemetery falls silent and black when Clarkson speeds away with Mrs. Kaye. My heart pounds in my throat as Sheriff Bottoms' hulking silhouette towers over me. I crawl backward on my knees. He steps closer, growling, "You make me sick."

He lunges for me and in one fluid motion I leap to my feet and make to run, only to trip over a low grave marker. I hit my head on a chunk of granite.

He grabs me by my shirt and pulls me off the grass. His fist smashes in my face. I reel, my ears ringing. I feel wetness on my nose. I'm on the ground again. I'm going to vomit.

He raises his nightstick and I pick up a rock beside my head and hurl it at him. Bull's-eye! He yelps and grips his forehead, his sheriff's hat sailing into the air.

No time to celebrate. I jump to my feet and sprint through the cemetery, weaving around tombstones and crosses. I hurdle the stone fence and disappear into the adjacent cornfield.

29

I haul ass all the way to her front door. The house is dark except for a light in the kitchen. I see, through the back door window, Vanessa at the Formica table, eating a sandwich and reading a novel, Pierre sprawled at her feet. I give a tap on the back door, startling her.

She lets me in. "My God! What happened to you?"

Before I can explain, she has me in the bathroom, where she washes my bruised and bloodied nose and treats it with rubbing alcohol. I feel *almost* lucky.

"Who did this?"

"Long story."

"Let's hear it."

She disappears for a minute, then returns with a small plastic bag full of frozen corn and tells me to hold it on my nose till the swelling goes down.

Back at the kitchen table, she sets a pitcher of water before me and I down the entire thing.

"All right." She sits across from me. "I wanna know everything."

And, with much squirming, I tell her about the whole sordid, uh, affair.

"I don't understand," she says. "Why did you sleep with your teacher for a year if you didn't really like her that much from the get-go?"

"She put a lot of pressure on me" drops pithily from my lips.

"And you took this girl Geraldine to the prom because her dad threatened to arrest your brother if you didn't?"

"I know this all sounds weird—"

"It doesn't sound weird, it sounds like you're blaming everyone but yourself for your actions."

This pisses me off. Big-time. "Vanessa, you have no idea what it's like to live in a small town. . . ."

"Now you're blaming the town?"

"Look, I didn't come here for a fucking lecture—"

"I just think that you'll keep getting stuck in these traps if you don't learn to say no to people."

"Yeah, well, what do you propose I do? Let my brother be arrested?"

"Your brother's an adult. You're not responsible for him."

This brings me up short. I've never thought of it that way.

"I think you'd feel a lot better about yourself if you stopped being a victim."

I push back my chair from the table. "Must be nice to have all the goddamn answers."

"There!"

"What?"

"Why can't you be that honest with everyone else in your life?" she asks.

"Because no one pisses me off like you do."

"Maybe that's because I expect more out of you."

God, she's so . . . I just . . . I have no response to this.

She stands and motions me into the other room. "Arty, I wanna show you something."

30

I follow her upstairs. Her uncle's snoring reverberates down the hallway. Her bedroom is at the front of the house. The room is spare: a small unmade bed with an old iron headboard rests on the polished hardwood floor, a plain pine dresser lurks in a corner. Over the bed there's an old-fashioned picture of a wolf howling at the moon. Piles of books clutter the floor. You'd never know a girl lived here. The wind blows the old, yellowed curtains as she closes the door behind us.

From the top dresser drawer she removes a stack of pictures and hands them to me. Black-and-whites of Pierre and me, taken at the old hospital, the Dog Lady's house, the air base, and the lake. I'm surprised how many are close shots of me. There're no "say cheese" corny smiles. I look totally natural and relaxed—hell, I didn't know I was being photographed.

"This one's my favorite." She hands me a profile shot of me staring intently out the upstairs window of the Dog Lady's house. It's the first picture I've ever seen of myself where I can see that I'm not halfway bad-looking.

She stands close beside me. "I love the look on your face here. Your eyes are so full of yearning, like you're wanting something that's far away, something you can't have. Reminds me of *Christina's World*."

"*Christina's World?*"

"You know, the Wyeth painting."

"Uh, sure." To deflect attention from my obvious ignorance, I say, "Didn't know you were taking my picture here."

"I'm going to title this picture *My Kansas Boy*. No, *My Yearning Kansas Boy*."

Is that how she views me? A boy?

"It's the best portrait I've ever taken. Of course, I had a great subject."

Her eyes move from the photograph to my eyes. We gaze at each other for a moment before I move in to kiss her.

She breaks it off before it gets too heated. "Join me for a cigarette."

We sit on the edge of the front porch, our legs dangling, while she smokes and tells me how she's freaking out about her mother's visit next weekend. I pet Pierre and think about what she said, about seeing myself as a victim.

She turns to me. "What do you think'll become of your teacher?"

"She'll get canned. No doubt about it."

"She knew the risks," she said.

The only sound is the squeaking of the windmill.

"I've never met her," she says, and comically raises an eyebrow. "But she taught you well."

"I'll send her a thank-you note. With a file." I lean over to kiss her, but she doesn't respond much.

"Something else on your mind?" I ask.

Vanessa tells me how she's leaving tomorrow for a two-day retreat to some Ozark lake with her therapy group. "They're letting me take Pierre," she says.

We talk about her sessions with her shrink, who sounds like a smart guy. "He thinks it's vital I don't return home after here," she says. "He thinks there's a cycle of dependency between me and my parents, and I agree."

Soon the sky lightens and the birds chirp. She stands. "I'll make us some breakfast."

In the kitchen, I set the table for three while she makes eggs, pancakes, and coffee. Around five-thirty her uncle comes down in his bib overalls and house slippers.

"Morning, Arty."

"Morning, Mr. Holtz."

"That's some shiner y'got there."

"Thank you, sir."

We eat breakfast. Afterward, her uncle heads out to the fields. Despite the coffee, I can't stay awake any longer. I go into the living room and collapse on the sofa. I don't wake until almost noon. I look around and find Vanessa in her bedroom, packing for her trip. She loans me her bike so I can get back to town.

"Do you realize we had an argument last night and we're still friends?" she says. "Maybe there's hope for us yet."

"Hope so," I say.

We kiss for the longest time, then I climb on her bike and pedal away.

31

I ride to the cemetery and peer nervously from behind a huge cottonwood tree. The Death Mobile is where I left it, keys in the ignition. There's no sign of Sheriff Bottoms. I put Vanessa's bike in the back and head into town, to face the nuclear meltdown that I know is unfolding.

I drive past Mrs. Kaye's house. Her car is in the garage and all the shades are pulled.

32

Reverend Hanky's Buick, along with Carrie's Corolla, is parked in our drive. I'm about to throw my car into reverse when Shirley and Dad scowl at me through the living room window. I park and trudge in to face my judgment.

"Just where in the hell have you been? Huh?" Shirley says with crossed arms.

"We thought you ran away." Carrie, on the sofa, dabs her seeping eyes with a tissue. "We were worried sick."

"Did you hear about Geraldine?" says Reverend Hanky, clutching a Bible.

I shake my head and Shirley thrusts a piece of pink notebook paper at me. Geraldine's overly curlicue handwriting reads, *I, Geraldine Renee Bottoms, have decided to end my life, for there is no reason for me to go on living. Arthur Milton Flood, my one and only love, has used me to cover up his affair with Mrs. Kaye. This is after he pressured me into giving him my cherished virginity!!!! I hope our Savior Lord Jesus Christ will take mercy on my soul!!!! I love you, Daddy. Never forget that and please forgive me. I hope to see you in heaven. Your beloved daughter, Geraldine.*

"She . . . she killed herself?" I ask.

"Not quite," Shirley says. "She drank eight bottles of Pepto-Bismol. Doc Hayes had to pump her stomach."

"Where is she?"

"Recovering at home."

Dad just sits in his La-Z-Boy, staring at the carpeting and looking confused and a little . . . curious? No one has asked me about my bruised, puffed face.

"You are a disgrace to this family," Shirley says.

For the next half hour, I lean against the fireplace mantel, trying to look repentant, while everyone talks over each other as to what they should do about me.

"He's eighteen, an adult now," Shirley says. "I say if he can carry on with a married woman, it's high time he lives on his own."

"No, Shirley!" Dad pipes up. "This is his home. He will always be welcome here."

"You're too easy on him, Milton!" she snaps. "That's why he's turned out the way he has."

Reverend Hanky suggests I be rebaptized in the lake; Carrie agrees and also believes I should be made a born-again virgin. Allen offers that my redemption lies in Pat Powers.

Finally, it's agreed upon that I am to attend church regularly, apologize to Geraldine, and deliver Meals on Wheels. Fine. Sign me up for all three.

"And," Shirley adds, "we're grounding you from your car until graduation."

"You can't do that."

"Oh, we most certainly can."

I turn to Dad for help, but he looks at the floor and mutters, "I think that's fair punishment."

"How am I going to get around?"

"You've got feet and a bicycle."

"Let us now bow our heads in prayer," says the Reverend.

33

Mrs. Watkins, the owl-faced substitute teacher, grades our English term papers at Mrs. Kaye's desk while everyone snoozes or studies for other finals. Yesterday the school board held an emergency session and voted unanimously to fire Mrs. Kaye for "moral turpitude." Judge Tate fined her two hundred dollars for public nudity as well as lewd and lascivious behavior on city property, and told her to go home and read her Bible. She's called my house a few times looking for me but I haven't called her back. I wish I knew what to say to her. Word has it her husband moved to Tulsa and filed for divorce. I feel awful about this but I keep reminding myself of what Vanessa said: she knew the risks. I'm not feeling like that's quite enough to absolve either of us, though.

Of course, my fellow classmates are buzzing. Guys at school see me as a stud, banging the "slutty" teach.

Between classes, I pass Geraldine in the hallway and she turns her face theatrically away. On Monday, she wrote me a five-page letter telling me how humiliated she is and how she can't continue in a relationship with an adulterer. The Ichthus crowd isn't speaking to me, either. Breaks my heart, let me tell ya. Sheriff Bottoms doesn't realize what a great service he's done me and her. I haven't seen or heard from him since that night in the cemetery and I'm petrified about his next move. The swelling has gone down on my nose, but it's still blue and sore.

Barry, trying to elbow his way into my spotlight, has been standing near me a lot while ordering people to "give Arty space." Yesterday, on my way out of the library, he gave me a searching look and whispered, "I understand, Arty. Guess we all have our needs." I'm not quite sure what he meant by that.

After school, I ride my ten-speed down Broadway. Allen, in tiny red shorts, white tube socks, and no shirt, jogs on the left side of the street. He's drenched in sweat and his gut jiggles over his elastic waistband like a hairy Jell-O salad, but he's giving it his all.

Every day Allen has been jogging, lifting weights, dieting, and cleaning our room—getting Pat Powered up for Renee.

"Go the distance, Rocky!" I yell, and speed past.

Too winded to speak, Allen gives me a thumbs-up and huffs on.

34

I rest my bike against the side of the Frosty. In her booth, red-faced Vernadell argues with Hal Denton. Darlene changes my dollar and I settle in front of Ms. Pac-Man, determined to beat Vanessa's high score. She gets back from her nutjob retreat in two days. Can't come soon enough for me.

I overhear Vernadell tell Mr. Denton that she's waiting on the check from the railroad and the moment she gets it, he'll get his money. He tells her he can't wait another day. Their conversation sounds eerily like the one Hal Denton had with the Stileses on the day of the fire. The ghosts kill me. Game over.

When Hal Denton leaves, Vernadell slides out of the booth and approaches me. "Y'wanna job for the night?"

"Huh?"

"Barry called. Said he's not coming in tonight on account of pageant rehearsal."

"Sure, why not?"

So it turns out that I'm not a half-bad waiter. Of course, it helps that I know the menu by heart—Zip Burgers, fries, two kinds of pie (chocolate banana and coconut cream), sundaes. After I get the hang of things, Vernadell leaves for her apartment, saying she needs a nap but will relieve me at midnight. It's just me and Darlene. The café gets busy around five and I only mess up one order during the rush. By seven it's dead quiet once again (in Harker City, we eat our supper by six-thirty at the latest).

I'm in the back studying for my biology final when the bell clangs. A stooped-over old man sits at the counter. I take a second look. Lord, would you look at that. It's Grandpa Kohl. Mom's dad. This is the first good look at him I've had in about four years. Whenever I run into him in town, I scurry off in the opposite direction. I have no use for a man who used his nine-year-old grandson to deliver vodka to his hospitalized daughter. He looks ancient, like the old drunk he is. His teeth are gone, his face sunken in. His hair (what little is left) and beard have gone white.

"What can I get you?" I look at the order pad, not him.

"Why, Arty." His breath reeks of whiskey and his words are slurred. "Sure good to see you, son. Shoot, I didn't know you worked here."

"Just filling in for a friend."

"How's Allen?"

"He's okay. Taken up jogging."

"Never see you boys no more."

"Know what you want?"

"Okay. Sure. I'll have a burger, no onions."

I write it down, stick the order over the grill. "Take care of him, will ya, Darlene?"

She nods and looks at me knowingly. In a small town everyone knows your stuff and sometimes that's not a bad thing.

35

For the next couple of hours business is slow, with the occasional railroader or bachelor farmer, and I get a lot of studying done. At twenty after ten, the phone rings and Mitchell Mann, the pageant director, who is staying in the honeymoon suite at the motel, places an order for room service. Darlene makes his two cheeseburgers and two orders of fries while I make his two vanilla malts—guy's a big eater.

I carry the fragrant bag to his room, where I notice Barry's Nova is parked. My hand is poised to knock when I hear Barry's unmistakable giggle inside. I lean forward and peer through the tiny gap in the drapes. Barry, naked and front side up, lies on the bed. Then the hairy bare ass of Mitchell Mann passes in front of my view. I step back, shocked, queasy, and weak-kneed. As the bedsprings *squeak-squeak-squeak* I set the bag in front of the door, knock once, and run.

"You okay?" Darlene says to me when I walk into the Frosty. "You're lookin' kinda pale."

I plop into an empty booth. How could I have believed all this time that Barry was straight? I can't get the image of the two of them out of my mind. Could this be Barry's first "experience"?

The front door opens and I look over my shoulder, fearing it's Barry. Two railroaders in striped overalls settle at the counter. I drag myself out of the booth and, all business, take their orders.

36

After work, I'm riding my bike home when I see a light on in the bank and Hal Denton's Mercedes in the empty lot. Mr. Denton has not yet responded to my requests, of which I've made four. And, of course, I'm desperate.

I peer through the glass front door and into the lobby. The drawn curtains in Mr. Denton's office are backlit. I knock loudly. A shadow moves across the curtains. I knock again, harder. The office door cracks open and Mr. Denton peers out. I wave and he makes a "go away" motion and shuts the door.

I walk around to the drive-up window and hold down the service buzzer. I see his office door fly open and Mr. Denton charges across the lobby. He glares at me through the glass. He looks awful, with at least a three-day beard growth and deep dark bags under his eyes. His armpit-stained shirt hangs half out.

"We're closed, for God's sake!" His voice sounds Martian-like over the speaker.

"It's important!" I shout into the little speaker.

"Who is this?"

"Arthur Flood."

"Come back during business hours, Arty." He heads back to his office. I press the buzzer again. He rushes over and yells: "Stop that, goddamnit!"

"I was wondering if you had a chance to look at my debt request form yet."

"Huh?"

"I was working for the Stileses. They owed me over a thousand dollars in back pay."

"Look, kid, they owed a lot of people a lot of money. Take a number."

"But I graduate next weekend and I really need that money. It's only one thousand—"

"If I had it, I'd give it to you. But I don't. And I won't have it anytime soon."

"Can you give me an emergency loan? I promise I'll pay—"

"No! Press that goddamn buzzer again and I'll call Sheriff Bottoms."

He stomps across the lobby and slams the door on all my plans.

When I step into our kitchen, I see Dad, in his flannel pajamas, sitting alone at the table, eating a bowl of Grape-Nuts and doing a crossword puzzle. He peers at me over his reading glasses and sets down his pencil. I've avoided being alone with him since the whole Mrs. Kaye thing went down.

"Hey, Dad," I say as I shut the door.

I go to the refrigerator, take out the milk carton, and pour myself a small glass. Not that I'm thirsty. I just don't know what else to do. When I turn around, he's still staring at me. Very disapprovingly.

"I expected more out of you, Arty."

I nod and hang my head.

"She's a married woman, for crying out loud."

"It was stupid of me."

"Shirley thinks I've been too easy on you over the years, and maybe she's right." He removes his glasses and looks about the room, as if searching for answers. "I must've certainly done something wrong."

"For—for what it's worth, I'm sorry."

"Hell, don't apologize to me!" He places his palms on the table and pushes himself up. "Apologize to her husband."

He drops the bowl in the sink with a resounding clang, and on his way out he says, "Thank God your mother isn't alive to know about this."

37

It's the following night, a quarter to midnight. Fifteen minutes before I get off work. (Barry's still "deep into rehearsals.") I'm counting my tip money (nine dollars and seventy-two cents) when the phone rings.

"Frosty Queen," I say.

"There you are," says Mrs. Kaye. "I've been calling all over town looking for you."

"You have?"

"Stop by after work. I have a surprise for you."

The line goes dead.

Twenty minutes later and here I am, knocking on her back door. In my head I'm repeating Vanessa's words like a mantra. But this woman lost her job and her husband because of choices I made. God, I hope her husband didn't come back. My pulse quickens at the thought. What if her husband has her at gunpoint, forced her to call me, and plans to kill us both?

"It's open," she shouts through the door.

I slowly turn the knob and peer in. The kitchen smells of freshly baked brownies. It's dark except for a flickering candle on the table where a woman with blotchy orange skin, spiky peroxide-blond hair, and red lips sits. If it weren't for the gap in her front teeth, I wouldn't recognize Mrs. Kaye.

"Well, what do you think?" she says, and runs her hands through her hair. "I know how much you like Annie Lennox."

"Uh, neat."

I look around. No sign of her vengeful sword-packing husband. I softly close the door.

"And the outfit," she says. "What do you think of the outfit?"

She stands and twirls. I've been so mesmerized by her face and hair that I've neglected to notice her new low-cut purple dress. The shoulder pads are gigantic and she smells of an expensive lilac perfume. My eyes adjust to the darkness and I note with a pang that her bottom lip is bruised and puffed up.

"What happened . . . ?" I motion to my lower lip.

She gestures for me to sit. "I made your favorite. Brownies with walnuts."

I lean against the sink. "Where's your husband?"

"He moved to Tulsa."

"Because of us?"

"Nope."

"But I thought . . ."

"He hit me when I found out about *him*."

I shake my head.

"He'd been on the road since yesterday and didn't know

I'd been fired. Then, last night, while the son of a bitch was down in his workshop, the phone rang. It was some woman wanting to speak to him. I asked her who she was and she told me she was his fiancée." She shakes her head and laughs mirthlessly. "Can you believe that? She had no clue he was married. He told her he lived with his elderly mother. Well, she gave me an earful. Seems they've been carrying on for over a year and she's seven months pregnant with his child."

"I'm sorry."

"I'm not; I'm glad it happened," she says with a fierce and deranged smile. "I really am. Now I can move on with my life. My mother always said I married beneath me.

"I filed for divorce today. After I left the courthouse, I decided to give myself a treat, so I drove straight to Topeka to that new mall on the edge of town. I got my hair done, bought this outfit, and spent some time in the tanning booth. I decided it's high time to start living again. Aren't you going to eat those brownies?"

"Thanks, but I'm not hungry."

"I'm sorry to hear that." Her brow furrows; she's genuinely hurt.

She reaches over to the counter, takes her pack of Virginia Slims, lights one, and exhales. "I'm moving to Chicago. Going to live with my sister till I can find a job and a place of my own. And I was thinking . . ." She blows smoke. "Why don't you join me?"

"You want me to . . . ?"

"We can leave after you graduate on Sunday."

Chicago. A real city. A giant city.

"Wow." I'm genuinely stunned. "Can I think about it?"

"What's to think about?" She taps the bottom of her Bic lighter on the Formica tabletop. "I'm offering you your heart's desire, a ticket out."

"But I'm broke."

"It won't cost you a thing. Once we're there, you can find a job." She reaches over and takes my hand in hers. "Trust me, baby, it'll be perfect."

38

"**H**ow was the Ozarks?" I say as I drop my ten-speed on the ground and step onto Vanessa's uncle's front porch. She's very tanned, very sexy. My blood pounds.

"Kansas Boy!" Vanessa leaps off the porch swing, throws her arms around my neck, and kisses me. "I missed you!"

"Me too!"

Pierre rubs against my leg and I pet him. Vanessa and I kiss some more, here in broad daylight, here on her uncle's front porch. God, how I've missed her smooth skin, that earthy smell, her soft lips. She's a highly addictive drug, this girl. My girl.

"C'mon." She takes my hand. "Let's go for a swim and catch up."

We pedal to the lake on our bikes. I tell her all about my car being impounded; she tells me about her New Agey therapy retreat. At the dock, she dives in smooth, legs together, and makes the smallest of splashes. I scramble to strip to my underwear and swim out to where she's treading water. The water is cool and it feels good, slick and natural. She splashes me and I splash her back.

Later, as we're lying on the dock, drying in the sun, she turns to me. "You seem distracted. As my therapist says, where are you right now?"

I take a deep breath and plunge in. "I know we agreed that we wouldn't make any promises beyond our time here together," I say. "But I graduate Sunday and you're leaving after this weekend and, well, I've been doing a lot of thinking. And I believe New York is the right place for both of us. You can pursue photography and I can get a job somewhere and support us. Then, later, I can take classes in illustration. What do you say?"

The air quivers between us. She is silent and looks at me.

"Arty. I like you so much." She is speaking slowly, deliberately. "The days we've spent together have been some of the best in my life. But I can't be responsible for a relationship after I leave here. I have to figure out what I'm doing with *my* life first. I have to figure out what I want, who I—"

"I understand you don't want to make a commitment right now," I break in. "That's totally fair. And I'm not asking for marriage or anything like that. God, no—no pressure here. But we can go to New York together, as a—as a team—"

Now she breaks in. "But I need time alone to figure these things out for myself. If we went together, I would be thinking of us," she says. "I'm not even sure if New York is where I want to end up."

"But maybe our being together is what you'll end up wanting. And if we don't try now, it'll be too late."

"Maybe," she says. "But I need perspective before I can make that decision."

She's right. She's sensible. But I have to leave with her. It can't be Mrs. Kaye. She closes her eyes, leans over, and kisses me on the lips.

"We have each other right now," she says softly. "Let's not think about anything beyond that. What do you say?"

I can't even choke out a response as my heart writhes in my chest.

39

It's around ten o'clock that night, and sprinkling, when I steer my bike into our drive and see Geraldine sitting behind the wheel of her Chevette. My first thought is to run. But I'm surprised she's sitting alone in our driveway at this hour. So unlike her. Why is she just sitting there? I pull up alongside and she looks at me with a blank expression. Something's up.

I get into her passenger seat. She stares out the windshield for a moment, then turns to me. "Arthur, my period's four days late."

I am too stunned. I lean back and close my eyes.

"You're sure?" I croak out.

"It should've come on Wednesday. It's never late."

"But we only did it once."

"Guess that's all it takes."

This is not happening. Not happening, not happening. I'm going to puke. I can't draw a breath. I'm going to die. Now. Please?

"If you are pregnant," I say, "we'll take care of it, right?"

"Of course we will, it's our baby."

"I meant we'll take care of the problem." I stare at her for a long moment, my brow creased in that you-get-my-drift way.

Her eyes narrow and her whole body trembles. "Abortion is a mortal sin!"

"So is premarital sex."

"I will not kill our baby, Arthur Flood! I hate you for saying that!" She bursts out crying and bangs her forehead on the steering wheel.

She bangs and bawls for the longest time and I just sit there, suspended in surreality. *This is a nightmare. I will wake up, right?*

Finally she stops, lifts her head, and leans back. I note that the top of the steering wheel has left a red, puffy, rounded imprint across her forehead.

"If I am pregnant," she says in a surprisingly level voice, "you will marry me."

"No, I will not."

Thwack! She backhands my nose hard, right where her dad hit me, and it stings like a bitch. The pain is almost a welcome relief.

I see my future. A high school education, a job on the railroad to support Geraldine and a child, regular attendance at the New Life Church, forced to become a Shriner or a Mason. A descent into numbness as I gaze into the TV and eat myself into high blood pressure and a coronary. Or maybe I'll find some drug to cope, to get through. A Flood family tradition. The classic Harker City destiny.

Ahhhhhhhhhh!

Then a thought.

"What if we put the baby up for adoption?" I ask.

This rates two slaps, but I successfully dodge 'em. Should've figured Geraldine, with her Cabbage Patch Kid collection, wouldn't go for it.

"Just think, what sort of life can we give the child?" I plead. "We're both broke, you're only sixteen."

"Maybe the Lord wanted me to get pregnant, like Mary. Maybe I'm carrying the Savior. Would you kill baby Jesus?"

"That was immaculate conception, and we weren't exactly immaculate out in that wheat field," I say. "Who else knows about this?"

"No one."

"Thank God."

"When Daddy finds out, he'll shoot you twice." I detect an unmistakable glimmer of spiteful glee.

"Please don't say anything to anyone until we figure something out. . . ."

She wipes her nose and eyes with her sleeve and starts the engine. "There's nothing to figure out. I'm keeping the baby and you're marrying me. I'll call you later."

PART THREE

1

I lie across the front seat of the Death Mobile and stare at the rain hitting the windshield. How can my life be over at eighteen? I haven't felt this exhausted since the night of the Stileses' fire. Marriage to Geraldine Bottoms. Should I climb to the top of the tower and end my problems in a leap? But what if I survive as a quadriplegic—and still have to marry Geraldine? I've got to talk to somebody about all of this. I need an ally.

Vernadell is not in her booth. Darlene, who is watching *The Thing* on TV, tells me V's at the motel, "dealin' with that fancy-ass Hollywood prima donna." When I don't find her in the tiny motel office, I call her name through the doorway that leads to her apartment. No response. As I turn to leave, the front door opens and Vernadell steps in holding a stack of pillows and blankets.

"I swear to God, that man's sendin' me to a not-so-early grave," she says, and charges past me into the apartment. I follow.

"Nothin's good enough for him," she raves, and stuffs the

pillows and blankets into a linen closet. "I've given him five—count 'em, five—pillows and there still ain't one soft enough for Little Lord Fancy Pants. Where does he think this is? The goddamn Ritz? Oh, and then there are the blankets. These here are all 'blends,' he says. He can only sleep under cotton. Egyptian cotton. Egyptian cotton! Seems that polyester don't allow his pores to breathe. Can you believe this?"

I've never been in Vernadell's apartment. A gray 1950s curved sofa faces a small TV with rabbit-ear antennas wrapped in crinkled aluminum foil. Snoopy and the Peanuts gang posters decorate her cigarette-yellowed walls. Who knew?

She sifts through a stack of blankets. "What're you doing here at this hour, anyhow? Y'look like you just saw death itself."

Even though no one else is here, I speak in a hushed voice as I tell Vernadell about Geraldine.

She shakes her head and says, "Them's the breaks, kid, them's the breaks."

"But what should I do?"

"Way I see it, there's nothing you can do. 'Cept pray she gets her period."

I expect some sort of advice or game plan from the wise and no-nonsense Vernadell, but she just shakes her head.

"You plan to marry her?"

"Hell no."

"Smart, boy. You two'd be miserable together. Wish I had something to tell ya."

"That's okay."

At least I know Vernadell won't tell anyone.

"Realize this might seem like the end of the world," she says. "But, believe me, it ain't."

2

I stand in front of Our Redeemer Lutheran Church. I haven't entered here since I was in the fourth grade and Mom was at the hospital drying out. The front door is unlocked and I step gingerly into the dark sanctuary, which smells of candle wax. The streetlamp outside illuminates the green, red, and yellow stained-glass window of Jesus holding up His right hand. I leave the lights off and try to tread softly. I don't want Reverend Vernon, who lives next door, to know I'm here.

I move down the aisle and stand before the altar. You're supposed to kneel, so I do. I look up at the statue of Jesus, pained eyes looking skyward, ever nailed on that eternal cross.

"Uh, look, Jesus, I know I've been a really crappy Christian. And I know this must look hypocritical, me coming here and asking you for help."

I look behind me, to make sure no one is listening. "Then again, God, I figure you kind of owe me on account of I begged you for your help with my mom and she died just a week later."

Shit. If God exists, have I already insulted Him? But in case I haven't, I continue. "I need your help. Just get me out of this mess. Please, God. Let her not be pregnant. Please do this one thing for me. Please, please, please. If you help me out, I'll do whatever you want me to. I'll even become a born-again. I will. Somehow." Did I just say that?

"Guess that's it. Thank you." I walk away. Then I stop and turn back. "Amen."

On my way home, I pass Mrs. Kaye's house. I want to blame her, Allen, and Sheriff Bottoms for what's happened, for forcing me to date Geraldine. Then I think about what Vanessa said, about me blaming everyone else for my mistakes.

Later that night, I lie on my bunk and stare at the cracks in the ceiling as Allen curls barbells in the dresser mirror and gives me a blow-by-blow account of how he has planned his date with Renee.

"I realize," Allen's voice puffs, "that as a stewardess, Renee has been wined and dined by all sorts of big shots. But when she's back here, I think she'll realize that by my staying here in Harker City, I'm making a difference too. That I'm playing an important role. I mean, as a mortician, you help people through one of life's most profound experiences. You help them say goodbye to a loved one. It's, like, a sacred thing."

Does everyone do this—convince themselves that their life has meaning? Do I?

"And if that ain't important," he continues, "I don't know what is."

"Jesus Christ, do you ever shut up?" escapes my mouth. "Shit, I'm sorry, Allen. I didn't mean that."

My brother looks like he's about to cry.

"I've just . . . got a lot on my mind right now."

"Just thought you of all people would understand," he says, swallowing a sob, and sets down his barbells.

"Please don't be angry."

"Who's angry? I'm not." He flops onto his bunk and turns his back to me. Vanessa is right. I am his only friend.

3

My bedside alarm clock shows 3:27 A.M. Allen's snoring is driving me nuts. Sprawled on the vinyl beanbag, I'm channel-surfing on Allen's black-and-white TV with the volume on low: a Juice Man Juicer infomercial, *The Munsters* (the episode where Grandpa creates a twin brother for Herman), followed by a lot of test patterns. Then an old movie. The only person I recognize in it is a young, thin, and very beautiful Elizabeth Taylor. The story eerily parallels what's happening to me: this guy (who kind of looks a little like Rob Lowe) accidentally gets this chubby chick pregnant, then he meets and falls in love with Elizabeth Taylor. The guy decides his only option is to kill the chubby chick, so he takes her out in a boat on a deserted lake, strangles her, and throws her overboard.

I switch off the TV. Why was this movie on now? Could this be the answer to my prayer? Why would Jesus, Mr. Turn the Other Cheek, urge me to drown Geraldine? Or did Jesus, who knows how undeserving I am, send my prayer straight to Satan, who arranged for me to see this particular movie?

I picture the whole lurid scene: late one night I take Geraldine for a "moonlight cruise" in a rowboat on Harker City Lake.

"This is so romantic, honeybunch!"

While she's obliviously wolfing down a hot fudge sundae, I steer the boat toward the spillway. Just as it's about to go over the edge, I leap out.

"Honeybunch!" I hear her voice echo and fade in the massive concrete funnel. Seconds later there's a resounding splash.

I enjoy this fantasy—that Geraldine's demise would bring hope back to my life—far more than I should, which scares me a little.

I switch off the TV and wander downstairs. The kitchen light is burning and I see Dad, in his flannel pajamas, doing a crossword puzzle and eating cereal at the table.

"Can't sleep, huh, Dad?"

He shakes his head. I pull out the chair across from him and sit. He wipes the milk from his chin and says, "Everything all right?"

"No."

"This thing with your teacher, it'll blow over."

I shake my head. "It's . . . worse than that."

Dad sets down his spoon and looks at me over the rims of his glasses, awaiting an explanation.

Here it goes. I take in a deep breath and say, "There's a good chance Geraldine's pregnant."

"This some sort of joke?"

"Wish it was."

"Good Lord, son!" He tears off his glasses. "Good Lord!"

Pushing his chair back from the table, he heaves himself up and paces the floor. After about a minute he asks, "You in love with her?"

I shake my head.

"Then you shouldn't marry her," he says, and sits back down. "That would be a mistake."

It's in this moment that I think I know why Mom drank.

"But how am I going to survive?"

He leans in and says very matter-of-factly, "You'll just have to get a job and start making child support payments. No getting around that."

"But I gotta get out of this town, Dad. You know I do."

"There's no law I know of that says you have to stay here to live up to your responsibilities," he says. "But y'might be surprised—your feelings toward sticking around might change once you have a little one. I'm not saying you'll want to be with Geraldine, but you're a loyal person, and there's a good chance you'll wanna stick around."

I want to reach over the table and kiss my old man. Thank him for not yelling at me, for not giving me a long-winded lecture about the importance of responsibility, for not calling me an idiot and a disgrace to our family. Instead, I smile and say sincerely, "Thanks, Dad."

He stands and starts out of the room. It's at the door to

the living room that he stops and turns back to me. "Let's not say anything to Shirley just yet, huh?"

I nod.

"And, son, are there any more surprises coming?"

I shake my head.

"Thank the Lord for that."

Once he's gone, I pick up the phone and dial.

"Hello?" Mrs. Kaye says groggily.

I tell her: "Count me in for Chicago."

4

Today is Friday, my last day of publicly funded education. I'm bombing my Spanish final. I haven't cracked a book or memorized one vocabulary word in here all year because Mr. Richards, our Spanish teacher and the only person at Harker City High who almost speaks a foreign language, doesn't give anyone less than a C. Mr. Richards once gave Eric Peterson an F. Eric's dad, president of the school board, threatened Mr. Richards' job if he flunked his son over a "spic" language. Since then, everyone gets at least a C in Spanish.

The bell rings and Mr. Richards wakes with a start. "All right, everyone, bring your tests up front here."

If I get 50 percent of the answers, it'll be a miracle.

In the hallway, I clean out my locker as all around me yearbooks are passed around for signing and someone plays Alice Cooper's classic "School's Out." A senior girl runs past, sobbing happily. I should be sobbing too, albeit for radically different reasons.

Barry struts up. I shake my brain to try to erase recent images of him.

"It's official. I've served my last slice of banana cream pie," he says. "I've quit the Frosty. Y'want my old job?"

"Sure, thanks."

"I can no longer be bothered with it," he says as he flings his right hand through the air dismissively. "It will only distract me from my career."

"Why are you wearing sunglasses inside, Barry?" I ask him.

"I auditioned for a surfer movie last night," he says.

I want to say, *Yeah, I saw your audition.*

"Mitchell wants me to go back to Hollywood with him once the pageant is over."

"That's great."

"It is. Remember, shift starts at four." He flounces off.

I approach Geraldine at her locker.

"Can you meet me in Harker Park in half an hour?" I ask. She nods. "What for?"

"I'll explain there."

5

Twenty minutes later, I'm on a swing in Horace Harker Park, sipping from a can of Dr Pepper and nervously waiting for Geraldine.

I finish the Dr Pepper and stare at the life-sized statue of Horace Harker. OUR BELOVED FOUNDER is etched in the marble pedestal below him. When Mr. Harker died in 1933, Grandpa Flood made the death mask that was used to create this statue. The problem was Mr. Harker was ninety-two and toothless when he died. The city fathers, obviously not wanting a statue of a shriveled codger, constructed a young, very muscular body for Mr. Harker, then stuck the toothless face on it. The result is a twenty-five-year-old muscle man's body with a ninety-two-year-old's face. They tried to fix this by putting on one of those Abe Lincoln top hats and a beard, but it didn't help much.

Too much Dr Pepper. Suddenly I have to pee. I look around for a bush or a tree, but right then Geraldine's Chevette sputters up and parks. I'll just have to hold it. I cross my legs tightly. My palms sweat and my heart acceler-ates. *You must do this, Arty. You must.*

She sits on the swing beside me. "Why, Arthur, how ro-mantic." She leans back, lifting her feet above her head. "Maybe we should get married in this park."

Do it, Arty. Now.

"Geraldine, the reason I asked you here is because I'm not going to marry you. I'm moving to Chicago, where I'll get a job and mail you child support every month. You have my solemn word on that."

I exhale. *There. Done.*

She scowls at me for what feels like a century. No words. I have to wonder how much of her dad's violent DNA is pounding through her right now.

"But I hope we can continue to be friends," I add, hating myself for saying that.

Her entire body vibrates and tears spring from the cor-ners of her eyes. "I have to go with you."

"No. I'm sorry."

"But I can't stay in Daddy's house! I can't raise a child there. He's so overprotective and paranoid, I'm dying to get out. Please let me go with you."

This surprises me. What happened to Daddy's adoring lit-tle girl?

"This is your child too," she says. "Don't you want to be a part of it?"

"Believe me, you'll thank me for this someday. You deserve better than me." I'm amazed at my own level of bullshit. Could it be that I mean what I'm saying?

"Hold me," she says. "I need you to hold me."

I put my arm around her shoulders. She embraces me at the waist, clutching me way too tightly. She sobs and her body jiggles. My bladder is at breaking point. She drops her hands and glares at me with her red, puffy, makeup-smeared face. "What did I ever do to you?" She swallows hard, her voice trembling. "I just loved you. All I ever wanted was for you to love me back."

"I'm sorry," I say. "But I don't."

"Maybe we can still make it work. You know, we can live like friends in the same house."

"Why would you want to be with someone who doesn't want to be with you?"

"Did you ever even like me?" Her voice is breaking up again.

"Of course—"

"Or was I always just a cover for you and Mrs. Kaye?"

"Please don't think that."

"I'm not stupid," she says. "I know Daddy forced you to take me out. But sometimes you were so sweet to me, like when you drew me that beautiful birthday card, that I believed you really loved me."

"Look, I like you. I just can't marry you."

She presses her bawling face into my lower stomach, further straining my screaming bladder.

"Uh, Geraldine . . ."

She mumbles something I can't hear.

"Could you please not push . . . ?"

She burrows her head into my gut, now while squeezing me from behind.

"Don't—I really have to pee."

"Why?" She repeatedly knocks her head against my stomach. "Why?"

I try to wriggle free, but she pulls me closer, tighter. "I need you."

"Geraldine!"

She looks up, stunned, and releases me.

I jump over the kiddy train tracks and behind the statue of Horace Harker, unzip my 501s, and am letting it pour when there's a gut-wrenching scream. I peer between Horace Harker's calves and see Geraldine, nostrils flaring, charging toward me like an angry bull. I bolt and piss all over myself.

She chases me around the jungle gym and spiral slide. "Betrayer! Liar!"

She runs out of steam and drops to her knees. I zip up my jeans.

"Why?" she cries, and falls forward, landing facedown in the grass. My jeans and Nikes are soaked and stinking. She

curls in a fetal position, tears streaming, beneath the statue of
our town's beloved creator.

"Arty, I'm scared."

I bend down and pat her on the shoulder.

"Me too," I say. "Me too."

6

I'm pedaling fast down Broadway, toward home, toward getting out of my soaked pee-wear, when there's the pinging of a little bell behind me. Vanessa is approaching fast on her Schwinn.

"Arty!" She pulls up alongside me.

"Oh, hey." I steer away in hopes she won't smell my piss.

"Why haven't you called me back?"

"I'm fine."

"What?"

"Huh?"

"Why're you avoiding me?" she asks. "And why're you practically on the other side of the road?"

"I'm kinda in a hurry. Let's talk later."

She cuts me off and pulls to the curb in front of the library. "Arthur Flood, if you value our relationship at all, you'll stop and talk to me."

I pull over and rotate my body so she can't see my wet pants leg.

She tilts her head and looks at me. "The thing is, I'm here for two more days and I'd like to spend them with you—"

Behind her, a car races up Broadway. Geraldine's Chevette. It flies through the intersection and swerves in our direction. I leap off my bike, grab Vanessa, and push her out of the way as the Chevette plunges onto the curb, knocks against a fire hydrant, careens into the front window of Duckwall's Five and Dime, and stops. Glass showers the sidewalk.

Vanessa looks stunned as I help her up. We cautiously approach the broken window. Geraldine bawls into the steering wheel. Mr. Fairberry, the store manager, stands frozen at the checkout desk, covered in dust. The Chevette's front fender can't be more than a foot from him. He removes his glasses, wipes the lenses with a Kleenex, and slips them on before dialing the phone.

Within ten minutes, Sheriff Bottoms and the whole town are there. Harker City's mother/daughter EMT team slap a neck brace on Geraldine and shove her into the back of the ambulance. Sheriff Bottoms' cruiser, lights flashing and siren wailing, escorts the ambulance away. Deputy Clarkson asks me what might have provoked Geraldine.

"I, um, broke up with her."

Vanessa throws me a puzzled look.

7

Once the crowd clears, Vanessa and I take our bikes and walk down Broadway toward the Frosty.

"You saved my life, Arty Flood," she says. "I thank you."

"I also caused your potential vehicular homicide."

"Yeah, what's all that about?"

So I tell her about my drunken one-night stand with Geraldine and its horrific consequences.

"Jesus. You really get around. You didn't use protection?"

"Obviously not. I was wasted . . . and stupid . . . and it was all over before I could take my Nikes off."

"Shit."

"Exactly."

And then, a sudden, shocking thought. "Um, you're definitely on the pill, right?"

"Told you I was. I had my own pregnancy scare back in California, remember? You know, this is . . . a lot to take in."

"Tell me about it. But believe me, you're the only one I care about."

"That doesn't exactly make me feel better. What if she really is pregnant?"

"Told her I'll send her child support but I won't marry her."

"Good call. Think she'll be okay?"

"Hope so. Anyway, I wanted to tell you that I'm moving to Chicago tomorrow."

"Chicago?"

"I thought about what you said and I couldn't agree with you more. We do need time away from each other. For perspective."

"Are you going by yourself?"

"I'll be with a, uh, friend."

"Who?"

"You don't know the person. Point is, I'm getting out." I do my best to sound cheerful, but her frown tells me she knows there's some bullshit in my announcement.

"Why won't you tell me who this friend is?"

"Told you, you don't know—"

"Arthur Flood, if you leave with that teacher, you'll regret it the rest of your life."

Am I that transparent?

"You'll be indebted to her and she'll never let you forget it. . . ."

I stop walking and turn to her. "Vanessa, she's my only ticket out."

"She's only *a* ticket out. When you leave—and you will—you should leave on *your* terms."

"Must be nice to have all the goddamn answers, Vanessa!

You know something? Some of us have to take opportunities when they come, no matter how compromised or pathetic they are. And what if I've knocked up Geraldine? I can't stay here. She'll never leave me alone."

"Running away won't solve that."

"Did I ask for your advice? You have no idea about my life—nobody does!"

I straddle my ten-speed but am unable to stir up much dust as I tear away from her.

8

Later that night, once everyone at home is asleep, I crawl up to the attic. Under the eaves, amidst sixty years of junk, I uncover Grandpa and Grandma's old lime green 1950s Samsonite suitcase. I lug it downstairs, dust it off, and resolutely start packing. I fold my shirts and underwear and wonder how I'm going to explain my leaving to everyone. Should I write a letter? I feel I should at least say something to Dad. I don't want him thinking I'm running off because I'm angry at him or that I'm shirking my responsibilities to Geraldine. And I need to tell him that I think he did a good enough job raising me and that I love him. But what do I write to Allen? God, how will he survive without me?

I hide the packed suitcase in the back of the Death Mobile.

I wake around 5:00 A.M. with a burning stomach. What did I eat last night? I try a glass of milk but it doesn't help. Around six, Dad gives me some Alka-Seltzer but it does no good. Tums, nothing.

By noon I'm in my cap and gown, along with the rest of my class, filing into the packed gymnasium, my stomach an inferno. I try to ignore the sight of Vanessa, seated high up in the packed bleachers, beside Vernadell.

I silently belch through Mitchell Mann's commencement speech about his road to success in Hollywood and the importance of dreams.

Barry, the valedictorian, delivers a long, heartfelt speech entitled "Life Is Like a Banana Split," during which I'm unable to stop a few farts from slipping out. Diplomas are handed out and all of us seniors rise and sing the school song, "I've Been Workin' on the Railroad," followed by the Kansas state song, "Home on the Range." Most of my classmates don't make it to the first chorus before their voices break and tears flow unashamedly. They hug and there's only one set of dry eyes in the class. Then it's mortarboards and tassels in the air.

Afterward, everyone gathers in the cafeteria to congratulate us and take our pictures. Vanessa gives me a big hug and I'm stiff but decent to her. Vernadell invites the whole family to the Frosty for free sundaes but I say no thanks. My stomach can't take it. Dad hugs me. "Proud of you, son."

"Thanks, Dad."

He hands me my car keys.

I park in front of Mrs. Kaye's house, near the FOR SALE sign. Suitcases are strapped to the Bug's roof and a small U-Haul trailer is hitched on the back. Her living room is empty, the walls bare. Only a few boxes remain. In the kitchen, Mrs. Kaye, on her knees, is clearing out the cleaning supplies from under the sink. A red bandana covers her hair and her tight jeans outline her ass. She looks almost sexy with her fanny in the air like that, God help me. She glances over her shoulder and says, "I'm almost ready."

"I'm not going."

She doesn't stop working. This makes me a little nervous. She reaches up for her pack of Virginia Slims on the kitchen counter, then turns and rests her back against the cabinet. She slowly knocks out a cigarette, lights it, and takes a deep drag, then stares at me as she exhales smoke. "You're not going."

"No . . . I'm sorry."

"It's the new girl you're running around with, isn't it?"

"This has nothing to do with her."

"She *is* cute, I'll give her that. And her ass is a lot tighter than mine."

"Please believe me when I tell you this has nothing to do with her."

She laughs knowingly and exhales smoke. "You'll never survive outside this town. You're too dependent on it."

"I'm gonna leave. . . ."

"Bullshit! If you wanted to leave, you'd be carrying these boxes out to the car." She takes another deep drag of smoke. "Face it, you're defined by this town. It's all you've got. You're exactly like your old man and your brother."

"Good luck, Mrs. Kaye. I mean it."

"Fuck you, Arty. And I mean that."

It's not until I'm behind the wheel of the Death Mobile that I realize my stomach is no longer burning.

9

I stretch out on the dock and stare at the stars and quarter moon. Rock music and laughter waft across the lake from over by the spillway. My fellow classmates are celebrating their graduation, their freedom, with a beer keg. Is Mrs. Kaye right about me? Deep down, do I want to stay in Harker City the rest of my life? Why else would I have unprotected sex with Geraldine? What did I think would happen? Did I set my own trap? Do I find it easier to feel sorry for myself, to do nothing, than to change my life? Would I cease to exist outside Harker City?

Then, in my mind, I hear Vanessa ask, *Are you going to let someone else define you?*

10

"**R**enee's plane's supposed to land this afternoon in Wichita," Allen explains. "Thought of surprising her at the airport, but then that might've looked like I had too much time on my hands. I'll just see her at the all-school reunion dance tonight."

I lie on my bunk and gaze at my brother, in his new leopard-print briefs, tweezing his nose hair in the dresser mirror. Allen's skin is bright pink from five days of sunbathing and running. He looks gaunt, tired, but determined.

"Her mom went to pick her up— Ouch! Shit!" He grips his nose and his eyes water.

He winces as he yanks hairs from around his nipples, then drenches himself with Aqua Velva.

"Allen."

He looks at me in the mirror.

"You don't want to asphyxiate her."

"Right," he says, and sets down the bottle.

He puts on the outfit he bought at a men's store in Junction City: lime green *Miami Vice*–inspired suit, white T-shirt, and white leather loafers. I have no idea how he paid for it.

He fastens his gold necklace and turns to me. "So, how do I look?"

It's his big day. "You look great," I tell him.

He exaggeratedly slips a Trojan condom into his wallet and winks at me.

"You going to the all-school reunion tonight?" he asks.

"Nah. It's too soon for me to reunite."

"Yeah, well, wish me luck." He sprays two shots of Binaca into his mouth.

"Good luck, Allen."

And with almost a hop in his step, my brother is on his way to meet Renee, his Ultimate Dream Girl.

I glance at the alarm clock. It's almost three in the afternoon, Sunday, and I have no compulsion to get out of bed. Ever.

Downstairs in the dining room, Carrie, on a stepladder, stretches to tack up a red streamer. A computer-generated banner hangs across the china cabinet proclaiming: FLOOD FAMILY REUNION '88. Balloons bounce on the ceiling. Personalized name tags rest on each place setting. Family photos dating way back stare at me from a large poster board attached to the wall. Grandpa and Grandma Flood's wedding. Black-and-whites of Aunt Sandy and Dad when they were kids. Our family portrait taken in '76 for the Bicentennial, where we're all dressed in red, white, and blue. Grandpa and Grandma Flood's golden wedding anniversary. Then I see a picture of Allen and me I haven't seen since I was little. It was taken in Old Abilene Cow Town and it's made up to look like it's from the 1800s. I'm about seven and wearing a Daniel Boone coonskin hat. Allen stands behind me in a big ten-gallon hat and fake handlebar moustache. We both look very serious.

"Don't just stand there," Carrie says. "Help me with this streamer."

In the kitchen, Shirley backcombs Gale Schneider's mountain of platinum. Tonight is the pageant dress rehearsal and Gale is Glinda the Good Witch.

I escape to the front porch and notice a white envelope stuck under my windshield wiper. I slip it out and tear into it. There's a note in Vanessa's handwriting: *Arty, I'm sorry you're angry with me. Nonetheless, I was glad to hear that you didn't go to Chicago. Anyway, you are cordially invited for breakfast Monday morning at my uncle's at 9 A.M. On this illustrious occasion, you can finally meet my notorious mother. Love, Vanessa.*

Mrs. Kaye's house looks empty when I drive past.

Dennis Dickers' butt crack greets me when I push open the Frosty's front door.

"Vernadell around?" I ask.

"She went to Salina to see about an emergency loan," Darlene says to the Royals baseball game on TV.

I'm on my second game of Ms. Pac-Man when the cowbell clangs. Barry saunters in wearing one of Mitchell's

Hawaiian shirts and sunglasses and plops down in a corner booth.

"What can I get you, Bar?" I ask.

He looks up from a script of some sort and smirks condescendingly at his old uniform on me.

"Just iced tea with a twist of lemon, waiter. I have to watch my weight."

I fetch his damn iced tea and bring it to him.

"Did you hear the news?" he asks.

I see my head shaking in the reflection of the sunglasses.

"Mitchell's going to cast me in the surfer movie."

"Congrats."

"Must be so derocatory to wait tables here after you've graduated."

"Barry?"

"Huh?"

"The word is *derogatory*. And yes, it is."

11

I'm in the back room, behind the Hobart dishwasher, when the front-door bell clangs. I peer out and see Sheriff Bottoms straddling a stool. *Fuck.* I inhale deeply, shakily pour a cup of water, and set it before him.

"What can I get you, sir?"

He stares at the cup and speaks slowly, menacingly. "Geraldine's home now. She has whiplash from the accident."

"I'm real sorry to hear that, sir."

He continues to speak to the cup. "Doctor said she'll be sore for a while." He looks up at me and in a deep whisper says, "Don't think for a goddamn second you'll get away with this."

The back door opens and Vernadell comes in, carrying her thermos. She looks tired; even her hair seems deflated.

"Any luck?" Darlene asks.

Vernadell shakes her head and fills her thermos with coffee. "I'm afraid the days of the Frosty Queen are fatally numbered."

The cowbell clangs and Sheriff Bottoms is gone.

"C'mon, Arty," Vernadell says. "We're leaving."

"Where to?"

"The lake. It's too nice an evening to waste in this rust bucket."

"Why ain't you takin' me?" Darlene asks.

" 'Cause someone has to work and you didn't just graduate from high school. 'Sides, you hate fishin'."

I sit on the concrete ledge below the spillway. Beside me, Vernadell rests on her lawn chair. We sip Buds and watch our corks bounce in the green cascading water at the base of the concrete funnel. So far we haven't had a nibble but the sky is cloudless and a bright sunset orange. Gnats hover like a fog over the water.

"Guess they ain't bitin' tonight," Vernadell says.

"Not yet."

I could be in Chicago right now.

"Truth be told, I don't care if we don't catch nothin'," Vernadell says. "I'm just glad to be out in the fresh air for a few hours."

I haven't seen Vernadell this relaxed in I don't know how long. Makes me glad. A small fish flops down the algae-covered spillway and splashes into Rust Creek. It reminds me of Geraldine and my murderous daydream.

"You all right?" she says. "You're real quiet tonight."

"I'm fine."

"Where's your girlfriend tonight?"

"Can we please not talk about Geraldine?"

"I meant your real girlfriend."

"I don't wanna talk about Mrs. Kaye either."

"I said your *real* girlfriend."

"Oh. She's not my girlfriend."

"Don't look that way to me."

"Well, she's not."

"I like her, you know. She's honest and smart."

"And crazy," I say.

"Hate to break it to ya, son, but we're all crazy." She takes a swig of her Bud. "She strikes me as a good one to let under your skin."

"She's not under my skin." I know I sound defensive. "Not really. Besides, she's leaving day after tomorrow. So what's the point?"

"You're too young to understand this now but when you get to be my age, you try to start enjoying every God-given day. Hell, you try to enjoy every God-given moment."

"Sounds exhausting."

She rummages around in her cooler, takes out another Bud, pulls off the tab, and sips. We sit in silence while I toss pebbles at the water.

"When my daughter was little— You probably didn't know I had a daughter, did ya? Well, anyhow, I used to bring her out here when her daddy came home drunk. I didn't want her to see him that way. She loved it out here. She could spend hours playing under the falling water. Guess I like to come out here 'cause it reminds me of her. I can still see her splashing and laughing."

I want to ask Vernadell what became of her daughter—if the rumors are true that they had a falling-out and haven't spoken in years. But I don't want to destroy the image of her little girl, splashing and laughing.

12

When I pull into our drive around eleven, Allen's Dodge Charger is not there. A good sign. Could things actually be going well for him and Renee?

In the living room, Dad sprawls in his recliner while watching the Kansas City Royals game and smoking his pipe. Shirley's nowhere around. My chance.

"Say, uh, Dad, can I talk to you a minute?"

He grabs the remote from the armrest and mutes the TV.

I lean in, hands on my knees, and say in a hushed voice, "I, uh, know things have been kinda tight lately, but, I, uh, was wondering if there's any way you could loan me five hundred dollars."

"Sorry, son. Just don't have it."

"Right. Well, thanks anyway."

I lie in bed but can't sleep, too accustomed to nodding off to the sound of Allen's snoring. The thought of my big brother being with a woman tonight, probably in a Junction City motel room, is too strange to contemplate. What if he moves in with Renee in a real city and gets a real job and leads a real life? I fall asleep to the novel thought of Allen becoming a happy human being.

My alarm clock sounds at 8:00 A.M. Allen's still gone, his bed still made! *All right!*

It's Centennial day. I shower, shave, and iron my dress shirt. In the dining room, Carrie is putting the final touches on the decorations. She hands me a FLOOD REUNION '88 T-shirt and tells me to be back by noon for the big meal.

On my way out of town, I pass Dad at the self-serve car wash, where he's waxing the hearse for the parade.

Pierre barks and wags his tail as I turn in to the Holtz farmstead. I knock on the front door and a girl who has Vanessa's small nose and dimples but is shorter and younger, with messy dyed reddish hair and braces, answers.

"You must be Samantha," I say.

"Who are you?"

"Arty."

She says nothing.

"Vanessa around?"

"In the kitchen." She unlocks the screen door and flops on the couch in front of a Road Runner cartoon.

I follow the smells of vanilla and coffee into the kitchen, where a middle-aged blonde in a low-cut red blouse sits at the table filing her nails. She looks up. She has the exact same blue eyes as Vanessa.

Vanessa herself is at the stove making pancakes. "Arty!

I'm so glad you came!" In less than a second, those blue eyes melt my waning resistance. She sets down her spatula, wipes her hands on a dishrag, and gives me a strong hug. "Meet my mom. Mom, Arty."

I turn to her mother and offer my hand. "Nice to meet you, ma'am."

Her mother smiles and shakes my hand. "You have to be Carla Kohl's son."

"Uh, yeah."

"Knew it the moment you walked in here. You look just like her, especially your smile."

"You knew my mother?"

"Carla and I were in the same class. In fact, we were great friends."

Is this what Vanessa will look like at forty-three? I could certainly live with that.

"You're just in time," Vanessa says as she sets the towering plate of pancakes on the table. "Sam, time to eat!"

"Do you need some help?" I ask.

"Nope. Just take a seat."

So I sit at the table as her sister shuffles in and sits sullenly across from me.

"Everyone, dive in before it gets cold," Vanessa says.

Samantha rakes three flapjacks onto her plate, then passes the platter to me. I take three and pass it to her mother. The steaming pancakes are sweet and fluffy.

"Good pancakes," I say.

"Delicious," her mother says. "Cooking is only one of Vanessa's many talents."

Vanessa raises her eyebrows.

I'm both disappointed and relieved that we're no longer talking about my mother. On one hand, it's nice to hear something positive about her for a change. Usually whenever people speak of her, they always end up shaking their heads and saying something like "What a shame" or "Poor Carla, such a tragedy."

"Vanessa tells me you just graduated from high school," her mother says. "Congratulations."

"Thanks."

"What're your plans?"

"Mother . . . ," Vanessa says.

"Actually, my main plan right now is to move out of Harker City the very second that's possible."

"Yeah. I couldn't wait to get out of here when I was your age," her mother says. "Everyone said I'd never leave this farm, but I scraped together a hundred bucks and headed straight for California. Never looked back."

"If you *never* looked back," Samantha says, "then why are we all sitting out here in the middle of nowhere?"

"Hey, your heritage is on this farm," her mother says. "It's important you girls know your roots."

"Yeah, well, if you love 'em so much, why'd you run away?" Samantha says.

Her mother points her fork at Samantha. "Don't get smart with me, young lady."

Vanessa turns to me. "Sorry you have to witness this."

I shrug and chew my pancakes. Truth is, I enjoy watching a family as bickery as mine. Especially if they're this luscious-looking.

Vanessa's mother lights a cigarette. "That Carla had a wicked sense of humor," she says, and flicks her ashes in the ashtray. "One time, she was being pursued by the Lutheran minister's son, who had slept with almost every girl in high school—"

Vanessa sets down her fork. "Mom, please . . ."

"I want to hear this," I say. "Go on."

"So she and this guy drive out to the lake and he thinks he's gonna get some action, right? Carla persuades him to get undressed, and when he's naked, she bolts with his clothes and drives off in his car. Poor guy had to walk back to town nude! She draped his underwear on the cross on the Lutheran church lawn—yep, Carla was a riot."

I like hearing about this unidealized side of my mother. My mom did have a pretty good sense of humor, from what I remember.

"You know," she says, pointing with her cigarette, "your mother and I had made plans to run away together."

"Run away?"

She nods and inhales. "We had made a pact our freshman year that the day we graduated, we were going to go straight to California and live on the beach. I was going to be an actress and Carla was going to be either an artist or a musician. She talked about wanting to join a band, like the Mamas and the Papas."

Why hasn't Dad ever told us this? All I ever knew was that Mom sang in the church choir.

Vanessa crumples her napkin on the table. "I have to get in costume for the parade."

"I'll do the dishes," I say as Vanessa runs out.

I can't help noticing her mother staring at me through her cigarette smoke.

"Geez, you just look so much like your mother. It's actually kind of frightening."

What can I say?

Mrs. Said shakes her head and stubs out her cigarette. "I'm glad you and Vanessa have become close. She needs friends like you.

"Vanessa—and I don't have to tell you this—is a very intelligent, capable young woman," she says. "I know she thinks her father and I are evil, that everything we do and say is wrong and bad. That's okay—I was the same way with my parents. And, truth be told, we're hardly Ozzie and Harriet. But I'm hoping that being out here in Kansas, she'll realize just what a splendid life her father and I have provided."

She smiles at me. "So how's your dad?"

"He's . . . good. Still running the mortuary."

"Tell him hi from me."

"Uh, Mrs. Said, do you think that if things had turned out differently, my mom would have gone to California with you?"

"No doubt about it. But then you wouldn't be here, now would you?"

I shake my head.

"You're welcome to come visit us," she says. "Make the move your mom never did."

"Maybe I will."

She stands and gathers up the dishes.

Ten minutes later, Vanessa bounds downstairs in her Dorothy costume: hair in two long braids, a blue plaid skirt, overly rouged cheeks, stuffed Toto in her arms.

"Got to go, Mom." Vanessa tugs my arm.

"I'm in the parade too," her mother says. "Why don't we ride to town together?"

"Don't think so," Vanessa says, and pulls me across the kitchen.

13

"**W**as I right about my mother?"

I steer around the big curve at the lake. "I don't know. She didn't seem so bad to me."

"That's because you don't live with her. Plus, she's on cloud nine this particular morning. According to her, she's the only one at her class reunion who didn't get old or fat. Of course, she's the only one in her class who's had a face-lift and a tummy tuck."

What's a tummy tuck?

"Any luck getting your money from the bank?" she asks.

I shake my head.

"That sucks," she says. "If I had the money, I'd give it to you."

"Thanks."

She says something I can't hear over the engine and the wind.

"What?"

She leans over and shouts in my ear. "Said maybe we should start looking for that missing guy they're offering the two-grand reward for on the radio."

"Monsieur Kleinstadt is long gone."

"What do you think happened to him?"

"He just took off, like any sane person would."

The traffic picks up toward town. People are pouring into Harker City like pilgrims into a holy shrine.

"Drop me off at the rodeo grounds," she says. "The floats start there."

I've never seen the downtown so full of cars, most of which have out-of-state tags, some from as far away as Idaho and Virginia. Broadway is blocked off with sawhorses and yellow tape. I can't even get close to the rodeo grounds. I have to park three blocks away!

"Thanks for coming to breakfast," Vanessa says, then leans over and gives me a quick kiss on the lips. "See you after the parade?"

"Break a leg, Ms. Gale." She gets out and is swallowed up by the crowd.

On Broadway, I push through the masses, 50 percent of whom I don't recognize. A cameraman from KACE-TV in Wichita films Old West gunfighters shooting it out with cap guns at the intersection of Main and Broadway. My brother-in-law, Rod, in a black cowboy hat and red neckerchief, hides behind a mailbox and fires away. Sheriff Bottoms, in a white hat, rides up on a horse and pulls out a pistol. "Stop in the name of the law!" Sheriff Bottoms shoots him with all due zeal and righteousness.

The gunshot startles me, it's so realistic-sounding. My

brother-in-law clutches his chest, groans, and drops dead. Applause, applause.

I shoulder my way onto our front porch, where a glum-faced Carrie slouches on the swing.

"What's the matter, Car?" I ask.

"Aunt Sandy called. She and Uncle Ed aren't coming."

"Sorry."

Carrie is wearing her FLOOD FAMILY REUNION '88 T-shirt, her makeup applied extra thick. I feel sorry for my sister, but I don't say so because I don't want her to cry all over me.

"Allen home?" I ask.

She shakes her head and looks forlornly down the street. Deputy Clarkson's cruiser, cherries flashing, leads the parade up Broadway.

"Mind if I join you?" I ask.

She scoots over and I sit beside her.

Mayor Fudge, hair higher than ever, sits in the backseat of a Caddy convertible and waves to the crowd like she's Queen Elizabeth. Harker City's only fire truck follows; Mitchell Mann waves deliriously from the bucket.

"Arty?"

"Yeah?"

"Why doesn't anyone care about our family reunion?"

Because most of us don't feel happy about who we are, I want to say. "Everyone's just busy, I guess," I tell her as I rest my arm behind my sister's back.

Geraldine, in a neck brace and her red, white, and blue polyester leotard, twirls her baton and leads the way for the high school band, which belts out the Beatles' "Yesterday." Behind the band, Shriners zigzag in figure eights with their miniature motorcycles and cars.

Carrie and I applaud Dad's freshly waxed hearse rolling down Broadway. He nods somberly. Tacked to the side is a homemade sign with old-time lettering: FLOOD FAMILY FUNERAL HOME. PROUDLY SERVING HARKER CITY SINCE 1922.

"You make that sign?" I ask Carrie, knowing full well she did. "It looks real good."

"You mean it?"

"I do."

Right away the Larsons' black limo and new hearse upstage Dad. Mr. Larson tosses bubble gum to the kiddies. Mrs. Larson, in her chauffeur uniform, tries to look friendly but professional.

Vanessa's mother rolls by in a tiara, a red strapless number, and a sash that says KANSAS JUNIOR MISS 1962. She waves big from the back of a pink crepe-paper-covered float being pulled by a John Deere tractor.

"Pretty lady," Carrie says. "Looks like a movie star."

A flatbed trailer carries Vanessa as Dorothy, Barry in a beard and stovepipe hat, Dale Clements in a scruffy-looking Cowardly Lion suit, Gale Schneider all made up and glittering as Glinda the Good Witch, and Shirley in a black hat and cape as the Wicked Witch of the West. A papier-mâché funnel cloud rotates on the back. Vanessa blows me a kiss and smiles. I stick my tongue out to catch it. She laughs.

The parade finishes after a group of veterans, holding flags and squeezed into old service uniforms, marches past.

"Thanks for sitting with me," Carrie says.

I smile at my sister. "Come on, let's get some lunch."

14

The delectable tang of grilled ribs wafts through the air, and Carrie and I follow the throngs up Broadway to Harker Park, where the barbecue is getting started. My sister heads to where her church has set up a big tent over by the swimming pool. A flimsy sign reads OLD-TIME REVIVAL TONIGHT AT SIX! MEET JES S. WHAT'S MISSING? "U" ARE.

Women in bonnets and long black pioneer dresses slice away at a hundred-foot chocolate cake. Over by the old cannon, Mayor Fudge judges the beard competition. Dad is a contestant.

Then I see it: the kiddy train running and Allen at the engine, unshaven and completely stoned. Why isn't he with Renee? Allen blinks several times, trying to keep himself awake.

"There you are," Vanessa says. She grips a slice of watermelon and her lips are wet. "Wanna go to the lake and cool off?"

"Okay. Sure. In just a minute."

"I've got to get out of here—Mom's starting to sign autographs."

Children scream. Everyone turns. The kiddy train, packed

full of panicked kids, speeds along its tracks going way too fast. Allen's slumped over the controls.

"Help!" a mother screams. "Someone!"

I rush over with several others. The train goes faster and faster. I yell, "Wake up!" at Allen but he's out cold. The little locomotive takes the corner too fast, flies off the rails, and smashes into the base of the Mr. Harker statue. Allen catapults out of the engine. Kids tumble and roll in the grass.

Hysterical parents run to scoop up their screaming children. They look okay, just scared shitless. Allen lies facedown in the grass, the pieces of the mangled locomotive littered around him. I roll Allen over. He reeks of alcohol. Thank God he's breathing. I shake him but he doesn't respond. I force open his lids and his glassy, bloodshot eyes roll to the back of his head.

I shake him. "Can you hear me, Allen?"

Nothing.

Parents curse at him: "Goddamn drunk!" "They ought to string him up!" "Where's the sheriff?"

I drag Allen by the arms across the grass, away from the angry crowd, to the shade of a tree. Dad runs over and splashes lemonade on Allen's face but he doesn't come around.

Sheriff Bottoms pushes his way through the crowd and hovers over him.

"You're under arrest!" He rolls Allen onto his stomach and takes out his handcuffs.

I push Sheriff Bottoms away. "He needs a doctor!"

"He's going to jail."

"No, he's not—"

Sheriff Bottoms whacks me in the right eye with the back of his hand, a powerful blow that buckles my knees. The crowd gasps.

"He was interfering with the law," Sheriff Bottoms yells to the crowd. "You all saw it. Well, didn't you?"

"You—you just hit him, you stupid thug!" Vanessa yells.

A siren wails and the crowd parts like the Red Sea as the ambulance pulls up.

The EMT team lifts Allen onto the stretcher and slides him in the back of the ambulance.

"You okay?" Vanessa asks.

"I think so."

"I'll go with you to the hospital," Vanessa says.

15

Dad and I take our cars and follow the ambulance to Abilene. It occurs to me that it must look pretty weird seeing two hearses chasing a screaming ambulance down the highway.

Vanessa squeezes my hand. "You look kinda shaken up. I can't believe that creep hit you."

"It's just his way."

In the hallway outside the emergency room, a doctor with muttonchop sideburns informs us that Allen has a concussion and that he's being admitted for observation.

"His blood alcohol level is dangerously high," the doctor says. "His drinking has clearly posed a danger to himself and others, which is the criterion for alcoholism; therefore I recommend he seek treatment right away. There's a good program in Salina. Should I call them for you?"

"How much will it cost?" Dad asks.

"Call them," I say.

The nurse wheels Allen out on a gurney. His eyes are closed and his head is wrapped in gauze. He mutters something about Renee but I can't make it out. My poor stupid, stupid brother.

We are walking out of the hospital when Carrie rushes up, bawling. "Is he all right? Is my brother all right?" As if Allen's not my brother too.

Dad tells her that he's fine and that we're to let him rest.

"I have to see my brother!" she says, and runs inside.

Rod, still in his cowboy hat, chaps, and holster, looks at us wearily and follows her inside, his spurs jingling.

"What the hell happened?" I ask Vanessa as we turn out of the hospital parking lot. "Allen was supposed to be getting it together. He was supposed to be becoming Super Allen."

"Maybe things didn't work out with Renee."

"He did a real job on that train, huh?" I laugh nervously, but she doesn't laugh.

"Maybe his accident'll be like mine," she says. "A wake-up call."

"Vanessa, I know you like to believe everyone can change. But not around here. Nobody and nothing changes around here."

"Well then, let's not go back to Harker City just yet, Arty," she says. "We both need a break from that place. Let's go somewhere and talk?"

"I know just the place." I turn the car around.

16

On the edge of town, I pull off onto a gravel road and park in front of the rusted chain-link fence that was once the entrance.

"Wait, what is this place?"

"Old Abilene Cow Town. Used to be an Old West tourist trap. They had a saloon that served root beer in a chilled mug. I loved it as a kid."

There isn't much left to love. It looks like a real ghost town now—most of the windows on the false-front buildings are broken out and the paint is worn off.

Vanessa the Trespassa gets out and squeezes through the gate. I look around to make sure no one is watching, then climb through.

The old stagecoach sits on its axle, the back wheels missing. She heads into the saloon.

I push open the swinging doors. It's dark and dusty but pretty much as I remember it: the long bar with the mirror behind it, the small stage where the cancan dancers used to be, and beside it the old player piano. Behind the stage, the wall mural of buffalo and Indians has faded but is still recognizable.

Vanessa pops up from behind the bar. "What's your poison, pilgrim?" she says in a John Wayne drawl.

I step up to the bar. "I used to come in here and order a cold beer in a dirty glass. And the nice old guy who worked here would pour me a root beer. Thought that was the coolest thing in the world."

Vanessa hops onto the stage. As Dorothy in her old-fashioned dress and braids, she fits right in.

"The day after Mom's funeral, Allen brought me here. He figured this was the one place that would cheer me up." Embarrassed, I clear my throat, pretending something is stuck in it. Vanessa sees right through me.

For the hell of it, I drop a quarter in the old player piano, and "Home on the Range" comes out on the thing, scratchy and warbly; the ghost's back at the keyboard.

"Imagine that." My voice cracks. "After all this time."

Without looking, I know she's still eyeballing me. I lean over the piano and watch the moving keys. "Used to think ghosts played this piano, no matter how many times Allen explained it to me."

A sob escapes, then another. *Shit.* I quickly wipe my eyes with my sleeve. "Sorry. God. Don't know what's wrong with me. . . ."

"Arty, it's okay," she says.

And with that I can't stop. I am a bawling, hiccuping, brokenhearted little kid.

I cover my face.

"I thought my brother died today."

She gathers me in her arms and hugs me so hard I feel my bones creak.

17

Seven o'clock that evening. Back to work at the Frosty. The place is dead. Everyone in town is at the pageant, except for Darlene, who's here watching *Lifestyles of the Rich and Famous* on TV. I'm sipping Dr Pepper and leaning against the Rock-Ola jukebox, listening to "Don't Go Breaking My Heart," Allen and Renee's song, when I see a familiar-looking car pull up outside. Geraldine's Chevette. Damn. She sees me looking at her and she motions me outside.

"You mind getting in the car?" she says as I approach.

I throw open her passenger door, set her baton on the floor, and sit.

Geraldine stares down at the steering wheel for the longest time, then says in a very quiet voice, "I was never pregnant."

I am too stunned to speak; my heart leaps.

"I told you I was because it was the only way I knew how to get you back," she confesses. "I know it was wrong."

I reach over and hug her tight. "Oh, my God! Oh, my God! You have no idea what a relief this is!"

"I knew that it would be. For you. I'm so sorry, Arty."

I release her and ask, "Geraldine, why in the world would you still want me?"

"You're sweet and kind—everything my daddy's not. You think I don't know my daddy's scary? Believe me, I know." She swallows hard. "Ever since junior high when I met you, you were the only decent-looking boy who was nice to a chubby girl like me. That alone was enough, and I . . . I convinced myself I wanted to spend the rest of my life with you. . . . I hope you can find it in your heart to forgive me."

"I do."

"Guess that's the only 'I do' I'll be getting from you."

"Why, Geraldine, that's downright funny. Now, can I make you a hot fudge sundae? With extra fudge sauce and sprinkles?"

She smiles and nods.

"Wait right here," I say.

It is my humble opinion that I have created the greatest hot fudge sundae ever at the Frosty Queen, with two Mount Everests of whipped cream topped by cherries, an ocean of hot fudge, and a blizzard of chopped nuts and sprinkles.

"Wow!" Geraldine says when I pass it through the window. "You gotta help me with this."

I get back into the car and we both eat the sundae until she glances at her watch. "Yikes! I'm supposed to twirl during intermission!" She turns the key in the ignition.

I jump out, she guns the engine, and Geraldine Bottoms is off in a blaze of dust and chocolate sprinkles.

I fall against the side of the Frosty and break down in tears of happiness. "Never again," I say into my hands. "Never again."

Energy pulses through me. I cannot, I will not, sit still.

I sprint down empty Broadway, which is decorated with candy wrappers, streamers, and paper plates, remnants from the parade. The distant sound of Vanessa and the cast singing "We're Off to See the Wizard" echoes in the still evening air. At the railroad crossing, a freight train is stalled on the tracks. I turn around and run back the way I came. I am George Bailey running through Bedford Falls after Clarence earns his wings.

I stomp on the air cord at the Dairy Queen and an electronic bell rings inside.

"Welcome to Dairy Queen. My name is Cindy. How may I help you this fine day—I mean, evening?"

"I'm free!" I yell into the microphone. "I'm free!"

"Excuse me?" she says.

As I pass Our Redeemer Lutheran Church, I shout, "Thank you, Jesus!" and hope He doesn't really expect me to become a born-again.

I jog all the way to school, scoot halfway up the flagpole, and sing "I've Been Workin' on the Railroad."

On the edge of town, I come to the HARKER CITY IS RIGHT WHERE YOU WANT TO BE! billboard.

"*No, it isn't!*" I shout.

I'm running out of town on Highway 76. The sun is

setting and the sky is an explosion of red and orange. Maybe I'll run all the way to Junction City! My heart pounds and I hear myself breathing. It's a good sound. It's the sweetest sound I ever heard. A semi whooshes past. I pull on an imaginary cord and the truck blows its horn. Haven't done that since I was a kid.

I run until the taste of hot fudge comes up in my throat and my chest heaves uncontrollably. I turn around and walk backward and take in Harker City—a silhouette of trees and rooftops with a silver whistle-shaped water tower and a chalky white grain elevator rising out of it. I catch my breath and start the journey back home.

18

Up in the bleachers, watching the pageant. Must be two thousand people in the audience. Who knew? A lot of folks sit on blankets or lawn chairs. Vanessa sings "Over the Rainbow"—a song I secretly love. I had no idea she could sing like this. It's just so corny and beautiful. Barry, as usual, emotes like crazy, and Larry Larson, the Cowardly Lion, can't carry a tune or follow a beat to save his life but still manages to be somewhat likable. The songs are just like in the movie, only they've replaced Emerald City with Harker City and the Great Oz with the Great Horace Harker. The audience applauds like crazy after each number.

Though I am loath to admit it, the pageant is fun. Everyone cracks up when the straw in Scarecrow Dale Clements' shirt almost catches on fire. The New Lifers shout amens and hallelujahs from their old-time tent revival in the neighboring field. Shirley, the Wicked Witch of the West, swings above the stage when her flying cables get stuck. She is suspended helplessly in the air and I can see panic in her face. Dad runs onto the stage. "Don't worry, honey, we'll get you down!" Within minutes, the city's cherry picker rescues her, to much applause, and the show resumes.

They get to the part where Dorothy wakes up and she's back in Kansas. "There's no place like home, Auntie Em," Vanessa says. "There's no place like Harker City."

I see a few ladies sniffling at this and some surprisingly watery-eyed men.

Suddenly, Mitchell Mann thunders out onstage in a shiny tuxedo and asks everyone to stand for the finale. A giant American flag rises on the pole and we all stand and sing:

> I've been workin' on the railroad,
> All the livelong day.
> I've been workin' on the railroad,
> Just to pass the time away.
> Don't you hear that whistle blowin'?
> Rise up so early in the morn!

Everyone vocalizes with such feeling that I find myself becoming a little choked up. Seeing all these people who have moved away and done other things but have come back to celebrate Harker City's birthday makes me realize that there must be something good about this place. Maybe Vanessa's right—maybe I will look back and remember my hometown fondly. If I can just get to the looking-back part.

Red, white, and blue fireworks pop and stream through

the night sky. Hoots and cheers. The cast members join hands and bow.

After the show, I rush up to Vanessa. "Guess what?"

"She's not pregnant."

"How'd you know?"

"It's written in the gleam of your eyes," she says, and hugs me.

At the carnival, we toss rings at the rubber ducks floating past but miss every time. I try to win her a mustard-colored dinosaur at the BB gun shooting gallery but she ends up winning it for me. After the Tilt-a-Whirl and the bumper cars, Vanessa holds our place in line for the Ferris wheel while I buy us some cotton candy. When I return, Kenneth Ray Schneider, the quarterback who gets every girl he wants and has often referred to me as "fag," whispers something to Vanessa.

"Don't think so," she says to him, then turns and touches her lips to mine. She opens her mouth and our tongues brush in a slow kiss.

She steps back. Kenneth stares, gape-mouthed. I'm too happy to react.

Vanessa slips her hand in mine. "Let's find some privacy."

"Wait! I totally forgot! I'm supposed to be at work!"

19

It's pandemonium at the Frosty. Every table, booth, and stool is taken and a line has formed outside. One middle-aged couple uses the Ms. Pac-Man machine as a table.

Vernadell comes around the counter holding two plates of fries. "Where in tarnation have you been?"

"Sorry. Had no idea people would be coming here!" I yell over the roar.

"Seems everyone who grew up in this town wants to relive their high school memories of this place."

The clanking of silverware on plates and all the voices drown out the jukebox.

I wonder if the creaky floor will be able to hold all the nostalgic masses.

I grab my apron and see Vernadell exchanging Vanessa's stuffed Toto for an order pad.

20

We work three hours nonstop. As packed as the place is, I recognize almost no one. It's weird being in Harker City and not knowing so many people.

Around midnight we run out of ice cream, but it's not until one-thirty that the last customer leaves. Vanessa, Darlene, and I collapse into the big half-moon booth.

Vernadell cashes out the register. "It's a record," she says, and tears off the receipt: $1,634.72. "Most money we've ever made in one night."

We clap and whistle.

"Might as well lock the door, Vern," Darlene says. "We're out of everything. You need to call the supplier first thing in the morning."

"No need." Vernadell throws a switch on the fuse box by the door, killing the red neon ice cream cone outside. "We're officially out of business."

"I'm not joking, Vern," Darlene says. "We're plumb out of everything, right down to sprinkles."

"And I ain't jokin' neither." Vernadell fills a mug with the last of the coffee and snaps off the machine.

We all gape at her, awaiting an explanation. She sets her coffee mug and a bulging Bank of Harker City deposit bag on the table and slides in beside me.

"I sold the business tonight," she says as she blows on the coffee.

"Get out of here," I say.

She arches her eyebrows and sips her coffee.

"Who's the buyer?" Darlene asks.

"Guy named Steve Bennett. Gray-haired fella, 'bout fifty, sat right in this booth most of the evening."

"I remember him," Vanessa says. "He left me a forty-dollar tip and pinched my ass."

"The sucker saw the crowd in here tonight, thought I actually had a good business, and offered me twice what this establishment's worth."

"Bennett," Darlene says suspiciously. "Never heard of him."

"Neither had I, but he sure remembered me. Said he grew up here but lives in Texas now, is in the computer business. Told me this place hadn't changed a bit and that it was comforting that some things in this world stay the same. Imagine that. When he sees this place, he sees the best years of his life."

"He going to be my new boss?" Darlene asks.

"Not unless you're relocating to Texas," Vernadell says. "He's moving the whole building to Houston. Said he's building a mansion there and wants to put the café beside his swimming pool."

"He wants a restaurant in his backyard? That don't even make sense," Darlene says.

Vernadell shrugs. "I asked him if he wanted the motel too, but he just laughed."

"How's he getting it to Texas?" Vanessa asks.

"Sending a truck to pick it up."

"It'll fit on a truck?" I ask.

"Son," Vernadell says, "it came on a truck."

Darlene folds her arms. "He was probably drunk, probably a wheeler-dealer, and you fell for it. . . ."

"I had my suspicions when he wrote me the biggest check I've ever seen right on the spot," Vernadell says. "So I called Hal Denton at the bank, who told me he's good for it. Said he donated two hundred grand to the Lutheran Home, where his mother lives."

There is silence as all this sinks in.

"So that's it," Darlene says. "No more Frosty."

"We were through anyway," Vernadell says flatly. "Denton planned to foreclose on us after the Centennial."

"Well, it still makes me kinda sad." Darlene looks away.

"Lookit." Vernadell's voice is uncommonly patient. "I owe a lot of people a lot of money. Even with Mr. Bennett's check, I'll be pretty near breakin' even."

"But how do you know someone local wouldn't buy it and keep it going?" Darlene asks. "Did you even try?"

"For your information, I did." Vernadell leans over the table and points her crooked index finger at Darlene. "I called everyone in this town and Abilene and Junction City who had two dimes to rub together, offering to unload it for close to nothing. And guess what? No one wanted it. Said it was too far from the highway, or it was too old, or we couldn't compete with the Dairy Queen. And who knows, maybe they were right."

The words hang in the ensuing silence.

"Darlene, honey, no one wanted to save this place more'n me," Vernadell says. "My daddy started the Frosty. It was his dream. I hate to see it go but its day's done. So let it end up some piece of nostalgia in some millionaire's backyard in Texas. At least it'll survive and give someone some pleasure."

"Well," Darlene says as she gets up and hangs her apron beside the grill, "I guess you did your best."

"Before you go . . ." Vernadell opens the deposit bag and counts out what looks like five hundred dollars, which she gives to Darlene.

Darlene takes the cash, stuffs it in her apron pocket, gives the place one final searching look, shakes her head, and walks out the back door.

"Looks like I ain't gonna win no popularity contests tonight," Vernadell says, and counts out three hundred dollars.

"She understands," I say.

She hands me the three hundred. "For your work here."

"Thanks," I say, and clutch the money in my fist. My escape money? My ticket out of Harker City?

She hands Vanessa fifty, then stands and goes to the front door and fumbles through her keys. She laughs.

"What's so funny?" I ask.

"Just realized that in the forty-eight years this place's been in business, it's never once been locked. I don't even have a key for the front door. Help yourselves to as much pop as you like and whatever else you can scrounge up. Just turn out the lights when you leave."

"What're you going to do?" I ask.

"Going to bed."

"I mean, now that you're out of business."

"I'll worry about that tomorrow." At the front door, Vernadell stops and turns to us. "Actually, I do know what I'm going to do. I'm going to sleep till noon. Something I haven't done since I was your age."

21

Vanessa and I are left facing each other in the booth. She stretches her hands across the table toward me. I reach out and meet them. Our fingers intertwine.

"Well," I say.

"Well," she says.

"How about a last dance at the Frosty?" I propose.

She smiles and nods.

I slide out of the booth, step over to the wall, and switch off the overhead lights. Except for the blue and red neon of the Rock-Ola jukebox, the café is dark. The old Frosty, in the dim, colorful light, has a kind of romantic old-movie quality. Vanessa slips three quarters in the jukebox and makes her selections. She turns around and we face each other. Spandau Ballet's "True" comes on the speakers.

I take her hand and place my left arm around her waist and she steps into me, very close. We dance slowly in the middle of the café, our cheeks touching. I can feel her legs, stomach, and breasts against me. We sway together but move no more than a foot or two. Soon she removes her cheek and looks at me before closing her eyes. She wraps her arms around my neck and we kiss. And it's as sweet and fresh as the first time we kissed in the rainstorm.

She rests her head on my shoulder, her arms now around my waist, and I inhale the outdoorsy smell of her hair. Nothing has ever felt so right.

The song ends but we continue to hold each other, still swaying. Soon Naked Eye's "Always Something There to Remind Me" begins. She whispers the words to the song in my ear as we dance on. More songs, more dancing, more kissing. Then, finally, the music ends.

She lifts her head from my shoulder. "Let's go to the lake."

I unplug the Rock-Ola and linger in the darkness. It's strange to see the café empty and silent. Feels weird knowing I will never see Vernadell in her booth again, or Dennis Dickers' butt crack at the counter.

"So long, you old rust bucket," I whisper. "Thanks."

22

Vanessa rides close beside me in the Death Mobile, her arm around my shoulder as she gently twirls a lock of my hair with her finger. We're almost to the lake when she says, "Wait, we need to stop by Uncle Roger's."

So I drive to the farm. Pierre waits for us at the end of the drive, like he knew we were coming. He jumps right in and goes apeshit licking us.

"Need your swimming suit?" I say.

"Got the one I was born with."

My heart accelerates.

At the dock, I kill the lights and engine. A bright full moon reflects off the lake.

Vanessa tosses a stick into the water and Pierre jumps in after it. Vanessa walks to the edge of the dock, unbraids her hair, and drops her skirt and blouse. No bra. She slips out of her panties and, for a moment, stands naked before me. Then she dives in, legs together. God is an artist.

I scramble to strip and swim out to where she's treading water. The water is warm and it feels good to skinny-dip.

The moonlight and her makeup give a ghoulish color to her face. She splashes me and swims off. I make chase.

We swim past the spillway, then along the dam. She's a fast swimmer but I catch up. Near the curve of the highway she stops and stands on something, up to her waist. Water drips off her nipples. I swim over beside her and my feet touch some sort of mossy, flat platform.

"What're we standing on?" I ask.

"Last one to the dock is a rotten egg," she says, and swims away.

I follow her to the dock, where she slowly pulls herself out of the water. Her wet naked body glistens in the moonlight. She smiles at me, then slowly walks to the Death Mobile, opens the back door, and crawls in. A lump rises in my throat and I climb out of the water.

23

A few hours later, we sit together on the concrete foundation, wrapped in a blanket, our arms tight around each other. We stare at the flames dancing inside the fireplace of our old house.

"This fireplace hasn't been used in nine years," I say, and throw the last of the sticks on the fire. I tell her how I remember hanging my Christmas stockings on the mantel and how, when I was six, we had our family portrait taken in front of it.

"It's a nice fireplace," she says.

"Dad did the brickwork himself."

We stare into the fire for the longest time, holding each other.

"My family never talks about Mom's death," I say. "Ever. Dad has never said so, but I know he feels responsible. On the day of the fire, he was supposed to be at home with her—she was only two days out of the hospital and Doc Hayes told Dad to keep her under constant surveillance. But Dad had a call to pick up a body over in Council Grove. Mom was sleeping when Dad left. What he thought would take one hour turned into four because of an unexpected blizzard."

She traces her fingers along the back of my hand. "Maybe it would be good for your family to talk about what happened."

"You don't know my family."

"Have you tried talking about it?"

"I know better."

"Would it hurt to try?"

"You know, it probably would."

We talk about everything but our futures until the sky tinges light blue in the east, meadowlarks sing their morning song, and a cool breeze blows off the lake.

She stands, drops the blanket, and crawls into the back of the hearse.

24

I'm sitting on the edge of Vanessa's bed, where she's packing her suitcase. Sunlight pours through the yellowed curtains. It's Tuesday morning. Her mom and sister are outside loading up the Volvo. Pierre sleeps at the foot of the bed.

There's no talk of staying in touch or whether we will see each other again. There's nothing to say, no plans to be made, and we both know it.

"Hand me those jeans on the dresser, will ya?" she says, and I do.

Vanessa closes the bulging suitcase and sits on it, and I help her zip it. She looks up at me. I take her face in my hands and kiss her, not too hard. There's a car honk.

"Vanessa!" her mother yells.

I pull back from the kiss. She gets to her feet.

"I have something for you," I say.

I grab my backpack off of the floor, reach into it, and take out the sketch pad she bought me in Topeka. Her eyebrows lift and she flashes me a surprised look.

"Open it."

She does. It's entitled *The Loch Ness Girl and Me*. It's a

comic strip of our time together: meeting at the lake, my searching for her, the time she pretended to be Italian and almost wrecked the Death Mobile, the old hospital and our falling-out, taking pictures at the Dog Lady's house, dancing in the rain, our making love. . . .

She smiles and laughs with every turn of the page. On the last page she looks up at me. Her eyes fill with tears.

"Vanessa! Let's go!" her mom yells.

Vanessa wipes her cheeks. I grab her suitcase and we walk out hand in hand.

Her sister and mom are already in the car. I load the suitcase in the back. She gives her uncle a big hug and a peck on the cheek, embraces Pierre, then walks over to me. She reaches into her back pocket and hands me an envelope. "Don't open this until I'm gone," she says. "Promise?"

"I promise."

"And only open it at the dock."

I nod and slip it into my back jeans pocket. She gives me a kiss on the mouth, then bends into the backseat of the Volvo. Her uncle, Pierre, and I watch in silence as the Volvo heads down the drive and turns onto a gravel county road. Soon the kicked-up dust fades and there's no sign left of Vanessa.

25

I decide to drive to Salina to see Allen at St. John's Rehabilitation Clinic.

Although he looks pretty tired and bruised, he smiles when I walk into his room. He introduces me to his roommate, a chain-smoking bag of bones from Russell who looks a little like Sonny Bono.

We go to the TV lounge, which is layered in a thick fog of exhaled tobacco smoke. Allen tells me all about the program here and says that Dad and Carrie have agreed to come for family week.

"We've got a lot of shit to work through as a family," he says. "Will you come?"

"I promise," I tell Allen.

"I'm not going back to Harker City," Allen says. "Think I'll make a new start of things here in Salina, where no one knows me. They got a nice vo-tech here—I'm thinking of maybe taking a course in car restoration and body work."

"You'd be real good at that. Sorry things didn't work out with Renee."

"It was never really about Renee. . . ."

I nod but don't press the issue. If he wants to elaborate, he can. I figure it'll all come out during family week.

We watch *Ripley's Believe It or Not* until it's time for Allen to meet with his counselor.

26

I drive around Salina for a while, grab a salami and cheese sandwich at Sub 'n Stuff. It's not until I'm flying down the empty two-lane Harker City highway that it occurs to me I have nothing to return for. Vanessa is gone, the Frosty closed. Allen has left. Barry left town with Mitchell Mann yesterday. Mrs. Kaye is in Chicago. The Stiles' Styles billboard comes up on my right: STILES' STYLES—BECAUSE WHAT YOU WEAR COUNTS! It seems like it was a hundred years ago when I worked there. I wonder if they'll ever nail Mr. Stiles for what he did.

Suddenly, smoke billows out from under the hood and my engine dies. I roll onto the shoulder but the engine won't start. This time, only serious and costly measures can revive the Death Mobile.

The cost of the tow truck, the new carburetor, and the labor comes to $280. I have exactly twenty dollars with which to escape my hometown. Make that eighteen-fifty after I get a Snickers, a Dr Pepper, and some Hubba Bubba.

As I ease out of Nordy's Full-Service Garage, it's hot as hell, even with the windows open. I see Vanessa's swimming goggles hanging on the rearview mirror and have an idea.

I find Pierre waiting at the end of the Holtz driveway. I open my door. He jumps in and I pet him vigorously. "C'mon, boy!" He sniffs the car for Vanessa.

I park at the dock. If I look long and hard enough, I can almost see Vanessa swimming toward me. Pierre barks and chases a frog into the cattails. I'm stretching out on the dock when I feel something in my back pocket. I sit up and remove the envelope Vanessa gave me.

The note inside reads: *Your ticket out is the platform in the lake.*

I strip to my underwear, put on Vanessa's goggles, and dive in. This feels so good, like I'm still with her. Over by the dam my foot touches the platform. I stand on it, catch my breath, and drain the water from the goggles.

Okay, so I'm standing on the platform. Now what?

I dive into the murky brown water and I can't make out much. Then I see a windshield. The platform is . . . the top of a car? I come up, catch my breath, and dive back down. It's too dark to see inside of the windshield but I swim to the rear of the car, where a thick slime covers the license plate. I run my fingers over it like a blind man reading Braille and make out the words BIG DOUG.

I break the surface and swim back to the dock, where I slip into my jeans.

27

I am speeding into town with Pierre. After I park in front of the courthouse, I take the stairs two at a time, the hot concrete stinging my bare feet. I shove open the door and make a beeline to the sheriff's office. Sheriff Bottoms looks up from his desk and stares at me over his bifocals. Deputy Clarkson puts down *Guns & Ammo*. I must look a sight with my wet hair and no shirt or shoes.

"I'm here to collect my two thousand dollars."

"What two thousand dollars?" says Sheriff Bottoms.

"The reward," I say. "I just found Doug Kleinstadt."

FIN